The Hypothesis of Giants

Book Two: The Change Agent

By

Melissa Kuch

ISBN: 1511731753
ISBN 13: 9781511731751

Dedicated to my beautiful baby girl, Lily — my little goddess.

"Difficulties break some men but make others. No axe is sharp enough to cut the soul of a sinner who keeps on trying, one armed with the hope that he will rise even in the end."

-Nelson Mandela

Chapters

Chapter 1

The Heart of Orion

Fifteen Years Earlier

Dark storm clouds swallowed the sky, casting their shadows over the town of Candlewick. The government building stood like a beacon of hope, its brick clad in white marble. A slogan engraved over the gold plated double doorway read *THE IDEAL HAS SPOKEN*; its curved script swerving and curving its way into the heart of the stone. A lone man stood bound in the center of a courtyard adjacent to the government building. His once strong and muscular frame had been reduced to skin and bones due to lack of nourishment and months of torture in Candlewick Prison. His eyes revealed his power as he gazed intently into the thicket of cameras awaiting his execution. He stood barefoot on the crumbling dirt that he would soon be a part of, "Ashes to ashes; dust to dust." He strained his neck upwards toward the sky for a glimpse of the sun he had not witnessed in the depths of the dungeon. How he longed to see it one more time...

The gilded doors swung open followed by bass drums pounding, *Thump... Thump... Thump.* Common Good soldiers marched single-file into the courtyard clothed in the Common Good Army uniforms; the fabric stained a vibrant indigo and orange. Inspector Herald stepped forward. Tall and majestic he stood out over the crowd, scanning the rejoicing faces with coal black eyes, his smile beaming as he waved to the camera. His chest was adorned with medals, each symbolizing a victory won over the religious protestors, who had been fighting for two years to restore their first amendment right, Freedom of Religion. The execution of David Xiomy would be the Inspector's greatest achievement. The crowd cheered as he approached the podium.

The Inspector's words flew from his mouth like venom, infecting the minds of all who listened.

"Today is a momentous day in our new history. Today we reset our calendars at year one and start a new beginning for our country. The leader of the religious protest, David Xiomy, better known as IMAM, has been found guilty of traitorous acts against the United States of the Common Good. He tried to beguile us with peaceful protests but with the Last Straw Protest, he was found guilty of taking innocent lives both by his hand and the hands of his followers. You all remember the pain and the wars that existed before the foundation of the IDEAL. You all remember the sacrifices needed for the betterment of the Common Good. It is for you, the people, that I stand here as the spokesman of the IDEAL. For the IDEAL contains the best of all of us and who we each strive to be. This man betrayed you all and with David Xiomy's blood we will restore peace in our country once again!"

Cheers erupted from the crowd and camera flashes brightened the gloomy day with their fluorescent light. The Inspector embraced the cheers, closing his eyes and holding his hands outstretched toward them. He stepped down from the podium, smirking to himself, as he walked towards the prisoner awaiting judgment.

"If only your God could save you now." Inspector Herald chided, clasping his hands in a mock prayer.

David's gaze was steadfast on the Inspector. "You know the role you played in the Last Straw Protest. You know that all I am guilty of is being a threat to you and your path to power. I united people from all religions to fight for their right for the freedom to believe in whatever they chose to believe. That freedom is the foundation of this country and those rights were taken away out of fear!"

"You killed people in cold blood because you were desperate," the Inspector's face was before him, his eyes radiated anger. "Your people are the ones who caused the towers of freedom to fall. Your people caused the subways to be blown to bits along with all the people within them. I was the one who acted. You were the one still living in a dream world that people of religion could live in harmony! Harmony came only after removing the religions that separated the people. I have created that peace and will keep it by any means necessary."

David's face stared into the crazed eyes before him, not recognizing the man he had once known.

The Inspector regained his composure and backed up, signaling a guard who approached with a blindfold. At that, David shook his head, preferring to look death in the eye. The crowd held its breath as the Inspector removed the silver plated revolver from his pocket. He held it up for all the country to see as he loaded a solitary bullet into the barrel. Only one was needed.

"David Xiomy, IMAM, you have been tried and sentenced to death. The IDEAL has spoken."

The drum roll began and a crow cawed in the distance. The Inspector raised his weapon, aiming for the man's head. He was about to squeeze the trigger when the gray clouds shifted. A pointed ray of sunlight streamed down and blinded the Inspector, forcing him to lower the gun in order to shield his eyes from the glow.

David Xiomy smiled as he beheld this sign and spoke loudly to be heard over the clamorous crowd.

"Fifteen years from today the prophecy will be fulfilled. Then one greater than I, will bring about a balance and restore freedom; a true giant among men who will restore hope and unite the people in a fearful world."

Through the sea of blank eyes, he could distinguish two hazel eyes that he recognized. They were unflinching, resolute and full of hope. There were no tears as her eyes met his. Fawn's long black hair was caught in the wind, gently and freely flowing over her face, a sight beautiful to behold.

The shot rang out to thunderous applause.

Present Day

Aurora Alvarez awoke with a start, her back aching as a tree root was jabbing into her spine. She sat up, massaging her neck as her eyes adjusted to the sun streaming down through the palm tree branches dancing above her. She had to remind herself that she wasn't in her home town of Candlewick or in her bed on Wishbone Avenue. Instead she was hidden away in the Amazon rainforest in what had once been known as South America. Fifteen years earlier this region had been acquired by Inspector Herald and the Common Good Army, declaring it a part of the United States of the Common Good. Aurora's father had confided to her that Inspector Herald believed it would be beneficial to acquire the entire North and South American continents to catch members of the rebellion fleeing beyond the borders to escape religious persecution. Aurora knew she wasn't safe here beneath the towering trees and over-grown foliage in the midst of the Amazon, but it was as if the trees themselves were rebelling, acting as Aurora's protectors from Inspector Herald's clutches.

The sun was at its zenith and Aurora realized she had slept longer than expected. Her thoughts were interrupted at the sound of Otus snoring loudly. He tossed and turned on the deep rooted ground and his green moss pillow. The snoring Otus, who was a thirty-foot giant, was the reason they were hiding in the middle of the Amazon Rainforest, since Inspector Herald and the Common Good Army wanted to capture Otus, and his companions, at any cost.

Aurora felt parched as her t-shirt clung to her curvy frame like glue. The humidity was intense and due to their close proximity to the equator, the temperature was well over 100 degrees Fahrenheit. She wanted desperately to take a shower to rinse off the sweat and dirt that was congealing on her skin. She had never felt so dirty in her life and she thought that her mother would have a coronary if she saw Aurora like this.

"You are not representing the Alvarez beauty," said her mother's voice in the back of her head, her thoughts mixed in her nickname "Fatty Alvarez" from back home in Candlewick. Even after all the running and the adventures of the past two weeks, she still felt humongous. She tightened her belt around her stomach that bulged despite the countless times she stretched and smoothed her shirt.

Aurora Alvarez's high school biology teacher, Mrs. Xiomy, was sun bathing on a log over a stream; her purple glasses resting over her big amethyst eyes while her blond hair cascaded down her shoulders. Though having the appearance of a normal High School teacher, Mrs. Xiomy was a fuse that could ignite at any given moment.

Aurora yawned and wondered where the others were. She stood up, stretched her arms over her head and caught sight of

Boreas sitting beside the stream. His jet black hair had grown over the past two weeks and was hanging stringy and uncombed. She watched as he washed his face in the stream, soaking his navy t-shirt in the process and cursing as a mosquito buzzed in his ear. He slapped at it, missed and looked up to catch Aurora staring at him.

"Well, it's about time you woke up!" He cried out. "Did you figure it out?"

The peace and serenity vanished in that very instant.

"Figure what out?" She called back in between a yawn.

"The Professor. Where the hell is he?"

Aurora yearned to go back to bed as she recalled the reason they were lost in this rainforest. They were in search of Professor Gassendi, the man who supposedly had the book regarding the ancient prophecy and the answers that Aurora and Boreas were searching for. Aurora didn't know how she got mixed up with this crusade. According to some ancient prophecy, she and Boreas were pre-destined to help Otus fulfill his mission of reaching the Aurora Borealis, also known as the Northern Lights. Somehow Boreas, Otus and herself had to miraculously stop the Geometric Storm–a cataclysmic natural disaster –from happening. How the hell they were going to do this was anyone's guess. They didn't even know when this storm was supposed to hit and the exact location in the Arctic Circle that they were supposed to be stationed at in order to stop it. They desperately hoped the Professor would be able to answer these questions, if they were ever able to find him.

Aurora removed the crumpled piece of paper from her jeans pocket and walked down the curved path that led to the stream.

"I told you he is supposed to be beneath Orion's belt," Aurora rustled the piece of paper in Boreas's face, showing the dots that when connected drew the constellation of the mythological Greek god Orion depicted with arrow in its hand.

"Well then, where is the Professor?" he exclaimed, splashing water at her and nearly getting the map wet in the process.

Aurora screamed in aggravation at the fifteen-year-old boy who was driving her crazy.

"Look Boreas, all your mother said was…"

"You mean that stranger who bore me and gave me some stupid shell to try to make up for missing 10 years of my life? Yes, what about her?"

Boreas sat cross-legged, haphazardly digging in the dirt with the small white conch shell with a hint of orange in its interior. That was the consolation gift from his mother, Fawn Stockington. For the past ten years he had believed his mother to be dead. Instead, she had built an underwater castle outside the reach of the Common Good government, naming it 'Plymouth Tartarus'. She had recruited followers from around the world who were not willing to give up their religious beliefs despite what the IDEAL put into law. It was illegal in The United States of the Common Good to follow any religion, punishable by either life in prison or death. Plymouth Tartarus had provided that religious freedom, but not anymore. It now was lying in pieces beneath the Atlantic Ocean. It had been bombed mercilessly by the Common Good Army led by Inspector Herald who had been in pursuit of Otus. Many had been killed as they tried to escape, and the survivors, including Aurora, Boreas and Otus, had found a way to the safe haven located hidden in the wilderness in the Hudson Valley. That was where Fawn created a new colony under the title of Plymouth Incarnate.

Aurora watched Boreas continue to dig with the conch shell and softened her tone saying, "Sorry. I meant, Fawn, the High Magistrate at the new Plymouth Incarnate. She said to connect the dots of the star map and we'll find the Professor."

"But the dots show Orion's Belt. There is no belt here."

"Well I thought this is where it's supposed to be," she said with growing frustration. "I'm not a star expert."

She threw her hands up in frustration, plopping herself down near Mrs. Xiomy who was soaking her feet in the water.

"This was a wild goose chase from the start," Mrs. Xiomy said, looking frazzled. "Fawn never intended for us to find Professor Gassendi anyway. Most likely he's been killed or is sitting in a prison somewhere."

Boreas cupped his hands into the stream, pouring the water over his head, combing his fingers through his thick hair and trying to spike the top of it like he was using hair gel. He stood up to his full height of 5 foot 9" showing his tennis player physique; tall, lean body with muscular arms and shoulders. Boreas possessed more of his mother's features with intense exotic eyes, a high forehead and though rarely seen, a big infectious smile that was still boyish in nature unlike his older and unworldly countenance. A long curved scar was visible right below the crease in his neck, as a reminder of where he had been cut by the Great Secretary in Plymouth Tartarus. He was lucky to be alive.

He suddenly charged towards Aurora, his nostrils flaring. "Give me that map!"

Aurora jumped to her feet and held the paper closer to her chest. "No, you can't read this anyway."

"Well, apparently neither can you!"

He grabbed the map but Aurora held on until it was a game of tug of war and the paper ripped in two. Aurora fell on her backside and Boreas flew back into the stream. Aurora looked down at the ripped map and jumped to her feet, outraged.

"Look what you did! Of all the people I had to get stuck with! I'm here with the biggest imbecile!"

"*I'M* the imbecile?!?" He cried out incredulously, standing knee deep in water, his clothes dripping wet. He stripped off his wet clothes until he was only standing in his boxers. "I hope you're happy now. You've probably been dying to see me take my pants off."

"Please, that is the *LAST* thing on my mind!"

He smoothed the clothes out on the grass to dry and held one half of the map in his hand. "You should have given me the paper like I asked you to."

"Fine! Here!" She threw the other half at him and shouted, "You figure it out!"

Aurora stormed off, kicking a stone that went sailing down a steep slope. She wandered further into the rainforest, zig-zagging her way through overgrown palm branches and entangling vines. It was so hot and she was so pissed off that she yearned to tear her thick, golden-brown hair out of her head. Of all the boys in Candlewick she had to get stuck with Boreas Stockington.

She would have preferred Jonathan, who was Boreas's older brother by two years. Jonathan had been her crush since the third grade. He was good looking, strong and his smile could melt a room. Of course he was dating the gorgeous yet malicious Hattie Pearlton, Aurora's arch nemesis, whose mission it was to make Aurora's high school life a living hell. Aurora sat on a boulder lost in her daydream. If Jonathan had heard the conch shell sound things would have been completely different. Instead she was stuck with his irritating brother.

"What are you two fighting about now?"

She whirled around to see Babs O'Hara, the seventeen-year-old Irish rebel who was, to Aurora's dismay, their appointed guide. The flap of Babs's dress was filled with hundreds of picked berries that matched her red lips. Aurora had secretly hoped she had been eaten by a crocodile while alone in the rainforest, but no such luck.

"Oh nothing, freaking Boreas just thinks that I got us lost. I swear Orion's Belt should be above us in the sky, unless I got the seasons mixed up or something."

Babs flipped her auburn hair that was tied back in a long ponytail.

"Don't ask me," she replied, chewing on a small berry. "I was stuck underwater in Plymouth Tartarus for the past ten years. I had forgotten what stars even looked like."

She handed over some berries that Aurora attempted to daintily eat, but ended up scarfing them down. The sweet juice was so appetizing and the taste lingered in her mouth, her stomach yearning for more. She licked her lips and wondered if she now had red lips like Babs did. Things like makeup were non-existent in the rainforest, so she would take all the help she could get.

"What did you expect?" Babs continued. "That the professor lived in a cottage and we could just go and knock on his door?"

Aurora stared at her mid-bite. That was exactly what she had thought.

Babs laughed and Aurora wished that Babs would choke on a berry.

"You don't know the Professor, he's as paranoid as men come. When I worked with him on the glass elevator in Plymouth Tartarus, it wasn't even easy to get a conversation out of him."

"How did you then?"

She shrugged, eating another berry. "I guess I just have a way with men… speaking of, what do you think about Boreas?"

"I wouldn't call Boreas a man." Aurora scoffed, then looked desperately for an escape route. The last thing she wanted to do was talk about Boreas with Babs.

Babs took another bite of berry and after swallowing asked, "You don't like him, right?"

A huge, spine-splitting laugh escaped from Aurora's mouth and a hyacinth macaw flew off its perch in fright.

Aurora regained her composure and said, "Absolutely not, we're just friends."

If they were even that.

"I mean, I didn't even talk to him until like the Independence Day of the Last Straw barbeque."

How friendly could you be in a few weeks? Except saving his life twice and him saving her life once... but who was counting?

"But he's totally not stable now anyway. I mean, he just found out his mom is alive after 10 years. How insane is that!"

Babs sucked on a berry and the juice poured down her chin as she shrugged, "he's a good kisser."

Aurora gave up. Boreas nearly got himself thrown into jail in Plymouth Tartarus over that kiss with Babs. A wave of jealousy swept over Aurora who never even had a first kiss. Spin the bottle in third grade with freckle-faced Marty Hutchinson did not count, since it was only on the cheek and anyway, she had to chase him around the yard 10 times until she caught him. Were all first kisses like that? Babs didn't have to chase Boreas around Plymouth Tartarus ten times until he kissed her. She probably didn't have to do anything but lean in, the way they did in the movies, all graceful and cunning.

Graceful, cunning and untrustworthy.

Aurora wondered what kind of a person Babs O'Hara was. She had kissed Boreas in Plymouth Tartarus even knowing that the law forbade an engaged woman from kissing another man. And yet she had kissed him. She claimed she was only trying to get out of her engagement with a man she didn't love, but Babs knew the law would punish Boreas and she let it happen anyway. Babs was someone who was going to get what she wanted at any cost, and now she was their guide to find the professor.

The thought made Aurora cringe, but she was the only one who felt that way. Boreas was enamored by her and Otus and Mrs. Xiomy were blinded with sympathy toward her. Aurora had to stay on her guard while reminding herself that this girl was Eileen's sister. Sweet, friendly Eileen who saw the good in everyone, but Eileen wasn't here in the jungle. Eileen had perished when the Common Good Army traced them to the ocean floor off the coast of Candlewick and bombed them. Aurora and about 300 others had narrowly managed to escape the destruction of Plymouth Tartarus, but too many others had died in that attack. Eileen as well as Babs's fiancé had died because of this mission and Aurora and Boreas were now entangled in a web of guilt.

"You didn't answer the question," Babs inquired again, gazing at Aurora as if wondering what she was thinking.

Aurora took a deep breath. She pictured Boreas and felt goosebumps prickle her arms. But she couldn't be feeling this way. She liked Jonathan. It had always been Jonathan.

She opened her mouth to say just that when something howled in the distance and both Aurora and Babs froze, utterly defenseless in that rainforest. Aurora thought she heard something rustle within the lush greenery around them and had a bad feeling, like someone or something was watching them.

"I think we should bring these berries to the others before we eat them all," Aurora said hurriedly, Babs immediately agreed, retracing their steps toward camp. Aurora wondered if Boreas was still putting the pieces of the map together, and she hoped he had his pants back on before Babs saw him.

✧ ✧ ✧

Aurora found Boreas exactly as she expected, still puzzled over the drawing of Orion and unfortunately still sitting there in his boxers, his naked legs causing Babs to giggle a little as they approached.

"Aren't your pants dry yet?" Aurora cried out, and went to feel the pants herself but they were still slightly damp.

Boreas turned mauve as Babs stared at him, grabbed his shirt and threw it over his chest.

Regaining his cool composure he said, "I am outnumbered at this chick fest. I need Otus to wake up since he is like 300 guys in one."

Aurora took the pieces of the map out of his hand and held them up again saying, "So where's the Professor, Mr. Know-it-all? I thought that you would have solved this by the time we returned."

"It's not my fault you ripped Orion's heart in two."

She was about to blast him with how it was his fault the page got ripped, when her lips froze mid-thought as she stared at the ripped page. Where the heart had been was in fact torn in two. A heart torn in two.

"What if it isn't a map after all? What if there's something I missed in the drawing?"

She held up the pieces together and there, sure enough, was a small dot that looked more like a speck than one of the other dots on the page. Aurora hadn't connected it to the initial drawing because it didn't have anything to do with the drawing of Orion. She now connected it and cried out in disbelief.

"There's another star here! A star not part of the Orion constellation. Does anyone know what this is?"

"It is the Antares!" Mrs. Xiomy adjusted her glasses, scrutinizing the page completely mystified. "The 15th brightest star in the sky. But that star isn't part of Orion. That star is part of the Scorpion."

"What?" Boreas exclaimed, putting his pants on.

"What if this star map has actually been a riddle all along," Aurora speculated excitedly. "If I remember correctly, the Greek myth says that the Scorpion chases Orion across the heavens because it's the Scorpion's sting that can poison Orion and defeat him. What if Orion symbolizes the Professor, and we are the Scorpion chasing the Professor across the country in order to find him?"

"Sounds like a load of crap to me," Boreas laughed, unconvinced.

"Yet, it does sound like something the Professor would think of," Babs chimed in, eying the drawing curiously. "And, no offense, but a map of Orion did sound way too easy."

"So wait...we are now the Scorpion?" Boreas asked, wrapping his head around this concept. "And this star Antares is where the Professor is?"

Aurora gave Boreas a huge hug and nearly kissed him, "Boreas, thank you for ripping the map!"

He scratched his head, still completely puzzled. "Wait...did you just thank me?"

"But it still doesn't help us," Mrs. Xiomy interrupted. "If Orion's Belt is supposed to be here, shouldn't the Scorpion constellation be here too?"

Aurora exclaimed. "I gotta wake Otus. Maybe he will know where we can find the Scorpion, and the star Antares."

Aurora jumped onto Otus's stomach; the rumbling from his snoring felt like an earthquake. "Otus, wake up!" She yelled. A loud snore erupted and then he was startled out of his slumber. Otus's big green eyes popped open and he let out a huge yawn that made Aurora stumble, only by clinging onto his blue overalls did she prevent herself from tumbling down. He grabbed her and sat up. He stretched his massive arms into the air and nearly knocked over a nest of bright red and yellow toucans with his spare hand. Startled, they nearly collided with each other in mid-flight. Aurora laughed at this spectacle. Otus was not a threatening giant; he was a peaceful and almost child-like one. According to Mrs. Xiomy, his features resembled an oversized Cabbage Patch Kid, with his curly hazelnut hair, round nose and chubby pink cheeks. He had ears that he could wiggle when he was thinking and he was a speed reader. Aurora had seen him read a 300 page book in less than a minute.

"What's all the commotion?" he finally asked, resting Aurora on the top of his head.

She leaned down next to his ear, saying, "Otus, we figured out that the star map is actually a riddle."

"All thanks to me," Boreas replied haughtily.

Just then something whirled in the air and burst open, inches from Otus's feet. Gas oozed out of the canister and Aurora screamed to the others to hold their breath, recognizing the substance being emitted as tear gas. More canisters exploded near the group. Otus attempted to kick some back toward the direction of where they were coming from, but more exploded left and right. Aurora's eyes were stinging and it felt like she couldn't breathe, choking and gagging on the gas. She tried to scream to the others to head toward her voice, toward Otus to get them out of this place, but her voice was paralyzed and only coughing fits ensued. Through the cloudy fog she spotted shadows, no...people, dressed in camouflage, wearing gas masks approaching them from all directions out of the woods like swarms of mosquitos. She spotted Boreas, also in coughing fits, swinging at one of the shadows, making contact. The shadow lurched backwards slightly and then punched Boreas in the stomach. Aurora felt utterly defenseless as Boreas was held down on the ground, and Babs was grabbed by another man with big muscular arms. Aurora slid down to the ground and was about to run to them, to do something, to help then, when something hard and metal and menacing was dug against her temple. A woman's voice whispered in her ear, "Resist and we will kill you."

The Common Good had found them.

Chapter 2

The Incan Trail

Aurora didn't know how long they had been walking. She still felt herself wheezing with each step, but at least she could breathe more naturally now that the gas was out of her lungs. Chains secured her wrists together and she was forced in line with the others. They had even found chains large enough to secure Otus's ankles and wrists and a majority of the guards had their guns focused on him. These guards did not wear the Common Good uniform of indigo and orange, which Aurora thought odd, but uniforms could be different down here in the rain forest. She couldn't believe that at the very instant they figured out the riddle to the professor's whereabouts, their entire mission was jeopardized. How were they going to get out of this mess? She turned around and met Boreas's gaze. It felt like just yesterday that they had been arrested by the Inspector and the

Common Good Army and thrown into Candlewick Prison. However, this time they didn't have Aurora's father to help them escape. They were on their own.

"Where are you taking us?" Mrs. Xiomy shouted, the only one of the group who hadn't lost the strength to fight against their captors.

"You'll soon find out," one of the guards with a bald head and tired brown eyes growled, pushing her along. They splashed knee-deep in mud and sludge as they continued through the Amazon. They only stopped briefly at a stream for some water to quench their thirst and for the guards to refill their canteens. It seemed like the guards were nervous as they continually stared up into the sky as if expecting to see patrolling Common Good planes.

Guarding them was a female guard named Molina who sat down next to Aurora, placed her gun on her lap and rinsed her face with water. She turned to Aurora and said, "I have never seen anything like him."

Aurora turned toward Otus, and knew it was true. All the guards were staring at him in awe. Aurora shrugged, "It's not every day you see a 30-foot giant."

"I didn't believe it when Romero spotted you on his radar. You should be lucky we found you before the Common Good."

Aurora nearly passed out. "I thought you were the Common Good."

The female guard laughed, "You thought…we were…"

Molina laughed and called out to her commanding officer, "Romero! They think we're working with the Inspector!"

Romero laughed hysterically, bent over so that his bald head gleamed at Aurora.

"Do we look like Common Good scum?" he scoffed.

"Then what the hell do you want with us?" Boreas called out.

Romero eyed his watch and said, "Just taking orders, kid. Now let's hurry, we're heading into the Andes and I don't like the look of those clouds."

Mrs. Xiomy's jaw dropped as she said incredulously, "You can't expect us to make that trek chained like this."

"What are you talking about?" Babs asked.

She pointed her chains upwards towards a path leading high into the Andes Mountains.

"Please say that is not where we're going," Boreas asked, straining his neck upwards toward the top of the mountain.

Romero smiled brightly, "Yep. Up the Incan trail we go. Get moving."

Aurora whispered to Mrs. Xiomy, "Where does it lead to?"

Mrs. Xiomy's eyes were wide with fear, "Machu Picchu."

Molina lifted Aurora roughly to her feet and Aurora felt something soft in her hand. When she opened her palm, a plantain was in it. She quickly scarfed it down before Romero could see. The sweet banana-like taste was invigorating as she chewed heartily, giving her strength again.

Molina whispered, "Don't worry. I know you're not the enemy. You just have to convince the IDEAL."

"The IDEAL?" Aurora cried out, startled. "The IDEAL *is* the Common Good!"

She looked at Aurora like she was a naïve child. "Don't believe everything you hear."

The temperature dropped as they headed up into the Andes Mountains, the rainforest below looking smaller and smaller as they ascended upward toward the gray clouds. Romero was right about the clouds. Aurora felt a drop graze her cheek and then another as rain began to pour on them, making their path slippery and treacherous, but Romero called out that they couldn't stop; that it wasn't safe. She felt cold, damp and muddy from head to toe and had to claw her way up the mountain at times when her sneakers started to slide backwards.

When the guards stopped to analyze the steep pathway, Boreas snuck close to Aurora. He smelled of sweat, and rain and mud were streaked all over his face apart from hazel eyes that gazed intently into hers. He whispered urgently, "What do we do?"

"The guard told me they are leading us to the IDEAL."

Boreas eyed her like she was crazy. "What? The IDEAL is here in the middle of nowhere? I don't believe it."

"We have no idea who or where the IDEAL is. We have never seen him. The Inspector just speaks for him, but maybe he is out here, hidden away."

"But then why did that jerk Romero say they don't work for the Common Good?"

Aurora shook her head, not having any answers. "I don't know. But it's not like we can make a run for it," Aurora raised her chained wrists, the iron digging into her chaffed skin. "Besides, maybe they don't know about the prophecy. Maybe we can still get out of this alive."

Boreas only said, "Maybe," then quickly hopped back to his position in line when the guards began turning around.

"It is steep and treacherous, but better than waiting for the Common Good to spot us," Romero called out, as rain streamed down his tanned face. "Look out for mud slides. If you start feeling lightheaded or sick that's due to the change in elevation. It could kill you but there's no turning back, so you better hope your body adjusts quickly."

Easier said than done, Aurora thought, as they headed up the steep stone trail. The pathway was badly maintained with over-grown stumps and roots. The elevation was affecting Aurora's breathing, causing her to take shorter breaths and her stomach to churn, but she ignored the symptoms. Like Romero said, there was no turning back. It was a slippery slope and she tried not to look down. Mrs. Xiomy's foot slipped and she got caught in a mudslide, her body slid down the slope and her leg banged against a tree stump. She was about to tumble off the cliff when Otus, chained and bound, reached out and grabbed her in his hand. He placed her carefully onto the ground as the guards raced toward them, guns drawn, threatening to shoot.

"He just saved her life," Aurora screamed out. "Don't shoot him!"

Mrs. Xiomy's leg was hurt and she struggled to her feet but then dropped back onto the mud, unable to move another muscle.

"If you are going to kill us anyway, just kill me now."

Romero stuck a gun against her left pupil but Otus's voice boomed over everyone, nearly knocking them off their feet with a shout of "NO!" "I will carry her in my pocket; no violence." Romero looked up at the gigantic face of Otus, confused by his kind gesture. He had assumed Otus was some monstrous beast looking to eat them, or something. Since Mrs. Xiomy was slowing them down, he finally consented, but Babs, Boreas and Aurora had to continue to climb on their own.

"And don't try anything funny or heroic, giant, or else you'll be attending your other friend's funerals."

"What's a funeral?" he asked, curiously. Romero looked up at him like he had three heads and Molina and the other guards laughed out loud.

"I don't think your threat worked like it was supposed to, Romero," Molina jabbed at her superior officer.

Romero turned beet red and then ordered everyone to shut up and keep moving.

"He can be such an egocentric jerk sometimes," Molina whispered to Aurora.

The wind was pounding on them like a relentless bully, and at this point they were high up in the Andes Mountains. Aurora couldn't see the sun through the gray clouds as it was nearly nightfall. Aurora took a deep breath and risked a glimpse at the 100 foot drop below her. Her feet were soggy and the poncho she was wearing was not enough to stop her entire body from shivering in cold. Her fingers were so numb that she had a difficult time trying to clutch onto the next stone step. Exhaustion was kicking in and she didn't know how much further she could climb. She turned around in time to see Babs nearly collapse. Boreas ran to Babs, ignoring the guards, saying that he would carry her the rest of the way. He put her chained wrists around his neck and lifted her small, fragile body onto his strong back. They continued to climb, Molina put her gun in its holster to help Boreas and Babs, fearing that Boreas would fall backwards down the slippery slope.

"Romero...they need to rest," Molina called out. Some of the other soldiers nodded in agreement.

Romero pointed up into the skies. "We are completely exposed. We cannot stop for camp."

"I doubt that the IDEAL will be pleased if you end up killing them."

Thunder roared, as if in response to Molina's statement. Romero eyed the young travelers, especially Babs, who was suffering from altitude sickness.

"We can stop there," Mrs. Xiomy shouted from Otus's pocket. Everyone turned and straining their eyes through the trees and rain they could make out what appeared to be an Incan ruin.

"It's Choquequirao," Mrs. Xiomy screamed down. "Its name means "Golden Cradle" and it is known as the sister site of Machu Picchu."

"Fine," Romero relented, feeling backed into a corner. "Only until the Sacred Hour, then we continue to Machu Picchu."

Another crash of thunder sounded, followed by a flash of lightning that was a little too close to Otus's head for comfort. They all hustled as quickly as they could toward Choquequirao. These ruins were originally built in the 15th century, consisting of stone buildings arranged around a central plaza, situated among steep mountain ridges that overlooked foamy and tumultuous whitewater rivers. When they were safely inside the citadel, Aurora turned and beheld through the gray clouds, shadows of the Andes peaks that reached up into the sky like New York City skyscrapers.

Romero ordered the men to surround the citadel and announced that he would radio into headquarters to let them know where they are. He then turned to the prisoners and shouted, "Don't you dare try anything funny and be sure to keep those detractors on your wrists. These ruins are not 100% safe from Inspector Herald's patrol planes but the detractors will keep you off their radar."

Molina handed them all water from her canteen and Aurora drank heavily. Babs rested her head against Boreas's shoulder and Mrs. Xiomy elevated her leg on one of the stone walls.

Once Molina left, Aurora and the others huddled together in the darkness. It was still unbearably cold and they had no materials and couldn't risk building a fire.

Boreas, his teeth chattering, whispered, "Otus, we must get out of here tonight, at the Sacred Hour."

Otus's stomach grumbled, not having eaten in two days. Aurora's stomach reciprocated.

"It's too risky," Mrs. Xiomy said. "I want to punch that guy Romero in the face, but I can tell when someone's afraid, and he sure is. Inspector Herald's men are out there. If Otus takes off, they will be able to pick him up on their satellite."

"You don't know that for sure," Boreas cried out, pacing back and forth, vapor escaping from his mouth. He threw off his wet poncho and then took a seat again besides Babs.

"If they're leading us to the IDEAL then we're all sunk anyway," Babs said slowly.

Aurora looked up into Otus's face and asked, "What do you say, Otus?"

Otus plopped himself down, the ancient walls shaking. "I think we should play a game."

"A game!" Mrs. Xiomy laughed, trying to stay warm as the rain continued to pour outside of their shelter. "Only you, Otus, would suggest a game at a time like this."

"How about guess the arachnid?"

He pointed to a spider inching its way up the far left wall, illuminated by a flash of lightning.

Aurora shrieked and buried her face in her hands. All of a sudden she felt something crawling on her back. She shrieked again, jumped up, and brushed herself off frantically. The others laughed uncontrollably. Boreas held up his hands in an itsy bitsy spider motion and she felt so humiliated. "Boreas, that wasn't funny."

She sat down, banging against him a little too hard and he immediately stopped laughing.

Otus was more curious than a child, wanting to know everything about human history. Aurora and Mrs. Xiomy filled his mind with knowledge as the night dragged on.

They were about to go to sleep when Otus asked, "Do any of you know what a bedtime story is?"

Mrs. Xiomy shook her head. Boreas didn't even respond. Babs leaned against Boreas and put her head on his shoulder. "I do, but I've never been told one."

Aurora leaned against Boreas's back, feeling his gentle breathing as if he were asleep, but she could tell that he was listening. She looked up at Otus who was fidgeting with a piece of wood and a knife, carving what appeared to be a horse.

Aurora cleared her throat and her voice echoed through the night.

"There once was a young girl named Indigo. She was all alone in the great blue sky looking down at the world from above. She was seen during the day but no one could see her at night. She thought that she must not be beautiful because, if she was, she felt that the moon would fall in love with her. So she decided to go on an adventure to search the rest of the sky for others more beautiful than she was to help her to become more appealing to the moon. Only with their help, she believed, would the moon notice her.

Indigo came across Red that was fierce, fiery and radiant and her heart palpitated when she saw her. Red gazed down at Indigo and smiled. 'Once I stand beside you, the moon will of course fall in love with you. He just can't see you now because you blend in with the darkness of the night; but with me by your side, how can he not gaze upon you?'

Indigo was happy to have found Red, but worried that it wasn't enough. She then found Yellow and Orange who were wholesome, sweet and everything warm like the sun. She asked them if they would come with her and Yellow agreed saying, 'With me by your side, how could the moon resist you? I am the color of the moon.' And Orange agreed saying, 'I am the color of the sun. With me you will be so beautiful that the moon could not help but fall in love with you.'

Along the way they bumped into Green. Indigo asked her to come with her and Green said, 'I am the color of the earth being born and of mother nature itself. The moon looks down upon my beauty with love every night. He will surely love you with me by your side.'

Last but not least they found the sisters, Blue and Violet; both were so lovely that Indigo begged that they would come with her too. Blue sighed and agreed, saying that she was the color of the sky that housed the moon. Violet interrupted her sister, singing, 'I am more than happy to come along since what is more beautiful than the Violet flower? The moon will love you forever and ever with us by your side.'

So Indigo brought Red, Orange, Yellow, Green, Blue and Violet back home with her and they waited together for the moon to show its face at night. Surely with all the colors together, the moon would realize just how beautiful she was! Night fell and the moon shone out over the world while the colors were lined up together, waiting for the moon to fall in love. They waited and waited, but the moon didn't see them amidst the darkness of the sky. Indigo realized that all of her efforts were in vain and cried, making it rain over the earth that night. But then something amazing happened! Her teardrops caused the clouds in the sky to cry too as they felt her pain over the moon not being able to see her. It rained and rained and the clouds began to disperse, allowing a ray of sunlight to shine through in the early dawn, right as the moon was falling asleep. He looked up, saw Indigo and her sisters high up in the sky and smiled at their beauty before fully resting, just as the sun awoke over the earth.

Indigo knew finally that the moon saw her as beautiful. She now waits eternally for the rain to subside for the moon to see her again; for with her sisters by her side, the moon will always be able to find her in the sky."

The rain had stopped and Otus was snoring loudly. Mrs. Xiomy and Babs had also fallen asleep. Babs's head was still nestled on Boreas's shoulder.

Just when she thought everyone had fallen asleep, Boreas let out a huge yawn, "Thanks for the girly story."

She sighed, closing her eyes and leaning against his back. "Glad you liked it."

The rain had stopped and the crickets were playing their strings, putting her in a sleep induced trance. She yawned, but quickly snapped herself awake, whispering, "Boreas, are you scared?"

"Of the IDEAL? If he's anything like Inspector Herald, then yes."

She took a deep breath. "I wonder what he looks like..."

Both of their hands were touching, as they sat back to back. His fingers found hers and gave them a comforting squeeze, "I guess we'll find out soon enough."

She held onto his hand, not letting go as she let dreams overtake her. She pictured herself in the sky beside the other colors of the rainbow, except in her dream the moon was the face of the Inspector. She felt her body go tense as he watched her. She tried to hide from his omniscient gaze but there were no clouds to shield her. He seemed to be moving closer to her, trying to engulf her in darkness when she awoke with a start, letting out a frightened gasp.

"Shhh."

It was Boreas.

"There are planes overhead," he whispered. Through one of the citadel openings they spotted a Common Good plane flying above with the indigo and orange flag mounted on the planes' sides. The planes were circling and Aurora felt her heart in her mouth. She desperately hoped that they hadn't been detected.

"Romero was right," she said in a fearful whisper.

"I hope these makeshift detractors work."

They were frozen in silence for what felt like hours until the planes moved on, heading due south. Aurora sighed in relief and just then Romero and Molina hurried inside their shelter.

"Get up. All of you. We need to move and we need to move now."

Aurora turned to Molina and said, "Do you think they will come back?"

Molina's face was pale and she clutched onto her gun, her knuckles turned white. "I think the best thing to do is get to Machu Picchu. There we will be safe."

The rain had finally let up and the clouds dispersed, the moon shining brightly as if guiding them the rest of the way toward their destination. Stars speckled the sky like sparkling fireflies and if Aurora wasn't fearful that each of those bright stars could be a Common Good patrol plane she could have actually enjoyed their beauty. She made a wish on the stars, like her father had taught her, hoping for a safe journey. She then made a separate wish hoping the IDEAL wouldn't kill them on sight.

Days passed by as they continued their arduous climb upwards into the Andes Mountains. When Aurora thought she couldn't walk any further, the path ended and before Aurora stood one of the most breathtaking sites she had ever witnessed with her own eyes. Through the early morning mist with the beautiful, lush green Andes mountains standing as the backdrop, stood a towering stone fortress; high gray walls lined the pathway and before them was a magnificent temple standing taller than Otus. As they stepped through the mist, the sun shone brightly overhead, streaming light across these ancient Incan ruins. Aurora could almost hear whispers of the past, of a people whose spirits still lived within these hallowed walls. They had reached Machu Picchu.

"Beautiful, isn't it?" Molina asked, watching Aurora's expression.

"Just to see this makes the entire journey worth it."

Molina laughed, "I thought the saying was it's not the destination but the journey that matters."

Aurora shook her head, "The person who wrote that must never have experienced Machu Picchu."

They followed Molina and couldn't believe that there were *MORE* steps they had to climb.

"You've got to be kidding me," Boreas whined, looking up the large steps, spaced at least 2 feet apart from each other, "Where's the elevator when you need it?"

Aurora's legs were rebelling but she forced them up the large steps advancing toward this incredible temple that had stood for thousands of years. They passed what looked like metal rods surrounding a perimeter and once inside the guards breathed a sigh of relief.

"What are those things?" Aurora asked, bewildered.

"Those distort the Common Good's tracking surveillance. This whole area is safe and off the grid thanks to the IDEAL's knowledge of the Inspector's equipment. It's a similar technology to the detractor bracelets, but much stronger."

They then walked into The Temple du Soleil, *The Temple of the Sun*, Aurora translated, mystified at why they were led to this place of all places. It was such an impressive structure with polished dry-stone walls and the dawn mist lifting above the sacred structure. The temple and surrounding architecture was fitted into the form of the mountains.

"Just in time," a voice echoed from the top of the temple. Looking through a telescope in what appeared to be an observatory tower was a very slim man in his early forties with prematurely white hair and dark sunglasses over his eyes. Very pale skin, an albino. Just then he pointed up into the sky where a dark shadow was beginning to make its way across the sun, engulfing it inch by inch. Everyone looked up, but Aurora quickly turned her gaze away, her mother always telling her not to look into the sun directly during a solar eclipse.

"Did you know," the eerily monotone voice echoed throughout the temple, "Solar eclipses used to trouble the Incan people, and they would even resort to human sacrifice as a part of their ritual to appease the sun god, Inti. They didn't understand why their god was angry with them, because to lose the sun, the source of their crop, their livelihood…well, they were willing to do anything to make the gods happy with them again."

The sun was now completely hidden by the shadow of the moon. There was complete darkness in the temple as the man started clapping; a 180 degree change in mood from the morbid lecture a few moments before. "Bravo!" he cried out completely animated, "To think that people were so afraid of something that we today know is nothing more than the moon passing between the sun and the earth. Incredible, isn't it?"

He removed his sunglasses to reveal red piercing eyes looking intently at them like a demon eyeing its prey.

"And then, like magic, it reappears again, and a life was wasted. By the wrath of a god? No. By the wrath of men. Those men and women were victims of nothing more than ignorance and fear."

The shadow had now begun to vanish, allowing the majestic sunlight to stream down upon them again. The sun was restored to its proper glory.

"Who the hell are you?" Boreas shouted, not caring to listen to the ranting of this madman.

The albino stood at the top of the stairs as the sunrays hit him, illuminating him like he was a divine presence in that temple of ancient history. "Just a man who knows about sacrifice. I think you have heard of me. I am the IDEAL."

"You're the IDEAL?" Boreas chuckled, "No offense but I was expecting someone a little, I don't know...less insane!"

The IDEAL laughed uproariously at the insult and Aurora turned to see Mrs. Xiomy trying to break out of her chains, the rage evident on her face.

"If you are the IDEAL, then you are a murderer!"

"Hello Rana Xiomy," he said, gazing at her, trying to fake sympathy, "I truly am sorry about your husband, David."

"No you're not!" She shouted, spitting in his face. He didn't even try to wipe it off. "You gave the order to Inspector Herald to execute my husband, after everything I did to try to save his life. I gave up protestors, my friends, to save him and instead you and Herald murdered him. You killed an innocent man in cold blood."

"No one said I was a saint," he bowed, "Besides, it was the Common Good that executed him. I am just the real man behind the IDEAL persona. There is no real IDEAL. Never was. It was something I thought up to give people something to believe in so they would flock to us out of fear. Fear is a valuable weapon, when used correctly. Hitler, Stalin, some of the great masterminds knew how to make fear look so enticing. Like them, we were here to protect, to save and to raise the superior race and country. Isn't that what Herald and I did? Didn't we accomplish that? The country is flourishing and thriving."

"Then why are you hiding away here in the rainforest?" Aurora shouted, surprised at her own courage.

He smiled at her, "I knew the Goddess of Dawn would be beautiful, but brains too...I am impressed."

Aurora's mouth hung open, "You know about the prophecy?"

"We all heard David preach about it right before he died; about a giant amongst men to save the people from a catastrophic disaster. And here is a giant, in the temple of the sun god. How are you?"

Otus held out his chained hand to shake his hand, oblivious to the fact that this man was dangerous.

Mrs. Xiomy shouted, "Do NOT shake his hand."

"I am not here to make enemies," Otus said, "I extend my hand as a gesture of friendship."

The IDEAL looked taken aback by the giant's friendly character. He held out his hand gratefully and his little hand was enveloped by Otus's, like the moon engulfing the sun just minutes before and then releasing the light; brighter and stronger.

He looked into Otus's eyes and said slowly, "I have seen so much darkness."

He then turned, and walked onto the altar as if he felt safer being off the ground. "If it makes you feel any better, Rana, I thought that David Xiomy died in vain. He was a good person. Like my wife was. She died when the towers of freedom fell, murdered by religious extremists."

"An eye for an eye doesn't make me feel better," Mrs. Xiomy snapped, her amethyst eyes were deadly, aimed at the IDEAL like they could shoot bullets.

The IDEAL smirked, "I can see why you would view it as revenge, but I prefer to think of it as justice. When I met Herald we vowed we would get justice. The best way to stop this from happening ever again was to ban religion entirely. That's what we vowed to accomplish, but it wasn't until David was executed that I realized I had killed an innocent man. I had become what I had been fighting against."

He turned to Mrs. Xiomy and said, "I understand your loss and your pain and I know you will never forgive me. But I hope one day I can find peace for murdering your husband. I just don't know how."

"Well for starters, why don't you let us go," Boreas said, holding out his chained hands that rattled as he moved them.

Romero and Molina both looked uneasy with that proposition.

"I don't think that would be wise." Romero said, pointing to Otus.

The IDEAL smiled at Boreas, "I like your attempt at negotiation, but I have to think about the safety of my people. I brought you here, against my better judgment, to keep you safe. The Common Good Army saw you on the radar screen, just as I did, and I knew that they would be coming after you in the Amazon."

"Why capture us then?" Babs cried out. "Why not just tell us that you wanted our help?"

"Well, you have a 30-foot giant and we had no idea how dangerous he was. Or any of you. Especially if you had your powers, which I am assuming you don't, otherwise you're hiding them very well."

Boreas laughed. "What do you think we are? Superheroes?"

"You're here to save the world, aren't you?"

Boreas bit his lip, avoiding looking the IDEAL in the eye. It was then that the IDEAL stopped, and grabbed Boreas's face, "Who are you?"

Boreas smirked. "If you're the IDEAL, then I'm the God of the North Wind. I can play the alias game too."

The IDEAL glanced at the conch shell around Boreas's neck, the orange interior glowing. He picked it up and rested it in his palm curiously.

"Who gave this to you?" he asked tentatively.

Boreas smiled and turned to the others amused. "Everyone, did you hear? The IDEAL has spoken!"

Molina snickered at Boreas's attack on the Common Good slogan. The IDEAL pretended not to hear as he looked hard at Boreas. Then, like he was hit by a spark of recognition, the IDEAL let go of the conch shell, took out a key and unlocked the chain binding Boreas's wrists. The chains fell and clanked against the ground. Boreas stood there free, unsure what to do.

The IDEAL observed the teen's uncertainty with a smirk. "We both would have killed each other by now, Boreas Stockington, if we wanted to, so I think we can trust each other. I am Max Radar, but you can call me Radar."

Boreas clutched his wrist, getting circulation back again.

"And just for the record," Radar added. "I didn't write the slogan *The IDEAL has Spoken*, but it has a nice ring to it. I think I still have some coffee mugs with that slogan engraved on them if you're interested."

Boreas jumped as Radar gave him an over-enthusiastic pat on the back. Radar then ordered the guards to release the others at once.

Molina excitedly took out the key and unlocked Aurora's chains. "Wow, the IDEAL is in a rare good mood," she smiled, "I knew we were all on the same team."

The guards released Otus but jumped back, afraid he would stomp on them.

Otus merely laughed, "I'm not like the giants in those books you read," but then added with a sly smile, "Unless you hurt my friends."

Babs asked someone for a bandage to wrap Mrs. Xiomy's leg. Immediately a medic was summoned with a medical kit and supplies. Mrs. Xiomy hollered that she would not accept any help from the IDEAL, but Babs told the medic to ignore her and nurse the wound so they led her to a room that would allow her to rest more comfortably.

Molina whispered something to Radar, whose red eyes gleamed and they asked Aurora and Otus if they wanted a quick tour of the grounds. Aurora, though feeling famished and exhausted, was excited to see the rest of Machu Picchu.

She ran to Boreas and Babs, who were huddled by one of the windows looking out at the picturesque view. She said, "I'm going to get a tour. You want to come?"

Boreas looked at her like she had lost her mind, "You're not going anywhere alone with the IDEAL...Radar, or whatever his real name is."

Aurora looked at him aghast, shocked at this protective side of Boreas. "I won't be alone. I'll be with Otus."

"And you'll be with Radar. I still don't trust him. I don't understand why he released me as soon as he saw Fawn's conch shell."

Babs narrowed her eyes, "I fear he knows that Boreas is her son. He may try to use us to get to her at Plymouth Incarnate."

Aurora felt queasy, she had not thought of that scenario. "We don't know that for sure," she replied. They didn't have any chains but they were still at the mercy of the IDEAL and his army.

"We should leave tonight at the Sacred Hour," he said, determined. "We can get into Otus's pocket and take off into the night before they can stop us."

"What if someone is able to track us out there?" Aurora asked, concerned. "They found us. What makes you think it won't be Inspector Herald next time?"

"We were out there for two weeks," Babs interrupted while trying to comb the mud out of her hair with her fingers. "We saw no sign of the Common Good or the Inspector's planes before the night we were captured. I say we take our chances and find the star Antares, and the Professor." Her fingers got stuck in her hair. She cried out in aggravation. "There's mud caked into my hair. I need a shower or a bath or something before we go back out into the wilderness again."

Aurora looked down and grimaced. She looked like she was in one of those mud spas that her mother frequented. She thought her mom would be proud that she was working on her complexion. Aurora agreed with Babs that they looked like hell, so she asked Molina if there was a place where they could clean off and change before the tour. Molina laughed down at Aurora from her impressive 6 feet in height. She removed her cap and long black curly hair trickled down her shoulders. "Believe me; I need a wash before our tour too. And deodorant is a thing that is so rare nowadays. I think Romero should get a biohazard sticker stuck on him."

"Tell me about it," Aurora laughed, recalling how badly the officer had smelled as they trekked through the rainforest.

Aurora and Babs followed Molina down the long flight of steps and into a sector with a row of houses overlooking a slope that had a peripheral view of the majestic Andes Mountains. Lush green forests dotted the slope of the mountain and far below her the water of the Urubamba River sparkled in the sun. Aurora couldn't believe how beautiful this was, yet a part of her wished she were back home in Candlewick where it was the Atlantic Ocean water sparkling and she would be walking along the beach with her parents on a sunny day like this.

She could not return to Candlewick, she reminded herself for the millionth time. It was no longer her home and her parents could be in jail for all she knew. Maybe the IDEAL would know if her parents were safe. That is, if they could trust him.

She went into Molina's house where she was standing in a trapezoidal-shaped room.

Molina said with pride, "Incan Ñustas or princesses lived here. I guess that's me now, though I am far from being a princess."

To their excitement, Molina showed them a separate bathroom with a shower, well, basically a hose attached to the ceiling with slits in the tile floor that acted as a drain, but it worked! Molina explained that there was no water source in Machu Picchu, however, in order for the Incan people to have built this palace for the Incan Emperor Pachacuti in the year 1450, the Incan people had to develop an irrigation system, an earlier form of plumbing. They built a canal to route water from a spring about 2,000 meters away from Machu Picchu where it feeds into 16 fountains, known today as the Stairway of Fountains. The water collects in a stone basin in the floor of the fountain, then enters a circular drain that delivers it through another channel for the next fountain.

"We added pipes to feed into our homes in order to have some modern conveniences, like a shower," she said, lifting her hands up to the shower with a huge smile plastered on her face. "But all in all, what the Incan people accomplished was a great achievement in civil engineering."

Babs, who couldn't wait to get the mud out of her hair, volunteered to shower first.

Aurora was fine with that since she was so in awe of Molina's house as artifacts that should be locked away in a museum were being used in her everyday life, like ancient pottery.

"This is incredible," Aurora said, picking up one of the vases and admiring the pictures on the clay pottery, "My father would be amazed at this."

"Is he a big history buff?"

Aurora nodded. "We both are. Every morning while eating breakfast he would read through a pile of history magazines. Though illegal, he had them stored in our home and would quiz me on certain historical facts."

Molina smiled, starting to unlace her boots. "Sounds like a good father."

Aurora asked, "What is your story? How did you end up with the IDEAL?"

Molina kicked off her boots, relieved, and then grabbed two papayas and tossed one of them to Aurora. Molina started peeling the outer layer of the fruit and said, "Not much to tell. Romero and I are from this area, lived in the town of Cusco at the bottom of the Andes Mountains. Once we were taken over by The United States of the Common Good, I joined The Common Good Army and believed in the cause, at the time. It was like we had won the battle but didn't really understand the war. It wasn't until we started seeing our friends and family vanishing that we understood that the Inspector would keep power with force, not love or peace.

Radar hit a breaking point. I don't think he ever got over the death of IMAM, well to you, David Xiomy. Radar tried to come clean about inventing the IDEAL persona to the public. He scheduled a press conference, but as soon as Inspector Herald heard about Radar's plans and knew that he would jeopardize all that Herald had worked for, he decided that Radar had to be stopped. He ordered Romero and myself to kill Radar, but we didn't. We knew that with the IDEAL, we had a chance to defeat Herald so Romero and I helped Radar escape. We came here to Machu Picchu and we've been building up our army ever since. We've been here now for five years or so. Not a bad place to hide out, huh?"

So Fawn and her people were not the only ones who were protesting or fighting the regime. Aurora wondered how many others were out there. If only they could all mobilize and band together, but that sounded impossible.

Babs came out of the restroom, looking like her old self in a blue hoodie and jeans. Her long hair was mud free and her freckles were visible on cheeks that were no longer covered in dirt. Aurora went in, closed the door, stripped off her dirty clothes and let the cool water cleanse her body. She watched the dirt and mud rinse off of her and down the drain in the floor. She felt so clean and rejuvenated, but the feelings dissipated as soon as she looked at herself in the mirror. Her eyes focused on the body fat, and how her body was not proportioned like the other girls, like Babs and even Molina though she was a little older. She quickly dug into her schoolbag and took out clean clothes. She covered her body with her sports bra, jeans and a loose black sweatshirt. After everything she had been through, she still looked at herself in the mirror and thought, *Is that really me?* The Goddess of Dawn should not look like this. A goddess should be beautiful.

Radar had called her beautiful earlier. Of course, he was a man who had helped manipulate the entire country's way of thinking. His words didn't mean much. *If only Boreas could think that way about her.*

She quickly removed that thought from her mind. *Get a grip*, she scolded herself. What did it matter if Boreas thought she was beautiful? It was Jonathan she cared about; Jonathan who was safely tucked away back in Candlewick, where she should be right now. Not stuck in this majestic wonder that didn't feel real, fleeing from Common Good patrol planes and being at the mercy of the second most feared man in the country. She should be in High School getting ready for 11th grade and thinking the worst thing in the world was dealing with Hattie Pearlton. She would prefer Hattie now   wow, she never thought she would say that. Hattie was cruel. She had humiliated Aurora at the spring formal dance by throwing fruit punch in her face. Hattie had thrown the drink in her face in front of Jonathan and everyone had laughed.

Yet it was Boreas, not Jonathan, who had been the one to help her that night, distracting the crowd by singing into a microphone. They hadn't even been friends at the time, and yet he helped her.

She opened the bathroom door and came out holding the dirty clothes outstretched in her hands with her schoolbag on her back. After Molina showered, they took their clothes down to the washing room, where some soldiers were already doing their laundry in a long wash bin. Aurora dunked her clothes in the basin, scrubbing them with soap and water. Babs said this was even worse than Plymouth Tartarus. "At least in Plymouth Tartarus, we had washing machines. I remember when the Professor helped install the first one," she said reminiscing, "It made all of our lives so much easier and it was fun hiding behind it when playing hide and go seek."

"I miss playing that game," Aurora said, scrubbing madly at the mud stains in her shirt. "I used to play with my friend Mary back in Candlewick when we were kids. She figured out all my hiding places in like 2 minutes. Did you play with Eileen?"

At the mention of her sister's name, Babs went quiet. "I think these are done," she said abruptly, squeezing the water out of the fabric, water flowing from her hands like a waterfall.

Aurora wanted to run after her, to apologize for bringing up her sister, Eileen. It was still too hard for Babs to talk about Eileen; she seemed to almost be pretending that Eileen was safe in Plymouth Tartarus, not dead at the bottom of the Atlantic Ocean. Aurora wanted to tell Babs that, for some reason, she still felt Eileen's presence; even here below the equator, high in the mountains, she felt Eileen was with her. She grabbed the cross that dangled around her neck, tucked beneath her shirt, and massaged her fingers over the gold form. It made her feel safe; strange that a piece of jewelry could do that.

Babs poked her head back into the washing room, calm now and called out with a smile, "Come on, Aurora. I know another game I used to play, let's race."

Aurora didn't give it a second thought. She ran after Babs and together they raced up the steep staircase toward the Room of the Three Windows. They both reached the last step at the same time. At that moment, winded and hearts pounding, they laughed with all the energy they had left. At that moment, they felt like normal teenagers.

Chapter 3

Room of the Three Windows

A urora and Babs were still laughing when they walked into the silent sanctuary of the Room of the Three Windows. The three windows were trapezoidal in shape and lined up side by side. The room consisted of only three walls on a rectangular base, covered by a roof made of adobe bricks, built from large blocks of solid rock carved in polygonal shapes. The roof was supported by a column of stone. Engravings in the carved stone represented the three levels where the Incan civilization divided the Andean world: the sky or spirituality (Hanan-Pacha), the Earth's surface or the mundane (Kay-Pacha) and subsoil or inner life (Ukju-Pacha). This temple was just as Aurora had envisioned and more. The sun beat down on them and

Aurora held out her hand to shade her eyes. She spotted Radar standing in the center of the room with Otus and Boreas flanking him, staring at large shelves covered with a tarp. Otus and Boreas looked pristine and clean, Boreas's long hair still wet and hanging loose down his shoulders, not tied back in a ponytail the way his brother was prone to wear it. He turned around to face them looking really handsome as the sunlight reflected off his face, illuminating his playful hazel eyes.

Otus's blue overalls were clean, although he still had a mud smear on his face, but it didn't seem to bother him. His sandy brown hair was extra curly and a pile of books was piled up in his arms. It was then that Aurora realized what was lined up on each of the shelves. There were rows upon rows of books that were forbidden in the United States of the Common Good. In fact, the only books the Common Good government deemed appropriate were textbooks they created to further their ideology. Anything outside of that was illegal, and even libraries were illegal.

"There you are," Radar called out in his obsequious tone. "Boreas was just telling me, Aurora, how you two broke into the Candlewick Library."

Aurora blushed, as all eyes turned toward her, including Boreas's.

"We had to get some information about Otus," she said slowly, looking down at her feet.

"Otus saved us in the end," Boreas said, noting her embarrassment. "He picked up one of the Common Good officers, who looked like he might pee in his pants."

"Wish I could have been there," Radar laughed, ushering Babs and Aurora to join them in the circle.

"Before we head down for dinner, I wanted to show you our library in the Room of the Three Windows. This room is our treasure trove. Books that I used to destroy with fire, I now treasure like a squirrel hoarding nuts in the winter. I am hiding them for the generations to come. Reading is a powerful weapon. One of the reasons we banned books was to prevent free thought amongst the people. This wasn't as hard to achieve as I had initially thought. Herald was the one to say that the people had already ceased thinking for themselves, but I had too much faith in humanity."

Aurora slid her fingers along the book binders, feeling the rough paper graze against her skin. "This is incredible," she said, afraid that she would wake up and find that this was all a dream.

"I told you she would love this," Boreas said with a huge smile. Otus was already done reading half of the books in his pile, whizzing through them like a hurricane. Aurora picked up one called *To Kill a Mockingbird*, by Harper Lee. She picked it up slowly and turned the pages and was already mesmerized by the words on one of the pages: *"That's what I thought, too when I was your age. If there's just one kind of folks, why can't they get along with each other? If they're all alike, why do they go out of their way to despise each other?"*

"This is powerful," she said to herself. Her hand then stroked the binder of a book with a title labeled *Star Charts*. Her heart stopped, remembering that they still had to locate the star Antares and figure out the Professor's whereabouts. Radar and Boreas were talking with their backs turned to the book shelf, but she had to move quickly. She held her breath, snuck her hand behind the tarp and grabbed the book from the shelf. She stuffed it into her school-bag and quickly zipped it up. Once she realized she hadn't been caught, she was able to breathe again, rejoining the others in the circle.

"I'm just borrowing it," she said to herself. She would return it as soon as she had a chance to read it later that night.

Radar clapped his hands. "So you all must be famished. I have arranged dinner for you in the main piazza. Mrs. Xiomy I have been told is feeling better and will be able to join us as well."

Otus saved them a trip from going back down the stairs, lifting them up in his hands and transporting them to the center of the piazza. Radar said that he could get used to having Otus around. Aurora thought how their journey up the mountain could have gone a lot smoother if Otus had not been considered a huge threat, but there was no use thinking about the past.

The scent of food wafted through the air. A long wooden table was set-up covered with all the local specialties. There was corn, potatoes, chili peppers, rice and chicken. They all sat at the table, along with the soldiers, including Molina and Romero.

Romero handed each of them a plate of food and made an attempt at a smile, which on him looked more like a scowl. "Sorry that I was hard on you out on the trail."

"That's the understatement of the year," Mrs. Xiomy snarled, taking the plate of food roughly out of his hands.

"I was just doing my job," he replied sheepishly, putting extra rice on her plate. "How was I supposed to know you were the good guys?"

Mrs. Xiomy dug her fork into the chicken. "Well if it makes you feel any better, I thought you were the bad guys too."

He banged his hand onto the table, squashing the mosquito that had been buzzing around her ear. Mrs. Xiomy smiled slightly as she took another bite of her chicken.

Romero sat down across from her and said, "I hear you're a high school teacher."

"Chemistry," she answered nonchalantly, taking a swig of water from the cup.

He smiled, "Before joining the army, I taught mathematics."

She nearly choked on her water. "I wouldn't have pegged you for a teacher. Obstinate egotist perhaps, but then again, so are most math teachers I've met."

He laughed and together they started to talk shop, comparing stories about unruly children.

Molina chuckled at the flirting taking place at the end of the table. She took a big bite of food and nudged Aurora. "Who would have guessed those two would hit it off?"

Aurora laughed too, taking another bite of potato. It felt so good to eat real food again.

After she finished her plate of food, nearly licking it clean, Aurora declared herself stuffed. She was eager to be alone so that she could read the star chart book in her schoolbag. Otus and a group of the soldiers were drinking and laughing heartily as the sun was setting behind him. Boreas was on his second plate of food and Babs was speaking with Molina about Plymouth Tartarus. Aurora took this opportunity to sneak away, to go back to The Temple of Inti and read before they took off at the Sacred Hour. She headed up the stairs when she heard her name being called out behind her.

She looked down to see Boreas racing up the steps toward her.

"I thought you were still eating," she said, watching his long legs clear the steps; he made it look so easy.

He reached the top and after catching his breath said, "I forgot my bag in the Temple of Inti. I figured I'd walk with you."

She smiled slightly and together they walked through the ghostly ruins as the sun set over the Andes Mountains. The vibrant colors of red, orange and yellow stretched out as far as the eye could see, like they were standing in the midst of the sunset.

It was quiet, except for their footsteps until Aurora said, "I know this is going to sound strange, but I feel like we were meant to find this place; like we were meant to find the IDEAL."

He shrugged, putting his hands in his pockets. "It feels like just a big coincidence to me."

She crossed her arms over her chest, hugging her sweatshirt closer to her body. It was getting colder as they inched their way through the corridor. "So you think we just found Fawn by accident in Plymouth Tartarus?"

"Believe what you want, Aurora, but I would have preferred to not have found Fawn and to instead think that my mother was still dead. Better than knowing that she abandoned me on purpose."

She bit her lip, not wanting to start a fight with him in this beautiful place.

He raised an eyebrow at her. "I know that look. What were you going to say?"

She laughed, her laughter echoing in that hollow chamber. "You do not know my looks!"

He then mimicked her face, looking like he was constipated. "OK... that's the one you do when you want to say something but think you shouldn't. Then this one," he did a pensive look like he was the model from Auguste Rodin's bronze sculpture The Thinker, "That's the one you do when you are deep in thought and don't want anyone to bother you."

She narrowed her eyes at him like she was going to hurt him. "And what's this one?"

He smiled; that infectious smile that caused those annoying goose bumps all over her arms. "That's the one when you pretend you want to kill me, but secretly can't stop thinking about me."

Her mouth gaped open and she cried out, "Please, like I could ever like someone like you."

Boreas stopped in front of her, the light illuminating his hair and his eyes. He smelled like soap and early morning dew.

"Why not?" he asked softly, leaning against the wall. His scar was visible on his neck. Aurora remembered how she had nearly seen him killed and how she had prayed for him in the Sacristy in Plymouth Tartarus. Not even sure who she was praying to, but praying to keep him alive.

He stood there waiting for her to answer. The goose bumps were still evident on her skin with him so close to her; her brain that usually was on overdrive stopped working.

"We want to kill each other half the time." She finally managed to sputter.

"But what about the other half?"

His eyes danced playfully and he took her hand in his. His touch felt so comforting, but this couldn't happen. She cared about Jonathan who was safe in Candlewick and didn't know that his mother was alive. Jonathan who wouldn't play these mind games with her. Jonathan who she wasn't afraid would break her heart.

She let go of Boreas's hand, her mind barely able to think straight again. "I think you'd better get your bag before it gets too dark."

He looked crestfallen as her words sunk in. He finally nodded. "The look you are giving me right now, that's the one look I don't understand yet."

He turned around and walked briskly toward the Temple of Inti. Aurora took a deep breath trying to analyze what just happened. She ran to catch up to Boreas as they walked into the Temple.

"I will be very happy when we leave here." Boreas called out, grabbing his bag in the far corner of the room.

Aurora sighed as the myriad colors of the sunset streamed through the windows illuminating the temple's grandeur. "I think I could stay here forever."

"I think you could too."

The voice sounded from up above them, like a voice from the heavens. Startled, Aurora and Boreas looked up and standing in the observatory tower was Radar, staring into his telescope.

"What do you mean by that?" Boreas yelled, throwing his bag onto his shoulder.

Radar looked down at them from the observatory tower. "I think the son of Fawn Stockington will be a valuable asset to my army, as well as Miss Alvarez here and that fiery rebel, Babs O'Hara and yes, a 30-foot giant to complete the package.

"I knew it," Boreas muttered. "I knew there was more to this when you freed us; trying to tempt us with food, showers, and forbidden books."

Radar pointed at Aurora smugly. "My temptations worked for Miss Alvarez here, didn't they?"

The way he called her Miss Alvarez sent shivers up Aurora's spine, reminding her of her encounter with Inspector Herald.

"You sound like him," she called out. "And you both have a telescope. I should have realized you were still as evil as Herald."

"I bought Herald that telescope. Glad to hear he still is using it. You hear about old friends re-gifting things nowadays."

She ran to the closest window and screamed out, "Otus!"

Radar laughed, "Why are you afraid of me? We are all on the same team here. I want to defeat Herald. I don't want to wait and rely on a prophecy to do it. We can do this together. Boreas, you know what I'm talking about. We need to take the country back by force. There is no other way."

Boreas remained silent and Aurora screamed out again for Otus, not sure if he could hear them from this distance with the roaring wind. She whirled back toward Radar and screamed, "We need to stop the Geometric Storm. If you don't let us go then innocent people will die."

"Innocent people die," He snapped. "That's life. We all have a death sentence, some sooner than others."

He came down from the Observatory deck, staring at them with those cold, red eyes. He turned to Boreas and said, "I won't force you to fight with me. But if you want to leave, you need to tell me one thing."

Boreas crossed his arms and smirked, "Fine. What do you want to know? I flunked out of Geometry last year and quit the tennis team to piss off my father, which worked. And I..."

Radar clapped his hands together to shut him up. "Let's start this again. Where is your mother hiding?"

Boreas looked at him like he was insane, "My mother is dead," he lied, putting on his best poker face. "She's been dead for ten years; died in the Candlewick Prison fire."

Radar pointed at the conch shell hanging around his neck. "Then how do you have that conch shell?"

Boreas held the conch shell in his hands, the sun now having completely set and the moon shining into the temple, their shadows lingering on the wall in this game of wits.

"I've had it as long as I can remember," he said, sounding sincere. Aurora just stood next to him, flabbergasted. He was a good liar.

Radar, however, was not convinced. "Good try, Boreas. Let me tell you another story, the real story. Your mother is alive, and you know it. She started a colony where she has been recruiting people from all over the world who want to be able to practice their beliefs freely. And you know where she is because she gave you that conch shell."

Boreas turned to Aurora and they both stared up at this madman before them.

"I need to take this country back, and I will have you and Fawn's people as part of my army."

"So that you can be the IDEAL again? That worked out great the first time around."

"I can make things better! Don't you see that?" he whirled around, knocking a vessel to the ground, splintering into a million pieces.

He held up a two-way radio in his hands. "Now tell me where she is or Rana Xiomy and Babs O'Hara will die."

He held up the radio in his hands, clicking it with his fingernails, nonchalant, even cocky.

"You know what your problem is, Radar?" Boreas said, confidently. "You underestimate your opponents. You underestimated David Xiomy, Inspector Herald and now me."

Before Radar could stop him, Boreas blew into the conch shell. Aurora heard the high pitched bellowing in the room, but Radar couldn't hear anything but silence.

"The shell is defective," he laughed amusedly. "You just cost your friends their lives, you stupid boy."

Suddenly a huge hand reached down through the temple opening and clasped Radar around his waist. Radar screamed out, calling into his radio for his men to shoot!

"Aurora? Boreas? Are you ok?"

"Yes," Aurora shouted, relieved to see Otus's face staring down on them. "Let's get out of here."

Otus reached down and he picked up Aurora and Boreas with his other hand and plopped them into his pocket. Babs and Mrs. Xiomy were there already, safe.

Radar screamed and kicked his legs, as he dangled high over the valley below.

"What should I do with him?" Otus bellowed.

Boreas clapped his hands, imitating Radar. "Drop him at the bottom of the trail so that he has to walk his way up like we did; should buy us some time."

Otus nodded and flew into the air, gunshots echoing around them. He landed at the bottom of the Incan trail and put Radar down.

Radar screamed out. "You are making a mistake! I swear the prophecy will fail and Herald will win. Two teenagers and a giant cannot save the world! You hear me?"

"Look out for mudslides," Mrs. Xiomy yelled down.

And with that Otus soared up into the air like a cannon ball while his passengers held on for dear life in the chest pocket of his overalls. He landed only moments later, having travelled 10 miles with one spring of his step, jumping again and again, as if avoiding walking on hot coals. He finally landed behind a huge waterfall to rest and figure out what they were going to do next.

"What happened?" Mrs. Xiomy asked. "I didn't even get Romero's number when Otus grabbed Babs and I and whisked us into his pocket."

"Radar was using us to get to Fawn and wanted to enlist us into his army," Aurora explained. "Borcas had the conch shell and was able to signal to Otus that we needed help."

"I didn't hear anything," Babs interjected.

Boreas smiled. "Only Aurora, Otus and I can hear it when I blow into it. It's like the conch shell that Otus had when he signaled us from the ruby-red house in Candlewick."

"Well, I told you not to trust the IDEAL." Mrs. Xiomy lectured. "So what happens now? He, as well as the Common Good, will be able to track us just like they did before."

"Not necessarily," Boreas said with a sly smile. He reached into his bag where he pulled out the four detractor bracelets he had stolen. "Put these on. Otus, you will need to hook this onto your pocket, like they did for you going up the Incan trail."

Aurora looked at him, impressed. "So, you were busy after you showered."

He smiled at her, "I told you I didn't trust that guy and I knew we had to protect ourselves if more planes are out there. But even so, I don't know how reliable these are."

"...Or even where we have to travel to in order to reach Antares," Babs responded, hooking the bracelet into place.

Aurora reached into her backpack and pulled out the star chart book.

"I am also guilty of stealing," she said, her cheeks turning red. Boreas, Babs and Mrs. Xiomy all looked at her like she was an imposter. "Don't look at me like that! I meant to just borrow it. And anyway, it's not the first book I've stolen from a library."

They opened the book and found a star map in the centerfold. She searched and found the star Antares, otherwise known as the red supergiant. Aurora pulled out the two halves of the riddle and Babs pointed to something inscribed on the back.

"What does 'estas' mean?"

Aurora translated it. "That means 'summer' in Latin."

"Who still understands Latin? Isn't it a dead language?" Boreas teased.

Immediately Aurora realized her mistake and now calculated the correct coordinates. Orion was not visible in Brazil in the summer season. It had crossed the Prime Meridian December 18th. This confirmed that they were to head from Brazil to Western Australia where Orion and the Scorpion were still visible this time of year.

"We need to go to Australia, around these coordinates," She called them out to Otus who nodded. "That is where the Professor will be hiding...if he is still alive."

"I think it's too risky for us in the air," Otus said at last. "...but, they won't expect us to swim!"

"Swim to Australia?" Mrs. Xiomy cried out, horrified.

"I can swim the backstroke and keep you all in my chest pocket. You'll have to hold on real tight."

Aurora felt a little panicked at the thought of swimming across the shark infested Pacific Ocean, holding on for dear life in the pocket of a giant.

Babs shook her head at the group. "I was appointed to be your guide and connect you with the Professor. I take that seriously and you have to be out of your minds if you think this will work!"

Mrs. Xiomy looked down, and on the ground was a business card to a diving store. "I guess people go swimming around here," she said excitedly. "I used to go scuba diving when I was around your age and I remember how cold the oceans got. If we are going to have any chance of surviving this swim, we will need wetsuits."

She turned to Boreas, handing him the business card, "You think you can commandeer us four wetsuits?" He examined the card and shrugged, "Only one way to find out."

Aurora's complexion was still pale at the thought of their upcoming trip across the Pacific Ocean. She looked up at Otus and said sternly, "You'd better not leave me as shark bait! If I fall out and you hear me scream, you paddle back ASAP! Promise me you won't be too scared to fight off those sharks?"

Otus laughed boisterously, nearly knocking them off their feet, his laugh like an earthquake, "Don't worry, Aurora. I think the sharks will be scared of me, not the other way around!"

Aurora looked to Mrs. Xiomy for her input, and saw that her gaze was turned toward the shadowy night sky.

"I think I'd rather take my chances with sharks than with the Inspector. At least I know the sharks will fear Otus. The Inspector doesn't feel fear, he creates it."

Chapter 4

The Proposition

*A*nalise Jones was cursing herself for being so stupid. *Why hadn't she kept her big mouth shut?* The reporter in her had thrown caution to the wind and had asked Inspector Herald a question. *Just a simple question!* And now here she was, locked in Candlewick Prison.

It had been a little more than two weeks since her arrest. Two weeks since the bodies had washed up along the shore in Candlewick with no answers, and nobody but herself had questioned the Inspector about the real cause behind the accident, if it really was an accident.

She was starving. The light flickered above her and she wished she was one of those proverbial flies on a wall, able to get up close and personal to the real story, and not be detected.

Two burly guards appeared outside her cell and ordered her to follow them. Analise gulped, fearing that she would have to face the Inspector.

She was led up into the penthouse suite of the Candlewick Government Building and pushed onto a black, plush couch. The room was bordered by windows that stood high above the town of Candlewick, the town she had grown up in; the town that she had lived in with her father until his death two years earlier.

She stood up from the couch and immediately the two guards jumped up with their guns drawn and pointed directly at her head. She cautiously put her hands up and sat back down on the couch, wringing her hands and staring aimlessly out through the windows at the beautiful Atlantic Ocean; that ocean that housed bodies just weeks before. Inspector Herald claimed it was a cruise accident, but there were no cruises set to embark in the waters that night or any night for the past month. She knew that there was more to the story than the Inspector was telling and she had to find out the truth.

Though there were countless TV monitors on throughout the suite, none of them emitted any sound. She watched the flashes of stories being reported, but none of them displayed Analise's arrest. She was scared to admit it, but her boss at Channel Four news was never going to intervene for her, a mere intern, even if he did know where she was. Analise hoped that this would be her break into real journalism. Though just seventeen-years-old, she was eager to prove herself and this was her big chance. She was now inside the government building and could get the story of her life to show everyone that she was a serious reporter. Of course, that is only if she made it out of this mess alive.

The private penthouse elevator doors swished open behind her and she turned her head, expecting and fearing to see the Inspector.

It was not the Inspector, shockingly, it was the First Lieutenant. He motioned to the guards to leave him alone with Analise. The guards hesitated, but when he yelled at them to remember who he was, they marched with heads down like sheepish school children, into the elevator and descended.

The First Lieutenant now turned his attention toward her. His uniform bore the indigo and orange colors of the Common Good, with the inscription "The IDEAL for Unity" written on his sleeve. A badge bearing two crossed saber swords, the insignia of a First Lieutenant, was sewn into the right shoulder of the uniform. Dark sunglasses covered his eyes and he wore a scowl on his handsome face. He walked with swift steps across the blood-red carpet, stopping directly in front of her. She noticed that his hand was on the hilt of his gun, peeking out of his holster.

He stared at her in silence for what felt like forever until he finally snapped, "Analise, what in the hell were you thinking?"

Analise jumped up, crossing her arms over her chest, "Nice to see you too, Jake."

"It is First Lieutenant Fray to you."

She turned and marched over to doors leading out onto a balcony where the Inspector's telescope was positioned to give her a clear view of the graveyard below. In his reflection in the window, she caught the First Lieutenant taking off his sunglasses and pinching the bridge of his nose with his fingers as if he were warding off a migraine. She smiled slyly at Jake's obvious distress.

"So...are you going to kill me?"

He put the sunglasses back on over his owl eyes, no longer the boy she had known on Wishbone Avenue, but the feared alter-ego.

"He doesn't want you dead...not yet. He wants more from you and you should be damn well relieved that I intervened when I did."

She whirled around, "Wait, what do you mean?"

"Analise, why did you have to open your big mouth? You know what kind of man he is. He will do anything he can to protect his image and the status of the IDEAL. At whatever cost necessary."

"So that's why those bodies washed up on the shoreline of Candlewick Park? To protect his image!?!"

Jake stepped back and took a deep, testy breath. "This is not an interview. I am warning you to do whatever I say or you will be killed. Do you understand me?"

She sat back down on the couch, feeling like the walls around her were closing in. The truth she had fought so long for was within reach, Jake knew and could tell her, but Jake was not the same person she had known.

"I understand. I have no choice but to listen to you, you hold all the cards."

He stood, towering over her and called into an intercom. A minute later a beautiful woman entered; tall with long auburn hair. Her piercing blue eyes stared at Analise in contempt as she walked gracefully toward them.

"Miss Thompson, this is the woman I was telling you about."

"Yes, First Lieutenant," which sounded more like Left-tenant in her British accent, her face void of emotion, "but do you think she will cooperate?"

"What is this about?" Analise questioned, fearful of what they wanted her to do.

"You will be the media spokesperson for the Inspector. You will deliver whatever story he gives to you. You will not ask questions."

"Why me?"

Miss Thompson glared at the First Lieutenant. "She has already failed. This girl will never pass the Inspector's test. He just wants a doll to play with, once he's done, he will dispose of her."

Analise stiffened, "I will not be his play toy. I'd rather die."

"You may not have a choice in the matter," Miss Thompson smiled mischievously. "A person in power likes to get his way and doesn't care about the consequences, especially if he wants a pretty seventeen-year-old girl."

Analise felt faint and sat down hard.

Miss Thompson, aggravated further, brought her a cup of water. "See, she doesn't have what it takes, Jacob."

Analise looked up into Jake's eyes, but he dodged her gaze. "This is not just to save my life, is it? You want me inside. You want me to gain his trust so that I can get on camera. There's something more to this, isn't there?"

Jake cracked his knuckles and the popping sound made Analise jump as her nerves were at their breaking point. Miss Thompson finally broke the silence. "This is your choice, Jacob. I have my reservations, but we are running out of time."

He appeared torn, like he was weighing his options and then nodded more to himself than to anyone in the room. Addressing Analise, "There's something happening out there. Did you hear about that fugitive, Aurora Alvarez, that everyone is searching for?"

Analise nodded.

"Well, she was here. She told me that there is going to be a deadly and catastrophic storm that will hit the United States of the Common Good. She said that she has to reach the Northern Lights, along with that boy, Boreas Stockington. She said that only they and their companion, a giant, could stop this storm."

Analise burst out laughing. "A giant! Wow, what are you drinking to believe that story?"

"There is a prophecy," Miss Thompson snapped. "Fifteen years ago in the graveyard below, I heard it declared by the traitor IMAM. He said that this would happen. I know it is hard to believe, but it feels like his prophecy is coming true."

"And the Inspector doesn't want to stop it or warn the people," Jake said, his voice rising in anger. "He doesn't care, and will stop at nothing to keep his people on a leash."

Analise got nearly in Jake's face and said emphatically, "Then stand up to him! Kill him! You are his closest ally, if you can't stop him, who can?"

"I can't!"

"Why not?"

"Because he has my family!"

He collapsed onto the couch, his face buried in his hands.

Analise was caught completely off guard. "He has your sister? Mary?"

Jake nodded. "And my Mom."

"I thought they moved to Iowa?"

"You should know better than anyone the role that the media plays with these disappearances."

Analise felt like her world was crumbling apart. The media, the one thing she had entrusted her life to, was tangled up with this web of lies. She looked up at the TV screens, taunting her with their stories. Were they all being spoon-fed stories by the Inspector? She wanted to put her arm around Jake, but he was not the same boy she had gone to school with. He was no longer the older boy who lived next door to her on Wishbone Avenue who had looked out for her so many years before.

It seemed so long ago, those innocent days, before Jake was drafted into the Common Good Army. She still remembered how excited he had been that he had been chosen, like he was going to change the world. Analise had been standing on the front porch beside her father, staring at Jake, who seemed so mature as his twelve-year-old self got into the Common Good vehicle to head off to basic training. Her father had turned to her then, his deep brown eyes concerned and fearful as he said, "He will not be the same person once they're through with him."

"What do you mean, Dad?" She had asked him with eyes full of innocence, twirling her braid in her hands.

Her father had put his arm around her and whispered, "I want to believe the country that I once knew and loved still exists. I want this to be a country you would want to fight for."

He had ruffled her hair then as he held her in his arms. "Promise me, Analise. Promise me that you will fight for the truth above all else."

"I promise, Daddy," she had replied, not understanding, but all was right with the world when she saw him smile.

Nine years later her father was dead, and the Jake Fray in front of her had changed, like her father had predicted.

Those memories were like scenes from a movie, the reel playing on a projector within the confines of her mind and instead of herself and Jake, there were actors portraying different people, different lives. Analise and Jake were both different, they had each seen too much to remain innocent.

Analise took a deep breath, "So after all this time, Jake Fray, whose side are you on?"

Mrs. Thompson appeared irritated by her question, as if she was purposely wasting time. "Don't you get it? We are breaking a million rules conspiring against the Inspector. What side do you think we're on?"

"How do you expect me to trust you? I mean...how can I?"

Jake held up his hand and she immediately stopped talking. A strand of hair fell out of place over his eye and for a split second she could almost still see that same boy that she had known and cared for like a brother, a protective brother who wouldn't let any harm come to her.

"I don't blame you for not trusting me. I wouldn't trust myself, but just know that I must play my part or else he will kill my family. I can't let that happen. You are our hope to infiltrate the media sector of the IDEAL. We need to find a way to get the word out to the people and we need to help Aurora on her mission. Will you help us?"

Analise felt the room spinning, the television screens blinding her and she leaned against the window, staring out at the waves with their foamy fingers crashing against the shores. She saw the graves lined up with more being dug as she watched. The dirt was piling up as the bodies of those who had perished from the 'cruise accident' were waiting to be buried in unmarked graves. For the first time in her life, she felt truly frightened that she would become one of those bodies, especially if she accepted Jake's offer. She felt like she was hyperventilating as she watched the gravediggers below and she reached for her heart, as if to ensure that it was still beating.

Promise me that you will fight for the truth above all else.

Her father's words lit a fire within her as she remembered her promise to him all those years before. She had lost him too young as he perished at the hands of the Common Good while performing a religious ceremony in the woods. His only crime was marrying two people who loved each other, yet he had been caught and executed without even a trial. Analise had to live without a parent because of the Inspector and the IDEAL's laws that went against everything her father had believed. If Analise wanted to find out the truth and find a way to avenge his death, this was her chance.

She licked her lips and with conviction coming from deep in her soul, said the words that sealed her fate.

"What do I have to do?"

Chapter 5

The Cavern

Otus's arms were like a propeller, spinning and whisking against the ocean water in a powerful and shockingly fast backstroke. Aurora and the others were strapped into the pocket of the giant's overalls by a rope wrapped around Otus's torso like a seatbelt. They were wearing the wetsuits that Boreas commandeered from the diving store. They had stood guard while he picked the lock and ran in. When he asked for their sizes, Aurora wanted to shoot herself when she admitted that she needed a large, compared to Babs's small. On top of that, the wetsuit was giving her the biggest wedgie and was so tight that everyone could see every bulge on her body, nothing left to the imagination. But at least her body was protected from the thrashing she was getting from the unyielding waves. Without warning, a towering wave splashed over them, the cold seawater stinging Aurora's eyes. She nearly choked on the salt water, the bitter taste burning her throat even after swallowing. Aurora dared not open her eyes again in fear that she would find herself face to face with another wave. She found herself clinging to Boreas's arm. If she became unstrapped from the leash that bound them, there was comfort in the knowledge that she would bring Boreas down with her.

Otus continued heading southwest, the current moving him along swiftly, seeming as though the waves were aiding him.

"We're nearly there," Otus shouted over the blistering wind as another wave crashed down on them. Aurora held her breath as they went under again. Just as she felt like she couldn't hold her breath any longer, Otus shot up into the air like a rocket. Aurora screamed as it seemed that Otus was about to do a belly flop that would kill his passengers when Otus did a flip in the air and landed feet-first onto dry land. He used his feet like brakes on a plane barreling into an airport runway, leaving screech marks in the sand. Otus tried to catch his breath as he unhooked the rope from around his torso and handed one end to Mrs. Xiomy. Mrs. Xiomy tied a knot in the hole of the pocket and Otus's passengers climbed down the make-shift rope ladder. They landed on the ground on shaky legs. Otus shook himself like a wet dog, spraying water like a sprinkler in all directions.

"I think I beat the world record for fastest swim across the Pacific Ocean," he bragged, as wet strands of hair hung over his droopy eyes.

Aurora sighed with relief that they had finally reached Australia. She looked up to behold the star Antares sparkling above them. A reddish tint encircled the star like a halo, living up to its nickname, 'Rival of Mars'. The shape of a scorpion was visible as if traced in the sky.

Once they regained their balance, they surveyed their surroundings and realized they were close to what appeared to be a farm. Aurora felt sticky and disgusting from the saltwater and sea-weed that were stuck to her wetsuit. Sand was like dandruff in her hair and all she wanted again on this journey was to find a shower. The scent of early morning dew and the musky earthiness of the land permeated the air. She spotted a lake and stripped the wetsuit off her body. It was much easier getting the damn outfit off than it was to get it on. She had a red bathing suit on underneath and with bare feet she walked down a narrow graveled pathway toward the lake, plunged into the lake, and the fresh water soothed her over-heated body. She rinsed the grime off her skin. She was followed by Babs and Boreas who nearly tackled her as they dove in.

Boreas sprouted up, squirting water out of his mouth.

"So where's this professor?" Borcas asked, eyeing the dawning sun warily, fearful strangers would soon be waking from their slum-ber. "Or do we want to sing him a wake up song of three teenagers, a loony teacher and a giant swimming in his lake?"

"Now I'm a 'loony teacher'!" Mrs. Xiomy splashed Boreas from where she sat soaking her legs and using her hands to rinse salt off her arms and face. She let her blond hair out of its bun, shaking the wet curls out. "I think we need to find Otus a place to hide first."

Dripping wet, but feeling revitalized, Aurora stepped barefoot onto the muddy grass that felt mushy beneath her toes. She strained her eyes to survey their surroundings. Leading off from the lake, there was a narrow creek that rushed over rocks that dug a trench through the farmland. A quaint covered bridge was situated over the creek, providing passage and adding charm to the vista. Beyond the bridge, a barn stood 50 yards from a red brick farm house framed amidst the green and yellow pasture. She pulled her sneak-ers out of her schoolbag and started to put them on her feet when she spotted Boreas dunking Babs in the water, Babs's auburn hair spilling down her shoulders. They were laughing together like chil-dren at a water park. She closed her eyes, trying to block out the distraction. She had told Boreas she wasn't interested in him. The only person to blame was herself.

Orange and yellow streaks were spreading across the black sky dissolving the stars. The sun was rising and the Awakened Hour was approaching. They were running out of time.

"Babs," Aurora yelled to get her attention. "Where do you think the Professor would be hiding?"

Babs stopped laughing, moving out of the lake, her purple bikini hugging her figure. "How would I know?" she said grabbing a towel and drying herself off. "You're supposed to find him; I'm just supposed to introduce you."

"Look," Aurora pointed at the sun peeking its head above the horizon. Paranoia started to set in on Aurora, they were in a strange country and the Common Good could be anywhere. "We don't have time for this! The only reason *you* are here is to find the Professor. I need you to tell me where he is NOW!"

Babs backed up, tripping as Aurora screamed in her face. Boreas scrambled out of the water, took Aurora by the arm and pulled her back so that she wasn't hovering over Babs like a predator.

"Look, she doesn't know, alright? We need to find somewhere to hide until nightfall. We can look for the Professor then."

Aurora stared at him, his wet shirt clinging to his broad chest as droplets sprinkled across his face. He pulled his shoulder-length hair out of his hazel eyes; eyes that seemed to change colors depending on what he wore. Now they were like mint leaves, matching the pigment of his shirt. He stared back at her so intently that she forgot how to breathe. She stooped down to finish lacing her sneakers. "Of course you would take her side," she mumbled.

"What is that supposed to mean?"

She didn't answer just stomped over to Otus who picked her up and whispered into her ear, "He has a point, Aurora."

"The only reason Babs is here is to help us find the Professor. And now she's playing dumb. If she can't help us what the hell is she even doing here?"

"Fawn said we needed her. You trust Fawn, don't you?"

Aurora nodded, twirling one of the wet strands of her hair between her fingers. Otus put her down and Aurora walked in stride beside Mrs. Xiomy.

"Teenage hormones at work," Mrs. Xiomy smiled mischievously at Aurora. "I think it's a bit obvious that you have a thing for him."

Aurora jerked her head toward her teacher. "A thing for who?"

Mrs. Xiomy turned around toward Boreas, who was walking with Babs behind them.

Goose bumps prickled her arms, but she rubbed her arms wildly to get them off of her skin. "He's the last person I want to be with."

"Then stop acting like a jealous girlfriend."

Aurora humphed and picked up speed, heading to the barn just in the nick of time. The sun rose fully in the horizon, the golden ball dancing in the sky. They could hide in the barn until they could figure out what to do next. It was a pine wood barn with a silo that stretched even higher than Otus's head. They quickly scoped out the area, but it appeared deserted. Otus broke the lock and they scurried into the barn and closed the door behind them. A loud banging noise echoed from within and they all scrambled behind Otus who they designated to go first to investigate. He walked over loose hay straddling the pine wood floors into the barn with Boreas and Aurora close behind him. The scent of manure was so repulsive that Aurora had to hold her breath, her nose craving the fresh air that lay behind the closed double doors. Otus peered down into the stalls and laughed outright at the source of the banging. Lined up in four stalls were four magnificent Australian Stock horses eating hay and swatting at flies with their tails. Behind the horses stood a chicken coop, with chickens still sleeping, nestled on their eggs.

Mrs. Xiomy rubbed her hands together and licked her lips as she exclaimed, "Eggs! Scrambled, fried, over-easy. You name it and I can make it!"

She ran from chicken to chicken and found six laid eggs that she carried in her arms, grinning like she had just won the lottery. It would be the first normal breakfast that they would have had since Candlewick.

"And this is real farm to table cooking," Mrs. Xiomy added with a wink as if she was doing a commercial.

"Just how are you going to make them?" Babs asked pompously, stroking the ear of the gray horse, "there isn't a pan or skillet."

Mrs. Xiomy imitated the girl and said in the same tone, "I guess we'll have to find one then, hmmm?"

Aurora giggled and Babs tossed her head, her braid flapping to the other side of her shoulder and continued stroking the horse that neighed in delight from the human contact. Boreas stayed back from the horses and instead went with Otus to ensure that the rest of the barn was secure. Each time the horse neighed, Boreas jumped while Otus watched him curiously.

"Don't tell me you're scared of those friendly creatures?" Otus nudged Boreas playfully.

Boreas slid over the hay strewed across the floor as if he was ice skating. "Horses don't like me."

"These don't seem to mind you."

"They will if I get too close. I was thrown from a horse when I was a kid. Ever since then I have stayed away from them because they seem to sense that I'm around and start jumping and kicking like they are possessed or something."

Aurora felt the sweat dripping down her neck and noticed the empty trough for the horses. She motioned for Babs to help her.

They grabbed buckets, made their way out of the barn and headed down to the creek where they filled the buckets with water. While there, they quenched their own thirst. They spotted Mrs. Xiomy snooping around the farmhouse, like a prowler with her face pressed against the window frame. Aurora realized that she was probably searching for something to cook the eggs with.

"She's going to get us all caught!" Babs hissed, picking up the heavy bucket and making her way back to the house. "And all for stupid eggs? Like she could make eggs better than Eileen anyway!"

Aurora froze at the mention of Eileen's name.

"Eileen did make the best eggs," Aurora added, wanting to put her arm around Babs, or something. But Aurora just wiped her hand against her jeans.

Babs sighed, like she was lost in her memories. "She would have liked this place. It reminds me of Ireland; green fields and views of the water. If we never were forced to leave that place, Eileen would still be alive."

Babs started running toward the barn and Aurora felt stupid just standing back there at the water trough. Every time it seemed like Babs was opening up to her, she took off. Aurora quickly picked up her own bucket and struggled to keep her balance as it weighed a lot more than what she was anticipating. She followed after Babs, feeling guilty for blowing up at her that morning about the Professor. She desperately tried to keep the water in the bucket but it was splashing all over the place. Didn't these people ever hear of plumbing?

They re-entered the barn and filled the trough with the big buckets of water. The horses dunked their heads into the trough and began drinking away. Otus apologized for not helping the girls but Boreas prohibited him from leaving.

"I am not going to have you off wandering around town like you are a tourist. We can get away with it, but you not so much."

Aurora sunk down onto the hay and felt extremely tired all of a sudden. She closed her eyes but she had a difficult time trying to fall asleep. Even though it felt like the farm was deserted, she had a funny feeling that they were being watched. And who was taking care of the animals? And more frightening, would that person come into the barn unexpectedly to find the place inhabited by a giant? Aurora shivered at the thought and hoped the Sacred Hour would come quickly so they could leave this place.

Just then a disoriented chicken came running out of the coop, its little red clawed feet running backwards and forwards as if it didn't know which direction to go. They laughed as the chicken hobbled over Otus's large feet and he said, "if we don't get eggs at least we could make a chicken tonight!'

Aurora and Babs glanced at each other simultaneously and ran to the door glancing across the farmland for any sign or trace of Mrs. Xiomy.

Without a word, they threw open the door and raced toward the farm house. Aurora found it difficult to keep up with Babs who sprinted like she was competing in a 50 yard dash. They reached the farmhouse and cautiously glanced through the windows. The place appeared deserted and for Aurora, it brought back memories of the little ruby-red house that housed a giant beneath a similar deserted facade. Aurora wondered if this farm house also contained secrets or if it was truly what it appeared to be. That nagging feeling of being watched lingered as she searched for Mrs. Xiomy through the mildewed window. The sun was beating down on her and she wished she hadn't just run in this heat. She wiped the salty sweat out of her eyes and yet couldn't see anything except an empty kitchen with a skillet on the stove. Her heart was racing as she whispered to Babs, "There's a skillet on the stove. Mrs. Xiomy must have gone inside to get it."

"But did she ever come back out?"

Aurora eyes followed a set of footprints straight from the barn and up the steps to the white painted farmhouse door that was still slightly ajar. She wiped another droplet of sweat from her forehead and wondered if Mrs. Xiomy had been so foolish to go into a strange house alone; perhaps her hunger and adrenaline took away her good judgment. Aurora ran to the front door expecting her teacher to emerge from there but no one came out the open door. There were only footprints leading in, not out. She heard panting and the sounds of someone creeping up behind her. The wind slithered over her body and goose bumps prickled the back of her neck. She and Babs whirled around ready to attack, only to find that it was Boreas who had chased after them.

"What happened? You ran out of there as if you saw a ghost!"

Aurora quickly filled him in on the disappearance of Mrs. Xiomy, who they were pretty sure was still in the house. Boreas's eyes were troubled but did not deny their assumption.

"Well then, ladies first," he said, motioning toward the open door.

Aurora smiled tightly as she walked past him, each remembering the last time they had trespassed into a red house. She pushed the door open further, slowly and steadily, keeping her eyes peeled for any sign of movement within. The house was definitely empty with hardly any furnishings except for a dusty and scratched up kitchen table, a bear-skin rug lying idly in the living room area, and a wooden rocking chair with a red, white and blue quilt hanging over the armrest. Aurora stepped forward and the wooden floor creaked beneath their weight as the group walked further into the house. Boreas was covering the rear, his knife drawn; the blade glistening from where the sun streamed through the open window. The only sound other than the sound of their footsteps was the wind rustling slightly against the house.

Aurora reached the dilapidated looking kitchen and whispered, "Mrs. Xiomy," her voice coming out more like a croak than a whisper. She paused and asked again, "Mrs. Xiomy, where are you?" Still no answer.

Aurora had reached the stove and turned left and right but there was no doorway or other room nearby for Mrs. Xiomy to have disappeared in.

"Help!"

They all froze. The sound was coming from underneath their feet! Aurora instinctively grabbed the skillet to use it as a weapon, but the skillet didn't move; it was stuck to the stove like it was glued on. The handle glowed under her hand like it was on fire, burning Aurora's skin and the floor boards flew out from under her. With a loud shriek she fell through a trap door. Aurora thought she was going to die, falling through the black abyss, fearing there was nothing to break her fall and then fearing that what did break her fall would kill her. Luckily, she landed in a ditch, her body cushioned by the gooey, muddy substance. She looked just in time to see a hand sinking beneath the surface. She grasped it and pulled with all her strength until Mrs. Xiomy's head rose above the goo, gulping for air, sandy particles covering her face although her glasses were miraculously still perched on her nose.

"Aurora," she gasped in between breaths, coughing up mud and sand. "Quick... sand."

Now Aurora felt it, her body was sinking and she couldn't feel any floor or ground below her. She moved slowly, remembering an old army tale her father told her of when he was stuck in quicksand.

"Mrs. Xiomy, don't panic and don't try to fight it. The more you fight the more it will pull you down. We need to get something to grab ahold of," Aurora shrieked, looking for anything that they could grab to pull them out of this deathly pit.

"There's nothing within reach. Where are the others?"

Boreas and Babs were still upstairs. She wondered if the trap door was the only way down. Aurora desperately looked around for another way but in the dim light, it just appeared to be a hollow cavern as their voices echoed when they spoke. The light was brighter in one direction and she could hear the distant sound of running water, but she didn't know how that could help them now. Her body was sinking more and more, dragged under by the weight of the muddy sand and she felt the fight or flight hormones kicking in. Mrs. Xiomy held onto her hand, attempting to calm her down.

"Aurora, now that we may not make it…"

"Don't say that," Aurora said, her mouth was nearly underneath the sand, the grainy substance resting on her lips and she feared even breathing would make her sink faster.

"…I just want to say, you're like the daughter I never had."

Mrs. Xiomy had her head tilted back as far as she could, her mouth trying desperately to speak without swallowing the sand that was inching closer and closer.

Aurora felt her eyes brimming with tears, her body tensing up, expecting the next breath to push them both down. Her mouth and nose was nearly beneath the sand and all she wanted to do was fight against it, but she had to stay maddeningly still and just wait for death to come. Their fate was sealed. *I'm sorry*, she found herself thinking. Sorry to her parents, to Otus, the world, to Jonathan… to Boreas.

The delusions started now, of an electric hum, of his voice calling out to her. *Boreas*, she thought, *I shouldn't have pushed you away*. But, wait, his voice was much too clear and nearby to be a delusion. She moved her head slightly and saw a shadow in the darkness that resembled the shape of a stick. Her eyes were nearly covered with sand but she was sure there was something there. With the last ounce of energy she could muster, she pulled her right hand out of the sand, still clinging to Mrs. Xiomy with her left while her body collapsed completely underneath the sand. Her outstretched hand searched madly for something to cling to, but her fingertips just grabbed air. Until, finally her fingers grasped something firm and strong. She clung to it with all her strength as the object started to jerk her body back toward the surface.

Her nose and mouth rose above the sand, coughing up all the muddy substance that she had swallowed; her lungs breathing in air. The object continued to pull them farther up and she could hear Mrs. Xiomy gasp behind her as her body also emerged out of the sand pit. They were pulled farther and farther until their bodies were completely on the surface. Hands rushed to their sides and helped them out of the pit.

"What the hell kind of freak house is this!"

Aurora wiped the sand out of her eyes and there stood Boreas, staring at her with concern written all over his face; his strong muscled arms still holding onto the wooden club that had saved her life. He knelt down beside her, resting his hand behind her neck and holding her in a sitting position. She felt so comfortable being held by him, as if nothing bad could happen to her while in his embrace. She stared deep into his eyes, his intense gaze making it feel like she was the only girl for him. She shook that idea off, like wiping the sand off her clothes. He didn't care for her; he liked Babs, who was busy helping lift Mrs. Xiomy to her feet; brushing sand out of her hair. Aurora struggled to her feet, resisting Boreas's help. She kept trying to wipe the sand off her clothes but the particles were clinging to her fabric like lint.

"Boreas, Babs, how did you get down here?"

"Babs thought of it, actually. Since you fell through the floor, Babs had the idea to try to find another entry under the house. We couldn't see one around the house itself, so we raced over to the bridge and sure enough, there was a tunnel that led in this direction. We followed the tunnel until we heard your voices."

"Boreas grabbed the club in case we ran into someone that he had to clobber over the head. But little did we know we'd need it to get you both out of quicksand. What the heck is that about, a frying pan booby trap?"

"I'm sure other objects are rigged too." Mrs. Xiomy stammered. "Whoever it is must be extremely paranoid about their things."

"Or out to kill anyone who comes snooping around," Aurora said, staring intently at Babs. "Who do we know who is extremely paranoid like that?"

Babs's thoughts were on the same wavelength as Aurora's, "The Professor!"

Boreas guffawed at the far-fetched notion.

"Either way, let's get out of here before something else happens!"

Mrs. Xiomy leaned on his shoulder and Boreas led her toward the cave when Aurora cried out, "Stop!"

Mrs. Xiomy and Boreas whipped around, expecting another travesty to have occurred.

"What is it?" Mrs. Xiomy's voice echoed back.

Aurora ran to their side.

"The cave will be rigged too. The only way out of here is to find the Professor."

"What's wrong with you? We just came from that way," Boreas exclaimed. "Now who's sounding paranoid?"

She shook her head and took Boreas's flashlight from his hands and shone the light beam back through the cavern. "The pot handle burned my skin when I touched it. It was an electric shock that triggered the trap door to open. I think you may have triggered something when you came through the tunnel. I thought it was my mind playing tricks on me in the quicksand, but I thought I heard something being turned on, like a generator or something."

She held out her hand and Boreas gave her the club. She threw it into the cave as far as she could. As if it was triggered by motion sensors, a flame thrower shot out flames, turning the club to a blazing crisp. Boreas, Babs and Mrs. Xiomy jumped back in fear and Aurora, though glad her experiment worked, was scared as she realized who they were up against.

"We'll never get out of here alive," Mrs. Xiomy cried out in horror.

"And this professor is supposed to help us?" Boreas whispered to Aurora as they gulped and headed cautiously down one of the narrow corridors leading away from the flame throwers and the quicksand, hoping they would have better luck going in the opposite direction. Boreas held the flashlight, which illuminated the rest of the hollow cavern. Large limestone and calcium deposits covered the base of the cavern resembling miniature sculptures created by nature. Hanging down from the ceiling were rocks in icicle form. They appeared frail, but deadly and Aurora worried at any moment that they would rain down upon their heads, impaling them with the sharp stone daggers.

"This must be one of the abandoned caverns," Mrs. Xiomy said, resting her glasses on the tip of her nose. There was a slight crack in the left lens, but other than that, they were remarkably intact after her near death experience. Her hand touched the wall of the cave and she licked her finger slightly, "just what I thought, limestone. The quicksand must have been planted in here, but you can't fake this entire natural wonder. I don't care what kind of a Professor lives here."

Something scurried past Babs's leg and she screamed. Boreas shone the flashlight in that direction and scurrying away was a raccoon. Babs buried her face in Boreas's shoulder and he embraced her, kissing the top of her head.

"Troglophiles," Mrs. Xiomy said, watching the raccoon scamper away. "They are the type of animals that can live in caverns;

raccoons, bats and even bears. They say that even the Australia Megafauna like the Diprotodon could live down here."

"Diprotodon?" Aurora asked, perplexed.

"They roamed over Australia 1.6 million years ago, before the Ice Age. They resembled giant wombats, some say they used to co-exist with humans until their extinction about 46,000 years ago. They have also found footprints down in these caves of the Tasmanian Tiger, a dangerous predator."

"Is this supposed to make us feel better?" Boreas cried out.

"Don't worry, the last of their species died in captivity many years ago."

Aurora froze, fearful that her footsteps would awaken the extinct megafauna from their graves. They were stuck in this cave, where most likely they would all perish.

"I think I would rather take my chances with Radar than with a Tasmanian Tiger," Aurora whispered, fearful her voice would awaken the dead down here in the depths of this chamber.

"Well, let's hope we find the professor before any giant wombats find us," Boreas said.

They continued slowly down the narrow, slippery path and Aurora wished they could signal Otus, but they were on their own. Mrs. Xiomy continued to provide them a geological lesson on the caverns, making it seem as if they were on a school field trip from hell.

Aurora folded her arms over her chest, trying not to shiver as there was a sharp decline in temperature as they headed further into the caverns. She envied Babs as Boreas had his arm around her shoulder, adding extra body heat to her lithe frame. Aurora felt her body tense, but had to remind herself that Babs just helped save her life. She should be thankful, not jealous. She tried to remain focused on:

A. Finding the professor
B. Staying alive

C. Not thinking about Boreas kissing Babs on the top of the head.
D) All of the Above.

So far, only B was successful, well, at least that was something!

Exhaustion and dehydration were starting to kick in. They had been walking deeper and deeper into the cavern and she was already tired after fighting the quicksand. Aurora knew that if they didn't find water soon, they would be in deep trouble, but she didn't want to state the obvious. Their steps became slower, their breathing weaker as they hugged the wall to keep from stumbling on the rocks lining the narrow pathway.

They wandered into another chamber, this one like a sparkling garden of jeweled flowers, with crystals lined up around a roaring river that cut through the center of the chamber. Aurora's eyes widened at this natural wonder.

How could something so beautiful live down in the depths of this abyss, completely forgotten by the world?

At the sight of water, they raced excitedly to the river. Boreas beat them there, cupped his hands and dunked them into the cold, wet elixir. He raised his hands to his mouth and was about to drink when Mrs. Xiomy shrieked for him to stop!

The water spilled down Boreas's shirt and he whirled around in annoyance.

"What's the matter?"

"The water is poisoned."

"How do you know?"

Mrs. Xiomy pointed to animal bones scattered around the river, "other animals have been here before us and unless you want to suffer their fate, do not drink the water. This professor thinks he's so cunning, but he doesn't know who he's messing with!"

Aurora looked down at the water horrified; the Professor was all around, waiting to drop the next test on them and dreaming up new diabolical ways to kill them. She turned to Babs and yelled, "Babs do something."

"What do you propose I do?"

"Yell, scream! Tell him that you're here, anything!"

Just then the openings in each of the four corners of the chamber were blocked by prison gates slamming shut. The group whirled around and horror struck them as they realized why they were being locked in. On the opposite side of the river, standing on four paws at a full two feet in height and six feet in length, was a wiry dark-brown tiger with black stripes extending from its shoulder to the base of its long stiff tail. The beast paced up and down, eying its prey – them. They huddled close together as it paced, looking at the four intruders and contemplating which one would be its dinner. It opened its jaw alarmingly wide and let out a gritty bark that made their blood run cold.

"A Tasmanian Tiger!" Mrs. Xiomy cried out in disbelief.

"I thought you said they were extinct!" Aurora stuttered while grasping onto her arm; digging her fingernails into Mrs. Xiomy's flesh.

"I guess they didn't count this one!"

They were horror struck as they realized that there was no place to run to.

"Maybe it's scared of water?" Mrs. Xiomy whispered, optimistic.

The tiger backed to the far edge of the cavern then ran at full speed, leaping easily over the river, landing facing the group.

Boreas cried out, "Guess not!" and took out a knife as four fire torches hung several feet over their heads suddenly lit the arena. The tiger looked emaciated from lack of food with bald patches spotting its brown fur. The humans were about to be a feast for its stomach and it growled in delight, sending shivers up their spines. The tiger raised its claws at Boreas who stepped back just in time, the claw only scratching his shirt, but tearing it to shreds. He waved the knife at the tiger menacingly and the tiger followed his every movement with its eyes. Again the tiger swung its paw and this time it smacked Boreas across the face, knocking him to the ground.

Mrs. Xiomy and Babs made a running jump, tumbling onto the other side of the river as Aurora made sounds and leapt about to distract the tiger. This gave Boreas time to jump back to his feet and slash the tiger across its left paw sending blood spurting from its skin as the tiger howled in pain. Boreas stabbed again, but this time the tiger anticipated the attack, turned and dug its claws across Boreas' exposed chest. Boreas fell to the ground, roaring in pain. Aurora studied the torches that were hung at least two feet higher than her head and wished again that Otus were here. She yelled at Mrs. Xiomy to distract the tiger. Mrs. Xiomy splashed and yelled in the water to try to draw its attention. The tiger merely glanced over its shoulder and growled; such pitiful attempts couldn't draw it away from his opponent. Before the beast turned back, Aurora grabbed and almost dragged Boreas back to his feet. Blood oozed from his chest between his fingers as he held his hand over the wound.

"Lift me up," she yelled as the tiger stalked toward them. Boreas hoisted her up on his shoulders and reached as far as she could, but missed the torch by just an inch.

"Grab it!" Boreas yelled at her frantically.

The tiger gained speed and right when it was about to pounce, Aurora clasped her hand around the torch's handle and swung the fire back and forth in the tiger's face. Petrified, the tiger took a step back and whimpered in fright. She continued to wave the fire at the tiger as it began to circle them, looking for a way around the flames. It came so close to them that Boreas could feel its hot breath on his face. The flame was dying and Aurora knew that only the fire could keep the tiger from killing them. Boreas was getting weaker as the blood continued to drain out of him, "I can't hold you up much longer, Aurora, do something."

The tiger circled them, dripping saliva off its sharp teeth. She knew it would try to attack them from behind. She watched in horror as the flame died down to just a faint glow hovering over the torch. She made eye contact with the tiger that appeared to be biding its time, waiting for the perfect moment to strike.

Suddenly a full and melodic voice began to sing from across the river. The tiger's face turned toward the momentary distraction of Babs' singing. She sang as loud as she could, her rich soprano tone echoing off the cavern walls. The tiger perked its ears to listen. Just then Boreas' knees gave out and Aurora toppled over him, rolling until her body landed face up directly under the beast. She looked up into a mouth full of sharp teeth and wild eyes as the last flame died out.

Chapter 6

The Professor

The tiger raised his paw, sharp claws poised to maul when a gunshot rang out. The gates rose and the tiger scampered off through hidden corridors within the cavern. Aurora didn't dare move as the image of the tiger's hungry face above her was still so vivid in her mind, her heart racing as if it would jump out of her chest. Her mind was yelling at her to get up, but her body was shocked frozen. Boreas also lay on the ground, clutching his chest, that sight snapped her out of her stupor. She hurried to his side and tore his shirt open, his bare chest revealing the claw marks deep in his skin. She pressed down on the wound with a portion of the shirt clumped together in her hand to try and stop the bleeding. Mrs. Xiomy and Babs were still on the other side of the river, anticipating another gunshot going off.

Boreas's voice screamed out, "If you're going to shoot us, get it over with, you coward!"

Coward! Coward. Coward...

That word echoed over and over again through the corridors. The aftermath of the echo was silence as they waited for gunshots as a response. Aurora continued pressing on the wound while peering over her shoulder for any sign of the person who had them held hostage.

A man's voice rang out, "I'm not going to shoot you, boy. Not yet."

Before their eyes, the river ceased flowing and drained out through tiny holes at the base to reveal an empty ditch. It was as if a drought had occurred in a matter of seconds and the gushing sound of water was now replaced with the heavy tread of footsteps approaching them from what had been the source of the water. Mrs. Xiomy clung to Babs as the footsteps came closer. From the shadows emerged a tall black man, with silvery-gray hair. He had a rigid nose, tightly drawn lips and thick wrinkles creased into his forehead. He wore a long, dirty, white jacket and dark pants, with dark black goggles fastened over his eyes. He inched forward step by step, tapping the ground in front of him with a mahogany-red cane.

"You're all very lucky I am nearly blind and not deaf. If I didn't hear Babs's voice I would have allowed my tiger to enjoy his meal!"

Babs ran up and hugged the man, he put his hands on her face and his cracked lips creased upwards into a semi-smile. She touched his goggles with her hands and shook her head in shock.

"Your...your eyes!" Her voice wavered.

"Old age and a little help from Multiple Sclerosis I'm afraid. I see only shapes and shadows, my dear. But I still have my brain and my hands. I've been stuck hiding down here from the Common Good, but they haven't come close in five years. You were the only ones to get past the quicksand. No one else ever made it to my good buddy Yoseph."

"The tiger has a name?" Boreas whimpered as Aurora helped him to his feet. The mysterious man tapped his cane until he came close to Aurora.

"Yes, and my name is Professor Gassendi."

"You're the Professor!" Aurora said in disbelief.

"No way," Boreas said frankly. "No offense, but I was expecting a little old French man."

"Not everything is ever as you expect," he said and pointed his cane at Boreas's chest. "I see that Yoseph has left his mark on you. Follow me to my chamber where I promise there are no more tricks now that I know I am amongst friends of Babs O'Hara."

Boreas nudged Aurora as they followed the Professor into the ditch and toward the neighboring chamber where they had to walk through a hole in the shape of a lion's mouth, where minutes earlier, water had flowed. It was almost unbelievable.

Babs walked ahead with the Professor, but turned back toward Boreas on occasion to make sure he was alright. Mrs. Xiomy grabbed Boreas's other arm and helped hold him up as they walked on the slippery limestone surface that was still wet from the mysterious vanishing river.

They walked into the Professor's chamber where the air quality was much lighter and they laid Boreas down on a sofa. They were surrounded by shelves set into the limestone that were lined with a huge collection of books. A small fireplace was set into the walls; the dancing flames emitting heat in front of a welcoming bear skin rug.

"I have spent the past five years of my life memorizing every book in this library and mastering my inventions."

"So you have just recently lost your eye sight?"

"It came on gradually, with the disease breaking my body down — one of the reasons, Babs, I couldn't stay in Plymouth Tartarus. My body, my eyesight and eventually my mind will be against me and I couldn't bring you down with me. I hid away here so that the Common Good could not benefit from my knowledge. As you witnessed, my inventions can be used as deadly weapons."

He searched in a cabinet, found gauze pads and other medical supplies that he handed over to Babs. Babs nursed Boreas, her hand moved over his chest, cleaning the wounds. He squirmed in fear as she sterilized the end of a long needle in the fire.

"Boreas, stay still," she said sternly. As she moved to stitch up his wounds, Boreas reached for Aurora's hand.

Surprised, Aurora took his hand and gave it a reassuring squeeze. His hand was calloused and cold as she massaged his palm with her fingers and smiled, "First you survive a knife wound and now a tiger. What's going to be next?"

"Don't forget the time a crazy teacher tried to strangle me with a scarf."

Aurora laughed. "Right! Why do these things keep happening to you?"

"I'm lucky, I guess."

Boreas tried to laugh, but Babs sternly repeated, "Boreas, don't move," and he obeyed instantly, clutching onto Aurora's hand a little tighter.

While Babs worked, the Professor took out some wine and some bread. He was about to serve it when he froze. "Wait... Boreas?"

"We didn't get a chance to introduce ourselves," Aurora said, releasing her hand from Boreas's grasp and held it outstretched toward the professor. "This is Boreas, our teacher Mrs. Xiomy and I'm..."

"I know damn well who you are." He threw the bread back into the pantry. "And I know what you want, but you can't have it! It's done! My ancestor, Pierre Gassendi, did not prophesize about you. He was a scientist. Naming the Northern Lights the 'Aurora Borealis' was his literary license."

"Prophecy or not, Boreas and I are helping Otus, who is a giant, get to the Northern Lights." Aurora stood up and threw the drawn map of Orion and Antares into the Professor's lap. "And Fawn said that you will be able to guide us on the next step of our journey."

"There is no giant," he stated matter-of-factly, "you're lying."

"He's back in the barn. We'll go up and show you."

He shook his head and went to the fire to warm his hands, rubbing them roughly against each other. "Leave immediately! All of you."

Mrs. Xiomy grabbed the Professor by the shirt collar and held him so that he was nearly raised off the ground, teetering on his tiptoes. "Look, I did not just travel thousands of miles in the pocket of a giant's overalls, nearly starve to death in the wilderness, suffocate in quicksand and almost get mauled by an extinct tiger to be told to leave! My husband was David Xiomy and he said that there's a book that can help us and you are going to give us that book or so help me I will feed you to Yoseph myself!"

The Professor's veins on his neck were bulging out of his skin as Mrs. Xiomy held him in her relentless grip. Boreas winked at Aurora; they were both very happy that she was with them.

"You of all people should know what the Common Good is capable of. Your husband knew and still died for it. I don't want to die for it, for them. I just want to be left alone."

She released him and he fell back onto the bear skin rug. "My husband died because they were afraid of what he was capable of. In two short years, he managed to rally people of all religions together, even non-believers, to fight for freedom."

"And look where he ended up, executed. You all don't realize what you are up against."

Aurora slowly sat down on the edge of the fireplace, feeling a brisk cold wind sweep over her body. They had been gone a while. It was most likely nighttime and Otus was up there alone, worrying about them. She began to fear that he would follow them into the cavern and fall victim to the booby traps the Professor had laid out. If only there was a way to reach him...

"Professor, one of us needs to go and warn our friend Otus that we are alright."

The Professor gazed at her through his thick black goggles and said hoarsely, "Your giant, I presume. Where is he supposed to be?"

"In the barn."

The Professor opened a cabinet to reveal what appeared to be camera surveillance equipment.

"Doesn't really help me much now with my eyesight as bad as it is, but there are cameras that cover the grounds and an intercom that will let you communicate with the different areas of the house."

Aurora jumped up and flew to the television set and sure enough, there stood Otus anxiously staring out the door for any sign of his friends. She grabbed the intercom, pressed the button and spoke into the speaker.

"Otus! It's Aurora."

Otus jumped back, whirled around in a circle and nearly fell over his feet. He wasn't able to see the source of the voice that sounded like an alien from outer space.

"I'm speaking through an intercom. We are alright. We are in a cavern and we found the Professor. Do not try to come down and find us because the cavern is booby trapped. Nod if you can hear me."

Otus nodded, still looking in all directions for where the voice was coming from.

The Professor quickly added, "Make sure he doesn't eat the horses."

"He's not that kind of giant."

Aurora shut off the intercom, relieved that Otus was alright. He had looked so worried and a part of her just wanted to go hug him to let him know that they were okay.

Boreas was stitched up and drinking wine out of the silver goblet that the Professor had handed to him. Mrs. Xiomy was surveying the books, searching for any sign of THE book they were looking for. She took out one book at a time, dusted off the name and then placed it back as quietly as she possibly could. The Professor calmly took a bite of bread.

"I have a powerful sense of hearing, Mrs. Xiomy."

Caught in the act, she replaced a book so abruptly that it thumped back into place.

"Well, we're not leaving until we get it. So you better get used to us, Professor."

He reluctantly said, "Well, since I'm a prisoner in my own home, let me tell you a little story about your husband, David Xiomy."

He sat back down on the rug and stared up toward the cave ceiling, where shadows danced from the flickering firelight. He removed his goggles so that his icy blue eyes were like two blank screens into the past. The others gathered around him to listen, even Boreas sat up on the couch to get a better view of the group on the floor below him.

"Sixteen years ago I was a Professor at the University in Candlewick. Inspector Herald entrusted me into his service as Head Scientist in the warfare department. I took the post enthusiastically, since it wasn't easy funding my inventions, and most Universities were not inclined to risk supporting me, due to the huge liability associated with my work. It was there that I uncovered my greatest invention — the soul extractor serum. This serum would dissect the deepest, darkest depths of your soul. If there is good and evil in someone, this will tear it out of them and force them to comply with that side of their being. Every human faces this conflict between good and evil and one will be the victor. With this, the person is forced to choose sides and the true nature of the soul is exposed. From that, I have proven once and for all that a soul does exist. The Inspector urged me to test it on our prisoner, David Xiomy, but I told him that it had to work on people that would be already on the verge of good and evil. He told me to test a higher dose then.

I am not a spiritual man, but I admired Mr. Xiomy's strength and perseverance to remain loyal to his cause and the people he stood for. I gave him a small dose of the serum and as I expected, there was little change in him. If anything, he became more outspoken and temperamental. And then on one of the last occasions, he said to me, 'Are you related to Pierre Gassendi?'

I was completely taken aback. Nobody, and I repeat, nobody, had ever made the connection before and I turned to him and said, 'How did you know?'

'It's funny', he said, his eyes twinkling and his body alert. 'But I think your serum is backfiring.'

He told me that from the moment I injected him with the serum it was as if he could read my thoughts. He asked me about the book, I was so shocked, I cannot tell you. I admitted to him that the book did exist. He nodded and then said, "Aurora Borealis."

I ceased injecting him from that moment on. I told the Inspector that the serum was not working on him, so we used it on other prisoners and got the result he longed for - innocent, peaceful protestors became murderers, rapists and madmen. When I told the Inspector that I wanted to publish my results, proving that a soul exists, he told me to wait until the rebellion was over to ensure that the serum did not fall into the wrong hands.

The day David Xiomy was executed I was in my lab and I felt that an innocent man lost his life. I went out to the graveyard after the execution, and when I saw his blood staining the ground, I felt responsible. Fawn Stockington approached me and told me that she wanted me in the underground rebellion. They needed me to continue David's work. I looked once more at David's blood stain on the floor, blood of this innocent man I had admired, and without hesitation agreed to join her. Together we made plans to build an underwater country. It took five years to complete Plymouth Tartarus. Fawn worked beside me in the lab where we used the government's own tools and resources to benefit our cause. She even picked the location right below Candlewick Park because she claimed that the Inspector would never think that his people would dare rebel right under his nose.

We continued to work for the Inspector, but changed my serum to minimize its effect and that's when he began to get suspicious. I was mixing more of the serum for the Inspector when my friend Pietra warned me that I was next on the list to be executed. They realized I had turned against them and were going to execute me after forcing me to disclose the serum formula. Fawn and I knew it was time to act. I told Fawn and Pietra to free as many prisoners as they could and to wait for my signal. I burned all of my notes and tapes and watched as flames engulfed the lab where I had made some of my greatest discoveries. As the lab burned, smoke filled the hallways of the left wing and I fled with a suitcase containing one last vile of the serum, so that I could replicate it if needed. The entire left wing was destroyed and all my career prospects and dreams vanished that day.

With the diversion, Fawn managed to free some of the prisoners and lead them through an underground tunnel out of the

Candlewick Prison. Other prisoners managed to escape in the chaos, but not everyone made it out alive. I found out that my friend Pietra was one of those who didn't make it. She had saved my life and I couldn't understand; why did I live while she died? Her sacrifice is what has kept me going. Inspector Herald had been brutally burned by the fire and was ruthlessly trying to sniff me out in order to get his hands on my weapons. Fawn was presumed dead, but instead became the leader of our undersea creation, Plymouth Tartarus. How is my famed undersea elevator? Is it still working properly?"

Babs put her arm on the Professor's shoulder and said slowly, "It was destroyed. It was all destroyed."

He took a shaky breath and put his goggles back on his head so that once again his eyes were covered by the mask.

"And Fawn? And the others?"

"Fawn and about three hundred survivors are at a safe haven they called Plymouth Incarnate."

He sighed and sat up, going into the back for his suitcase. "I told you, it's all hopeless. All of it."

He grabbed a book and flung it against the wall. He grabbed another and another until he cleared an entire shelf. "Damn it! It was all for nothing!"

His goggles appeared blurry and Aurora knew that beneath them, he was crying. "It's not all for nothing, Professor. Otus is our last hope. We need to get him to the Northern Lights…"

Boreas laughed darkly and it echoed throughout the entire chamber. His hand was holding his chest as he struggled to his feet. "Aurora, it's over."

She glared at him. "What do you mean, over?"

He pointed at the Professor accusatorily, "He may be blind, but you are all deaf! All of this is ludicrous and it's about time someone says it. So I'm saying it."

"What are you saying?" Aurora felt herself fidgeting with the golden chain around her neck and quickly stopped. "Are you saying that he's lying?"

"I'm saying that we're being played, Aurora! You and me. Come on, he's right! How are we going to stop them? The Common Good! They have guns, bombs, and an entire army! Need I state the obvious that both of us are unarmed with a giant who wouldn't hurt a fly if it was buzzing in his ear! I mean, don't get me wrong, I love Otus, but the Professor is making sense, it's hopeless!"

The Professor eyed Boreas suspiciously, "Who are you?"

Boreas threw up his arms in disbelief. "Great, now you're senile too. What's next?"

"He's Fawn's son." Babs said slowly, and Boreas eyed her as if fire was shooting out of his pupils. Aurora enjoyed that look a little too much.

The Professor nodded, staring at Boreas a bit too long, seeing the resemblance. Boreas's face went rigid and he sunk back down on the couch, grimacing.

Aurora stood up, feeling the same desire the Professor had, to start flinging things across the room. Feelings of exhaustion and frustration were overwhelming her as she slumped against the side of the cave.

"Professor, we just want the book and then we'll leave. That's all we came here for. Hopefully there is something in there that will explain how we are going to fight against the Common Good Army."

Boreas scoffed at this, but Aurora ignored his outburst. The Professor looked at her for a long time and then reluctantly opened his briefcase and took out a glass canister. He explained it was a sleep serum that would leave the victim unconscious for up to 48 hours. He then took out an old withering book with French writing on it and a cover made out of lamb skin. It was the book they had been searching for! Lastly, he removed a vial filled with a neon-green substance.

"This is the last remaining dose of the soul extractor serum."

"Looks more like a drug to me," Boreas said, picking up the vial and turning it onto its side so that with the slightest twitch of his hand, the liquid slid from side to side.

The Professor snatched the vial out of Boreas' hands and cradled it as if it were a baby. "This is my proof that a soul exists, you creaton. Imagine what this would mean to Science and to Religion. You would think that the Common Good would welcome this discovery with open arms. But no, instead they branded me an enemy of the state and sentenced me to death. That's when I realized they didn't want people to know about my invention, they wanted to keep people in the dark so that they would conform to the Common Good's agenda. That is what is going to happen with the Geometric Storm, they will keep people in the dark. It's about power and once people begin to question the Common Good government, they will crumble."

Aurora eyed the neon-green substance with disbelief that something so small could do so much damage.

"We are not here to fight the Common Good government. We are here to stop a Geometric Storm from killing people."

The Professor pointed his walking stick in her direction and smiled his crooked smile, his golden tooth shimmering in the light. "Same thing, my dear. Same thing."

Chapter 7

Prophecy Revealed

urora's ears popped as they ascended through the cavern walls on an elevator contraption that the Professor had designed.

"That was my second prototype," he yelled to be heard over the whooshing sound as they rode through the dark narrow tube, splashing through a pool of water. Completely caught off guard, and soaked, they watched as the Professor opened a door leading them into the basin of a well. They jumped out of the elevator and into the well, and they climbed one after the other on ladder rungs to find themselves once again back on the farm. The Professor dripped out of the well, then pressed a button on his watch and the elevator descended back down into the cavern.

They all stared downwards as it disappeared from view.

"It's all about illusions," the Professor beamed.

"You are either a mad scientist or a magician," Mrs. Xiomy said, scrunching water out of her golden locks.

It was past midnight and the stars shone brightly above them, including Antares with its reddish halo, haughtily staring down at them, knowing it had helped them reach their destination. Aurora wished that star could have forewarned them of the dangers they had encountered. Exhausted and having narrowly escaped death, they all walked slowly back toward the barn that appeared so welcoming and warm in the distance. Mrs. Xiomy was watching the Professor like a hawk as he carried the book and vile in his suitcase. They all agreed to read the prophecy with Otus present since it primarily pertained to him. The Professor continued to use the walking stick, but seemed to learn how to orient himself on his own land while building his cavern bomb shelter/fun house.

They opened the doors to the barn and were immediately met with the intense odor of manure and chickens. They were never so happy to smell anything so uninviting. Otus immediately jumped up, nearly knocking his head against the roof planks of the silo and holding up the light to make sure they were his friends and not his foe. Upon recognizing his friends his smile stretched from ear to ear.

"I am so glad to see you!" Otus called out. "I was so worried!"

"You had good reason," Boreas said, bandaged up and Otus stared at his wound in horror.

"Aurora said that you were alright!" Fury escalated in Otus's voice like a boiling tea kettle. "Who harmed you? Answer me!"

"Calm down, Otus," Aurora said, beseechingly. "Everything has been straightened out. We found the Professor."

"And he has the book," Mrs. Xiomy quickly added.

Otus's face resumed its natural complexion, "Well, where is this Professor?"

In the excitement, they hadn't noticed that the Professor was hiding at the door, his back frozen against it, staring up at the magnitude of the man that stood before him.

"It's not possible. It is against all natural order that you should exist. Your body structure and brain capacity must be ten times the average human being."

"Which makes him a giant," Boreas said, helping the Professor with the words.

"Yes. Yes of course. A giant. How did you come into this world?"

Otus shrugged. "I don't remember anything about my parents. I remember bits and pieces of my past, mostly running and hiding from humans, until I befriended Mrs. Taboo who found me and led me into the basement of the ruby-red house in Candlewick."

"Fascinating. And are there more like you?"

"That's what we were hoping you would tell us."

The Professor scrambled with his briefcase and took out the old and withered book and carefully opened it. Aurora and Mrs. Xiomy cuddled up against Otus's knee and Boreas lay down in the straw, his head resting on Babs's lap. The Professor continued standing but dropped his walking cane so that it clanged to the floor. His face appeared menacing like an insect with just the candlelight flickering around him.

"This is the chapter Pierre Gassendi wrote regarding the Aurora Borealis. This is the only copy and it has been passed on from generation to generation in his family. I am now the rightful and most likely last heir of this family line. Since I can no longer read due to my poor eyesight, I will recite the passage from memory. He writes, 'I had a vision as I approached the beautiful array of lights streaming across the sky in the Arctic Circle; a vision of Boreas, the God of the North Wind, blowing a gust of wind across the sky and of Aurora, the Goddess of Dawn, bestowing the rays of the morning light through her fingertips. Together they encircled a giant as tall as the stars who reached into the lights and moved the colors as if by command. A large and dangerous ball of light was aiming for him but, with the help of the other elements, was able to engulf the ball and swallow it whole and protect it from hitting the ground.

The Goddess of Dawn will inherit her powers beneath the water of the French explored lake. She will be tested in the hour of darkness and her powers will grace her being when she shines a light in the eyes of the one who cannot see.

The God of the North Wind will inherit his powers by fighting against death and riding a black stallion to the tallest point in Hyperborea, a land of eternal spring which on this day will be touched by a cold wind. He will conjure up a gust of wind that will save the person he loves most. Many will perish beneath the mountain of snow.

And the giant is destined to make a choice to decide if what he cherishes most in this world is truly worth fighting for. His choice will come when the Geometric Storm hits'."

The Professor picked up his walking stick and started to draw something in the dirt, his stick being used like a carving knife into wood. He shone the light over the carving and everyone peered at the ground once his shadow stepped aside.

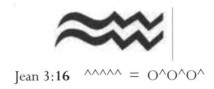

Jean 3:16   ^^^^^ = O^O^O^

Aurora stared at the pictures depicted in the mud and they were triggering something in her mind as if she had seen them before. Like images from a dream that are trapped in the unconscious realm and hidden from reality once awakened. Otus leaned back and closed his eyes letting the book's prophecy settle in; Aurora wondered what he was thinking.

Boreas dug into his bag and pulled out his leather jacket and then zipped it up over his chest. He curtly said, "That was the biggest load of crap I've ever heard."

Otus tried to grab him but Boreas avoided him and dashed to the other side of the barn.

Mrs. Xiomy called out, "Boreas, this is not the time or the place."

He pointed dramatically toward the drawings. "Are these alien signs? Crop circles? Are we cryptologists? Hold on everyone as I blow a giant gust of wind and knock this barn down like the big, bad wolf. Unbelievable!"

The Professor scoffed, fixing his goggles on top of his head, "And you call yourself Fawn's son."

Boreas threw his bag onto the ground and shouted, "Just shut up old man! You don't know anything about me, so just shut up! I am done with this!"

He stormed out of the barn and Babs shook her head at the crew, her crafty manipulative eyes dancing in their sockets. "It does sound a bit far-fetched to me. But that's just my opinion."

She ran off after Boreas and Aurora sank down to her knees holding her head in her hands as the whole room started spinning. She couldn't remember when she had eaten or drank water or slept a full night without waking up in nightmares. She was freezing and looked to find her sweatshirt, digging into her backpack until she located it and threw it on.

Mrs. Xiomy stood up and grabbed the book out of the Professor's hands and started sifting through the weathered pages.

The Professor said, "No wonder Fawn left him, the boy's a coward."

Mrs. Xiomy slammed the book shut. "You are forgetting that he is fifteen-years-old! Both of them are."

"He's a liability, Rana. You don't need me to tell you that. For you were a liability to your own cause. Maybe you both should leave together before you jeopardize all of our lives!"

Otus's eyes sprang open and he stomped his feet on the ground so hard that the entire barn shook like an earthquake. Mrs. Xiomy grabbed onto a beam to steady her balance and the Professor clutched her arm. Mrs. Xiomy immediately tried to shrug him off like he was a cockroach clinging to her skin.

"We've all been chosen for this so let's stop yelling at each other so that we can try to figure out what on earth those drawings mean. For all we know the Geometric Storm is going to happen tomorrow and we're here squabbling like those chickens!"

Aurora looked up at Otus who was towering high above them, his shadow stretched out over the two adults who were now hugging each other for dear life in the face of the giant's wrath.

"Aurora, go talk to Boreas and bring him back here."

"But Babs is…"

"Go and bring him back here now!"

Otus sprayed her with saliva and she wiped her face with the back of her arm to clear her eyes. She reluctantly marched past the drawings and through the double barn doors in search of Boreas.

The Sacred Hour was nearly over and the grass rustled softly as her feet swept over the ground. A coyote howled in the distance and she walked a little faster trying to make out two sets of footprints in the mud. She heard voices and she sunk down and tried not to make a sound.

"You need to get out of here while you still can."

It was Babs whispering in her melodic voice and Aurora saw her sitting beside Boreas against a tree stump, the arms of the weeping willow tree nearly covering their silhouettes from view.

"I can't lose you like I lost Eileen!"

Aurora froze as she saw Babs lean in and kiss him on the mouth, deep and sensual, holding him close in her embrace. He stroked her auburn hair and caressed her back as she leaned in closer and kissed him over and over again.

Aurora felt her blood boiling and her heart racing as she quickly turned to retreat back to the barn, when her foot stepped on a twig, cracking it in two. Boreas quickly separated from Babs and stood up in a defensive stance.

"Who's out there?"

She couldn't run and cursed under her breath for being so fat and loud. If Babs was in her shoes she would have slithered through the brush without making a sound, her sneakers just like moccasins. Aurora whirled around and pretended she had just reached them and hadn't seen a thing.

"Oh there you are. I've been looking for you. Babs, can you go back to the barn? Otus needs to talk to you."

"It sounds like you're trying to get rid of me." She rose to her feet and gave Boreas's hand a reassuring squeeze. As she walked past Aurora, she whispered menacingly, "Don't talk him out of this."

Aurora waited for Babs to be out of earshot then walked closer to Boreas. He stood behind the flailing arms of the weeping willow tree, revealing his face between its fingers, astute and annoyed.

"I know what you're going to say, so just say it."

She laughed, and grabbed the weeping willow vine and stepped behind it so that she was face to face with him underneath the canopy of falling tear drops.

"You have no idea what I want to say to you right now."

He turned his back on her and started walking to the opposite side of the tree trunk.

"Babs wants me to go back to the safe haven with her. She agrees with me that this entire mission is absolutely crazy!"

"So you are abandoning us!" Aurora cried out.

He shot her a look as he leaned back against the trunk. "You make me sound like my mother."

She followed him under the weeping willow tree exclaiming, "How can you think of abandoning us! You were the one who came chasing after me back in Candlewick, remember? You said that we had to help Otus, your words, Boreas."

He banged his head against the trunk. "That was before I knew about…Why are you even here? Can't you leave and tell Babs to come back. At least she cares about me."

She sat on the opposite side of the trunk, her hand picking up a fallen leaf that she twirled nonchalantly in her hand. "Yeah, cares that she has a travelling companion back to the safe haven."

"You never liked her since day one. Admit it!"

"How could I not like her? I mean, she saved my life today. Of course I don't know why she couldn't have sang before the tiger nearly ate me for dinner…I mean, singing can be really difficult," she said sarcastically.

He scooted his way over to her side, but she got up and stood towering over him. It was too dark to make out how he was looking at her, but somehow she sensed it.

"You're upset about the kiss."

She grabbed the weeping willow vine that was flapping into her face and tore it from the branch. "What kiss?"

"You know what kiss. You were standing there, so stop pretending like you don't know."

"Oh, *that* kiss! You know Boreas, that didn't upset me. Nope. The thing that upset me is that ten minutes ago you stormed out of the barn like a freaking child after we were being told that, yeah, we are going to have to save the world. And you go making out with that manipulative flirt and totally don't care about Otus, or Mrs. Xiomy…"

"Or…you."

"Yeah, or me! So, that's why I'm upset, Boreas. Because all you care about is yourself."

She started to walk away, but he grabbed her by the shoulder and whirled her around to face him. The sun was beginning to rise over the horizon with a ghostly hue cast onto the meadow, illuminating his face. His thick eyebrows were squinting down and his cheeks were flushed from the wind chill.

"Look, it's not that I don't care about you guys. Because I do. But I've gone through my entire life being told I am not good enough. Never could meet my father's expectations. Why can't I be more like Jonathan? Jonathan can do no wrong. And I'm the one here on this mission. I thought finally, I can do something that Jonathan can't. I was chosen for this. And, after all this, I still feel I'm not good enough. That Jonathan is better suited for this mission than me. He should have been chosen."

The Awakened Hour had approached and the rooster crowed as the sun highlighted the fields like golden blades of grass swaying in rhythm with the wind. She tucked a strand of her hair behind her ear, thinking about Jonathan and wishing he could be here with her in this beautiful field and kissing her under the willow tree. How different things would have been if Jonathan had been chosen. Boreas eyed her curiously as her mind drifted like the willow seeds floating and encircling them in that meadow. He watched her and his eyes opened wide in realization, as if finally putting the pieces together.

He shook his head at her. "You also wish Jonathan had been chosen, don't you, Aurora?"

She shook her head in disbelief, "What? What are you talking about?"

"After everything he did to you. That's who you fall for?"

"Boreas. It's just a crush. You know that I don't wish…I mean…you were chosen for this. Not Jonathan."

His fingers rose to his temples and he lurched his head back and laughed darkly at the clouds hovering overhead. "Maybe you like being called Fatty Alvarez. Maybe you like it when he puts you down and lets Hattie make fun of you in front of him. You probably live for it and can't wait to see him again so that they can throw more punch on you like at the dance. Next time, I won't distract him. Next time I'll throw punch in your face too."

She slapped him hard, her hand imprinted on his right cheek. Her hand stung from the impact and Boreas rubbed his cheek, his eyes scowling at her.

"I'm leaving! Goodbye, Aurora."

He brushed past her and she stood there, breathing heavily and holding back tears. She wouldn't let him see her like that. She sunk down onto the grass and lay there like a wounded animal, feeling so humiliated. She didn't know how much time had passed, lying on her back in that field, looking up at the sky moving though she knew she was going nowhere. Clouds whirled past her in fragmented discourse and oh, how lonely she felt, so lonely and so afraid. She put her face in her hands and tried to block out the sun; wanting desperately to disappear.

Chapter 8

The Gift

Boreas snuck to the back door where Babs was supposed to meet him. He whistled and put his ear to the door, waiting for her to signal back, but no signal sounded in the morning air. Instead, a giant hand reached down, grabbed him around the waist and held him upside down, the blood rushing to his head as he looked down toward the ground. Otus hung onto his legs and swung him back and forth as he headed back into the barn. Boreas yelled for help, but he spotted Mrs. Xiomy and the Professor sitting there keeping a keen eye on Babs who mouthed, "I'm sorry."

Otus held him upside down, close to his mouth and his massive tongue stretched out of his mouth and nearly licked Boreas across the face. He licked his lips and said, "You know, I've never eaten a human being before, but I think today might be the day."

"Otus, stop it and put me down!"

"Where is Aurora?"

"She's outside. Damn it Otus, you can't stop me from leaving!"

Otus threw him up in the air until his flying body was right-side up, then grabbed him again in mid-air, squeezing Boreas until he could hardly breathe.

"Just watch me."

He slammed through the barn door and cried out, "Aurora, where are you?"

Boreas was desperately trying to pry himself out of Otus's fingers but they wouldn't budge. Just then, Otus spotted Aurora walking towards them slowly, her clothes dirty and her face pale. Boreas turned his face away from Aurora, his face still stinging where she had slapped him.

"Boreas still thinks he's leaving."

"Let him leave," she said, disheartened. She didn't even look up at Otus when she walked past and sat down huddled with her knees pulled up to her chest and her sweatshirt pulled down over her legs.

Mrs. Xiomy ran to her side and said, "What on earth are you two ranting and raving about this time?"

"Why can't you take a hint and leave me alone!" She grabbed a piece of straw and started chewing on it from the side of her mouth.

The Professor was wiping his goggles with his shirt sleeve as he added, "Can we please get back to the pictures?"

Boreas kept on fighting to get free from Otus's grasp but Otus held him tighter, like a treasured doll.

The Professor adjusted the goggles back over his eyes and again took out his walking stick to draw in the dirt. "Now then, my ancestor, Pierre Gassendi, was both a physicist and a mathematician. Most likely this is a formula of some sort. Not sure if they teach you kids atomic theory in school, but these little circles could very well be atoms."

"It's all nonsense," Boreas yelled, his voice sounding more like a pipsqueak as Otus was cutting off his oxygen supply.

"Is there a mute button on that kid?" Mrs. Xiomy put her hands behind her head as she laid down on the straw patch, shutting her eyes for some sleep.

Aurora took off her sweatshirt and used it for a pillow, patting it down and putting it under her head. "I think we should all get some sleep. We need to be refreshed to leave here and start heading back to the United States of the Common Good toward Lake Champlain."

"Why there?" Otus asked letting out a giant yawn.

"Because the United States of America was still unexplored while Pierre Gassendi was alive and the French explorer Samuel de Champlain lived in the early 1600's too. Champlain's noted explorations were Lake Champlain and Quebec, so Pierre would have likely heard about them. I am truly hoping that Lake Champlain is the right area because at least there will be cover for Otus to hide in. If it's the city, we'll have to come up with a more brilliant idea."

Boreas's ears perked up at the mention of Lake Champlain. His father had a cabin out there. He remembered they used to all go there when he was a boy. If he could pretend to comply a little while longer, he and Babs could escape one night and make a run for the cottage. From there, they could escape this mad expedition.

Otus stared down at him and said, "No fight on this one, Boreas?"

"No," he said firmly still avoiding Aurora's gaze. "I think it's a good place to start."

☆ ☆ ☆

Aurora ran down the turquoise steps of her house in Candlewick, passing the black and white pictures of her grandma on the wall and wandered through the maze of collections piled high toward the ceiling. At the end of the maze sat her father, looking content and clean shaven, absorbed in reading his history magazines. Her mother was wearing a red robe and her hair was in curlers under a hair-net. She wasn't wearing makeup, revealing some slight wrinkles that revealed her age that she kept hidden from people during the day. She was drinking her cup of coffee, smiled as Aurora approached and said, "Aurora, you look beautiful today. Have you been losing weight?"

"Thanks, Mom," she said, kissing her on the top of the head.

Her mother asked Aurora if she wanted some pancakes.

"Blueberry is your favorite, isn't it darling?"

Aurora followed her mother to the stove to help her prepare the batter. She started mixing the ingredients in a silver bowl until the batter was creamy and all the flour had been absorbed into the mixture. Suddenly there was a loud crash and something smashed through the living room window. Horrified, Aurora watched the ivory draperies catch on fire. The fire engulfed all their collections, burned the baseball cards, the beanie babies, and ate away at the leather covers of the books, the pages shriveling up and turning to ash. The fire was crawling along the ground, inching its way toward the three of them in the kitchen. The silver bowl dropped out of her hands, the mixture drizzled out, leaking into the cracks on the wooden floor. Her parents were oblivious to the danger present in their house, her father was still reading the magazine and her mother was still preoccupied with flipping the pancakes. Aurora yelled and screamed for them to get out, but they didn't listen and continued laughing and smiling as smoke and flames enveloped them.

Aurora jumped up with a start, dripping in sweat and her body shaking. She looked around frantically for flames, but there was only darkness. She heard the soft pitter-patter of rain on the roof and realized she was still in the barn. Her neck ached from sleeping on it the wrong way and she cracked it, letting out a sigh as she did so.

"Dreaming of Candlewick?"

She whirled around toward the voice, coming from the stables. With wrists tied firmly to a stable spike, Boreas sat. Otus had tied him there to ensure he didn't try to make a run for it while the others slept. Babs was locked in the chicken coop, despite her protests that she wouldn't run away or help Boreas escape. Of course they didn't trust her. Aurora felt so thrilled when they turned the lock and she secretly hoped one of the chickens would lay an egg in Babs' precious hair.

She stood up and walked past Boreas to get a drink of water. Her mouth was so parched and she drank heartily to satiate her thirst. She then dunked the ladle back into the bowl, carried it carefully over to Boreas and put it against his lips.

His lips wrapped around the side of the ladle and he gulped the water down, his Adam's apple bobbing as he swallowed.

"Thanks," he said slowly, his voice raspy after sleeping. Beside him a horse neighed, and he immediately tried to shift away from the animal out of fear.

Aurora enjoyed watching Boreas like this, looking so vulnerable. She stood up to pat the horse on the top of the head. She caressed its mane slowly, feeling hot air blowing out of the horse's nostrils in delight.

"It's a cruel joke tying me to the stable, knowing how much I hate horses."

She continued petting the creature and said, "If I had my way, I would have tied you to the horse. But then he'd trample you and we would have way too much mess to clean up."

"I deserve that."

Boreas uncrossed his legs and as if sensing his motion, the horse neighed and panted heavily. Boreas inched as far away from the horse as possible. Boreas was right. For some reason horses didn't like him.

"Aurora, I want to apologize."

She squatted down, hugging her knees for support, "I don't want to hear it."

"Look, I was angry. When I found out that you liked Jonathan, I got so…anyway…I shouldn't have said what I said."

"But you did say it, Boreas! You really think you have it so hard and you don't even think that maybe, I've had it hard too."

The pitter-patter of the rain drops pounded stronger against the roof, hitting with swifter strokes. Boreas's words from the night before played over and over again in her mind; she wanted to drive them from her memory, but she couldn't forget.

He was struggling with his bonds. His hair was sticking up and she couldn't help herself, she reached up and smoothed it down with her hand. He looked up at her with eyes so tender and soft, staring into hers. She fought the trance and backed away quickly.

Aurora took a deep breath, "When all the kids at school picked on me because of my weight, or because I was different, I used to have a dream that a boy, the only one who ever smiled at me, would like me. That was Jonathan. That may sound stupid to you and I know he doesn't even know I exist, but you can't help who you fall for."

Boreas closed his eyes then they flickered open, staring intently into her own. "But what about us?"

Her fingers stopped combing through his hair as the goose bumps prickled her skin. She leaned away from him, crossing her arms over her chest, "There is no us, Boreas."

"But after everything we've been through…"

"After everything we've been through, I really thought that we were friends. But I think that was just another stupid thought for someone like me." She paused and took a deep breath, clutching onto the bar for support. "A friend doesn't turn against you when things get rough. That's not the way this works."

He leaned forward, biting his lip like he was fighting something within him. A ray of moonlight streamed through from the skylight and rested on his face, illuminating the features that she had memorized throughout their journey. The way his eyes squinted a little when he was thinking; those eyes that now stared intently into her own, like they were reading her mind. He whispered, "You can't deny there's something here. I thought it's just that you didn't like me, but you are so fixated on Jonathan that you're not seeing what's right in front of you."

"You're with Babs."

"Because you're in love with a guy who doesn't know you exist!"

She pulled the knife out of her pocket and flipped it open so that the blade stuck out. She put the sharp edge against the twine and rocked it back and forth until the twine gave way, releasing his wrists.

"No, Boreas. We're just the answer to a prophecy. We can't be anything else."

Boreas massaged his wrists, letting the blood flow back into his veins. Aurora put the knife back into her pocket and stood up. She peered out the window and noticed that it was almost the Sacred Hour when they would have to leave this place that had felt so safe and so far removed from the dangers that lay ahead.

She headed over to the chicken coop to let Babs out when Boreas cried out, "Aurora, I..."

"Can't a man sleep without all this racket?!?" the Professor hollered out.

Boreas immediately turned and pretended he was packing up his stuff.

"I swear things were so much quieter when I was in the cavern. The only racket was my friend Yoseph. Now poor Yoseph is stuck fending for himself."

Aurora opened the latch of the chicken coop to find Babs gathering eggs from the chickens and putting them into a wicker basket.

"Since the Professor is not trying to kill us anymore, he won't mind us using his stove to make eggs."

Aurora's stomach growled and she smiled at the girl that the night before she wished would have egg yolk stuck in her hair. Mrs. Xiomy was thrilled to use the skillet and they all migrated to the farm house where she cooked them scrambled eggs, eggs over easy, poached eggs and they all sat down to their first full breakfast in a long time. Otus burped and everyone laughed as the Professor told them stories about his other experiments. There was research to find cures for cancer and even the common cold. He had found ointments that healed even the worst mosquito bite in less than 2 minutes. He had been a druggist for many years until the war came and no one had money to spend on his ointments and medicines. They were too busy spending money on weapons. The only thing they were concerned about was surviving a bullet and his medicines couldn't bring the dead back to life. So he realized that in order to make a living, he had to abide by the basic principle of supply and demand. He went to University to try to come up with a resurrection drug and in the process that is how he developed the soul extractor.

"Sometimes one road leads you down another and only the brave will follow it to see where it will lead."

It was drizzling now and Aurora watched Boreas get up from the rocking chair and take a plate out to Otus who was standing outside the house since he couldn't fit inside it. She hadn't said another word to Boreas since their morning talk and vice versa. She preferred it that way.

Her words replayed over and over again, "we can't be anything more."

Did she believe that? Did she want that?

She took the last bite of her scrambled eggs, chewed it slowly, savoring each morsel. She washed it down with some water and realized this could be the last breakfast they had together for a while.

She looked through the blurred window pane and spotted Boreas and Otus immersed in conversation, seemingly planning something and ignoring the raindrops pouring down on them. She saw Boreas hold out his hand to the giant and Otus took the little hand in his and shook it. It felt like yesterday she had made the same gesture with Otus back in Candlewick Park, promising to not give up on him. They were in this together. Like the Professor said, some journeys lead you down a road you never expected, and only the brave will follow where it leads. She looked around at the people in her life, people she never expected to be a part of her journey. And here they all were in this brief moment of time, defying all logic and reason and searching for magic in an ordinary world.

Mrs. Xiomy snapped her out of her trance by calling her over to help with the dishes. Mrs. Xiomy, while busy scrubbing a pan, said, "I never leave a pot or pan in the sink back home and wouldn't do so in a friend's house either—even if this is the same booby-trapped pan that sent us falling into a quicksand pit yesterday."

Otus peeked his head through the small door, calling out, "All aboard!"

The Professor said, "All aboard what?"

Mrs. Xiomy took his arm and led him toward Otus and pointed at his overalls pocket.

"We're travelling by pocket?" The Professor cried out. "That's something in all my years I've never done."

Otus lifted them up to the pocket and carefully deposited them inside. Babs and Aurora jumped on the next palm and rode it up and Aurora looked around for Boreas. She then heard him holler from above her. She arched her neck up and could make him out sitting in Otus's ear cavity.

"What is he doing?" Babs cried out. "Boreas, come down here now!"

Boreas waved back, not looking the least bit disconcerted. All of a sudden Otus jumped high into the air, the Professor shrieked while the barn and house disappeared from view. Otus perched his legs on top of the mountains, like a hawk surveying its surroundings, and the scenery before them was breathtaking. The majestic snowcapped mountains reached high into the sky, their peaks hidden by puffy dove-gray clouds. Emerald hills stretched as far as the eye could see and the sun peeked its way through the clouds, causing the mountains before them to glisten. Aurora leaned over the side of the pocket and nearly fell out as a rainbow appeared over the mountain range, the colors blended together as one, cascading over the mountains like a waterfall. Her heart stopped as she beheld this beautiful picture before her eyes, remembering the bedtime story she had told Boreas and the others back in the wilderness, about the rainbow and Indigo, who wished to be seen as beautiful in the eyes of the moon. Aurora looked up just in time to see Boreas slide down Otus's jacket sleeve and land in the pocket besides Babs.

"It was your idea to bring us here, wasn't it? What a beautiful gift!" Babs said hugging him, and holding him close to her chest.

Aurora continued to stare at the rainbow and smiled to herself, knowing full well that the gift was not for Babs, but for her. She had heard about guys giving necklaces, cards and other presents to show how they feel, but this was a new one. Boreas had given her a rainbow.

Chapter 9

The Ambassador

The media press room in the Candlewick Government Building was bustling with activity in the late afternoon. Analise was beyond anxious, typing madly on her keyboard, careful to meet her deadline. The Inspector would not be happy if this story didn't make the airwaves for the 6 o'clock news. It was crazy that she was now feeding stories to her old boss at Channel Four news instead of being the lonesome intern begging for a story. She felt on top of the world, though of course she was playing the role of press secretary for Inspector Herald. However, as the days progressed, it was getting more difficult discerning truth from fallacy.

Miss Thompson plopped something on her desk, eyeing her with an irksome glance and fixing her glasses on the bridge of her nose.

"They've located an enemy compound at Machu Picchu. The Inspector believes the two fugitives, Aurora Alvarez and Boreas Stockington, are hiding there. The Inspector wants you to report that they are almost in custody."

"Is that true?" Analise asked, biting the tip of her pencil.

"If the Inspector says it, then it's true."

Miss Thompson turned her back on her. Analise gave the head secretary a dirty look behind her back.

She tweaked the press release and emailed it out to all the major networks and leaned back in her chair, relieved it was 5:55pm. She had just made deadline with five minutes to spare.

"Don't get too comfortable," Miss Thompson called out to her. "The Ambassador Ball is in one hour."

How could Analise forget? It was what everyone was talking about for the past three weeks, the night when Inspector Herald would introduce a new IDEAL Ambassador to promote the IDEAL's policies throughout the world. In other words, be the poster-child for the IDEAL. Analise wondered who would be brainwashed enough to volunteer for this role. She kicked off her flats, put on her red high heels then dragged herself into the bathroom to make herself beautiful.

She looked at herself in the mirror. She fixed the tight black dress she was wearing with the low neckline. The bright ruby necklace that the Inspector had given to her as a welcome present hung loosely around her neck. It was like the ruby was a constant reminder that if she failed, there was a one-way ticket back to the Candlewick Prison with her name on it. How did Jake talk her into this? She hurriedly fixed her eyeliner and applied lipstick to her trembling lips. She took the makeup brush and hurriedly applied pink blush on her dark-skinned cheekbones. Her hair she had straightened the day before so she felt presentable. If only this was real, she thought. But, like the mask she was wearing, it was all a mirage, for the Common Good.

She laughed to herself and exited the bathroom, banging right into Jake Fray. He looked so handsome yet severe in his First Lieutenant uniform, his hair gelled back, but there were no sunglasses hiding his eyes from the world this time. He looked startled and out of character when he recognized Analise, then apologized politely.

"Would you like to make a statement?" She cried out quickly when he was about to walk away. "About the Patrol Planes that nearly caught two teen fugitives?"

He excused himself from his fellow officers and walked up to Analise. "I hear the Machu Picchu discovery made deadline," he said in his cold manner. She shivered with him so close to her.

"You know it." She replied haughtily. "Made some tweaks as per the Inspector's request."

He nodded like he was semi-listening. He then looked down at the ruby necklace dangling from her bare neck. "Really beautiful, a present from the Inspector, I presume?"

She smiled tightly, "He knows how to thank a girl for a job well done."

"I bet." He didn't look amused, but continued on like they were business associates. "The new ambassador, you will want to schedule an interview with her. Prevent her from answering any questions."

"So the new ambassador is a *HER*," Analise asked, perking her interest, "Anyone I know?"

His eyes looked deeply concerned and troubled, but he merely responded in his strong voice, "Yes."

They stood there looking at each other in silence, when Analise finally asked, "Sooo…are we just going to keep staring at each other or are you going to be a gentleman and escort me into the ballroom?"

His eyes lit up for a moment, but then returned to their hollow coldness. "That wouldn't be wise."

"Stop being wise for one moment and be human," she laughed, taking his arm, something he wasn't used to, and he tensed up. "There's nothing wrong with escorting a beautiful woman into a ballroom. Pretend like this is our prom."

"A prom," he laughed nervously, like the word was foreign to him.

"Yes, look at what a good person I am. Helping you to live out quintessential events you missed from high school."

"Missing a prom is not something that keeps me up at night." He paused. "Did you go to yours?"

"Yes," she replied abruptly. "A complete disaster, as most proms are from what I hear. My date showed up late and then ended up leaving with a different girl. But I got my first story published in the Candlewick Times about life at Candlewick High afterwards, so it wasn't a huge waste."

"The guy was an idiot," he said plainly.

"What guy? My date?"

He turned to her and smiled, "He shouldn't have left you. Tell me his name and I'll take care of him for you."

She laughed, "I think that's a little extreme, but I thank you for the offer."

Two soldiers stood at attention as they approached, saluting the First Lieutenant with a sign of respect and then nervously opened the doors. Jake didn't even acknowledge them. Jake and Analise walked into a beautifully decorated room, the same one that Analise had been supervising that entire week with vendors and decorations to ensure that everything was just right for the new ambassador unveiling. Jake clutched onto her arm a little more as if he was protecting her as they made their way down the red-carpeted staircase. Inspector Herald was standing at the bottom of the staircase and gazed up at Analise with rare affection. He was a tall man, wearing a white tuxedo and a black top hat covering his bald head.

Some foundation was applied to his skin to help hide some of the burn marks on his face. His eyes were coal black and though some of his face had been distorted during the fire, he stood with confidence that demanded the public's attention.

"Why Miss Jones, you look absolutely radiant this evening."

He took her hand and kissed it tenderly with his lips.

"Thank you, Inspector," she answered, still linking arms with Jake, as if unsure who should let go first.

"First Lieutenant," he acknowledged Jake fondly, as Jake saluted him, but the Inspector took his hand and put it down to his side. "None of those formalities tonight. This is a rare night to celebrate, isn't it, my young friends? Miss Jones, may I escort you to your seat?"

Analise turned to Jake who immediately unlocked his arm from hers. Instantly she felt empty as he took a step away from her. The Inspector put his arm around her waist, leading her to his table.

"I know the First Lieutenant recommended you for this position, but I didn't realize you were friendly toward one another."

Analise fixed the strands of her hair over her right shoulder. "We were neighbors growing up in Candlewick. It was nice catching up with him."

"He's a good soldier, and a good man," the Inspector said with admiration, "the type of man who could take my place one day."

Analise bit her lip, thinking of how Jake was conspiring behind the Inspector's back.

"You did a decent job on the Machu Picchu story," he said, in his charming voice as they promenaded through the crowds of people.

"Thank you, Inspector," she said, as he handed her a glass of champagne from a waiter's tray. "Any new developments in the chase?"

He smiled, "You're always in reporter mode, Miss Jones. Relax tonight and enjoy."

"Just looking forward to writing that story," she replied, taking a sip of the bubbly liquid.

"I tell you Miss Jones, I thought my biggest victory was killing IMAM fifteen years ago. But I think I will feel even more victorious after I have captured those two traitorous teenagers."

"And the giant?"

He looked at her unsteadily. "Did Jake tell you about that?"

Her mouth went numb. "No," she quickly stated. "I just do my research, like with any story. You see I got my hands on the tracking surveillance pictures from the chase and saw something that looked kind of gigantic, so just assumed."

They reached the table and he slid the chair out for her to sit.

"I think we can keep the giant piece off the record, don't you agree," he whispered in her ear.

She took another sip of the champagne, feeling so stupid for letting that slip out of her mouth, nearly putting Jake into danger. Too much was counting on them. The Inspector was deep in conversation with some of the High Ambassadors so she surveyed the room searching for Jake and found him speaking with Miss Thompson in the far corner. She was about to get up and try to warn him about her slip-up when the lights dimmed and the room fell silent as Miss Thompson walked up to the podium dressed in a floor-length ivory gown. Her glasses were still glued to her face and her voice soared through the room.

"This man needs no introduction since he helped free this country from religious tyranny that had caused such devious acts as the Towers of Freedom bombing. This man, along with the IDEAL, have given us hope when we thought we were lost in an embittered world of constant fighting and wars. He freed us from ourselves and I am so proud to be a part of The Common Good. Here he is, the spokesperson for The IDEAL and our leader, Inspector Herald."

Everyone in the room jumped to their feet, including Analise. Clapping sounded as Inspector Herald shook hands and walked up to the podium like a politician.

He cleared his throat and took a sip of water. "Thank you!" He silenced everyone with a wave of his hand. "The IDEAL and I could not be more pleased with how far this country has come in 15 short years. Our economy is flourishing, Common Good protesting has been eradicated since we came into power, and we have made the future brighter for our children and our children's children."

More applause sounded and Analise eyed Jake who was not clapping in the shadows by the stage curtain.

"But this is just the beginning. True some have said my methods are Machiavellian, but there is a price for freedom, and we all know that price. Many of us have lost loved ones through the rebellion and even earlier when the religious zealots were constantly at war with each other. We have, as a people, helped abolish those religions from our shores and I swear I will do everything in my power to ensure we keep this country safe from anyone who is illegally practicing these dangerous beliefs behind closed doors. Just recently, as you all have heard, our very own library was broken into by two teenagers, and they were helped internally by one of our own legal councils, Charles Alvarez. He has been tried and incarcerated for helping his daughter Aurora Alvarez and her traitorous accomplice, Boreas Stockington, escape from Candlewick Prison. The Common Good Army is in hot pursuit of these traitors and will stop at nothing to bring them to justice."

More applause and people cheering on their feet.

"But there is one who will stop at nothing to help us bring the IDEAL's policies to fruition. One who will speak across the world to highlight the IDEAL's words and vision, help us bring peace, and stop the protestors from rising. She alone can help make Aurora Alvarez and others like Aurora see reason. She has been given a second chance, for her family's sake, and for the sake of people like her who think that the IDEAL has forgotten them, believe that the IDEAL has persecuted people unjustly. This woman has seen the light, that we have not abandoned her; that we are the voice of the people. She possesses the willpower and the strength to promote the truth. Her love of her country and the people in it will help us continue to rise in the years to come."

He paused and smiled for the cameras. "Without further ado, please welcome the new ambassador for the Common Good…. Norma Alvarez."

Applause and gasps erupted throughout the ballroom as Norma Alvarez, wearing a stunning black frilly dress with her hair in large curls that cascaded down her shoulders. Her face beamed in the limelight like she was born to grace that stage. She gave Inspector Herald a big hug by the podium as cameras flickered and the spot-light was on her.

"Thank you," Norma Alvarez spoke out through the micro-phone, bright red lipstick accentuating her full lips with every word. There was not a twinge of nervousness in her tone. "I accept this great honor and I hope to continue to speak the IDEAL's words and teachings to all who are willing to listen."

People started calling out, raising their hands with questions when Analise jumped to her feet and found her way to the stage. She quickly told Miss Thompson to lead Norma Alvarez off the stage then hastened to the microphone, "Mrs. Alvarez will not be taking any further questions tonight. I will have an in-depth inter-view with the new Ambassador later this week that will air on all major channels. Thank you and the IDEAL has spoken."

She hurried off stage where Mrs. Alvarez stood, now looking fragile without the limelight to boost her courage.

"Congratulations, Madame Ambassador," Analise said, taking Mrs. Alvarez by the arm and leading her into the backroom, feeling pissed off that Jake or the Inspector hadn't warned her about this media circus. "Now the media is going to want to ask you loads of questions but you will just say 'No Comment'. You will stay with me and Miss Thompson until the interview at the end of this week."

"Herald didn't mention anything about an interview," she said, nervously biting one of her perfectly manicured red nails. "I don't think....I think I have lived up to my side of the bargain...agreeing to this ambassador gig."

"Look," Analise said sternly, careful that no one was able to cavesdrop. "I don't know what Herald has in store for you, but I am on your side and want to look out for you...and your daughter."

Mrs. Alvarez looked up at the mention of her daughter. "My daughter and my husband are the reasons why my world has fallen apart. This is the only way I can think of to protect them. But you, Analise Jones, must never say that you are protecting my daughter out loud again unless you want to find yourself thrown into Candlewick Prison. I will not warn you again."

And like that she whirled around, her curls bouncing behind her, as she sashayed out the door, the fragrance of rose petals still present in that room.

✫ ✫ ✫

Jake took a shot of whiskey. The ballroom had emptied, leaving only him and the bottle in the empty auditorium that had turned the night upside down with the introduction of Norma Alvarez as the new Ambassador for the Common Good.

He had sat there watching Analise take charge of the situation. And he had also observed how the Inspector had watched her closely, like a hawk pondering its prey.

"May I join you?"

Startled, he jumped to his feet. The alcohol made him feel woozy as he made out the features of Inspector Herald before him.

"Inspector!" Jake cried out, horrified. His uniform suit jacket was hanging loose on a chair and he looked disheveled. "I didn't know…"

The Inspector laughed. "You remind me of myself at your age. No need to apologize. May I?"

Sitting back down on the bench, feeling awkward in that large room, he poured the Inspector a glass of whiskey, the brown liquid dribbling into the glass.

They clinked glasses and embraced the burning sensation as they swallowed the liquor.

"Puts hair on your chest, the IDEAL would tell me," The Inspector said, cradling the glass in his hands. "This reminds me of the nights on the campaign trail when we would just be drinking, contemplating the day… how far we had come."

"Where is the IDEAL now?" Jake asked, taking a swig of the whiskey, knowing he was testing the waters, but the alcohol was clouding his better judgment.

Herald turned to his young protégé. "I want to tell you the truth, Jake. The IDEAL is in me, in you, in all of us. The IDEAL is the best of what we yearn to be. It's an idea."

Jake stared at him, thinking he had misheard him. "So there is no IDEAL?"

Herald started cackling, grabbing the bottle and pouring himself a second glass. "Feels so good to get that off my chest after all these years. No, well there was someone who thought of the

IDEAL. Max Radar, my compatriot, ran the campaign. Him and I…well let's just say we didn't see eye to eye after a while."

"You disposed of him?"

The Inspector drank heartily and closed his eyes. "No. The job was never completed. He's still out there biding his time, but he was all brains, he didn't have the backbone for the execution. He's not a man like us."

Jake sat there, straddling the swivel chair and rocking back and forth, feeling a little nauseous as all of this was sinking in.

"That reporter friend of yours, she's going to be too much trouble, I fear. She mentioned something to me tonight about a giant."

Jake went into robotic motion, bringing the glass to his lips, sipping on it, swallowing, afraid to make any sudden movements.

The Inspector continued, "Did you mention anything to her about a giant?"

Jake's insides did somersaults but he banged his glass against the table, the glass shattering and whiskey spilling all over his hand. "That is strictly confidential information," he yelled out, feigning insult. "I would never tell a living soul not involved with the mission and if she dared to say I had anything to do with it…"

"First Lieutenant, calm down!"

Jake realized he was shaking, shards of glass had cut his hand and he just ignored the bleeding.

"I am sorry, Inspector. It's not like me to lose myself like that. It must be the alcohol. I will turn in."

"I think that's a good idea."

Jake took a cloth napkin and wrapped it around his hand. He saluted the Inspector and said good night.

"First Lieutenant…" the Inspector called out, his voice echoing in that empty auditorium. "That old saying is that it gets lonely at the top. It's…it's not easy staying true to what you believe in. And the long list of friends I had at the beginning of the journey, has been reduced to two men. One being you and I don't want to scratch your name off that list."

Jake turned around slowly, staring at the man before him who looked just as helpless as any human being. This man had changed the world and was now counting the names of his friends on one hand.

"I hope you'll never have to."

Chapter 10

Division

"Read it again?"

The Professor cleared his throat and repeated from memory the passage Aurora requested.

"The Goddess of Dawn will inherit her powers beneath the water of the French explored lake. She will be tested in the hour of darkness and her powers will grace her being when she shines a light in the eyes of the one who cannot see."

They were at Lake Champlain and Aurora wrapped her mauve sweater tighter around her shoulders. They were in the Adirondack Mountains at the edge of where the lake bordered Vermont and New York. Autumn was upon them as the leaves from the trees were already changing, transforming into a collage of colors. Some leaves were already drifting toward the ground, succumbing to the hands of the wind. They landed gracefully into the placid sapphire lake that stretched outwards for miles. They found a safe clearing in the woods to set-up camp where Otus could remain hidden from fishermen and tourists.

Soon Boreas was snoring lightly with Babs leaning against his chest, her long hair draped over his body like a blanket. She was now wearing a sweater dress that hugged at her knees with full-length leggings. Mrs. Xiomy was wearing another indigo and orange concoction with a matching beret that held her golden hair back off of her face while she played cards with Otus. Aurora stood at the foot of the lake waiting for a sign or something to happen that would magically transfer powers to her. She stood there, but no great manifestation occurred, she was still just plain Aurora. In frustration, she kicked a rock with all her force that sailed through the air and plopped into the water. She gazed down, watching the circles expand outwards until they faded back into the fluidity of the lake and still, nothing happened.

She screamed out in exasperation, scaring two robins that flew wildly from their tree branch. Boreas awoke with a start, his eyes blinking open as he stretched upwards, yawning deeply.

"Did you get your powers yet?"

He said it mockingly and Aurora was too frustrated to even argue with him.

If she was the right Aurora, then something was supposed to happen. *Why wasn't it happening?* She figured that the blind man who would see was the Professor, but as far as she could tell he was still mostly blind and they had been sitting at the edge of this lake for weeks now. The robins chirped in harmony above as if they were laughing at her, she was feeling lost and bitter as she tossed her oily hair over her shoulders. Her stomach ached; she had been living off of nothing but berries, rabbit and trout since they arrived at the lake that she couldn't remember what carbohydrates tasted like. Despite all the running and eating meager meals she still felt like she was a huge beast compared to Babs and Mrs. Xiomy.

But then, two nights ago while they were making camp, like they always did, Mrs. Xiomy came behind her and whispered, "I think you need to pull your pants up a bit."

Aurora couldn't understand what she was talking about, but she yanked her pants up anyway, thinking she needed to cover her mid-section. "These pants fit me," Aurora said out loud.

Mrs. Xiomy was insistent when she said, "You can't have your pants falling down and your shirt hanging off of you, you don't want these boys to get a free show." Aurora did feel like they were falling off and she started to feel like the shirt was a bit baggier than when she had started this journey; then it had been snug. But when she looked at her body, all she saw was the same frumpy girl she had always been.

She woke up yesterday morning with a shirt and a pair of pants beside her in indigo and orange. When she tried on the clothes, surprisingly they actually fit. It was nice not having to keep pulling up her pants every 5 minutes. Mrs. Xiomy beamed when she saw her come out from behind the girls changing quarters (which was behind two big oak trees).

"How do I look?" Aurora asked sheepishly, feeling self-conscious, like these new pants must cling to her chubby body or worse that they would rip at the seam and she'd never hear the end of it from Boreas.

"Really pretty!" Mrs. Xiomy gushed. Aurora dropped her chin but her teacher lifted it back up and said, "I am not an idle flatterer."

"Sorry," Aurora feigned a smile. "I'm just not used to it that's all."

✡ ✡ ✡

The days and nights had started to blend together and there were still no powers or anything that appeared remotely supernatural. It seemed like any other place, ordinary, except Aurora was confident that the prophecy meant this lake. Despite the group complaining that it was a lost cause, she stood her ground and Otus stood beside her to silence the others. Even Boreas had quit complaining; sensing his complaints were falling on deaf ears, but Aurora still spotted Boreas and Babs whispering in corners when they thought she wasn't watching.

Aurora sat down beside Otus who ruffled her hair with his thumb. His shadow loomed over them and stretched to the shoreline of the lake, providing them with some shade from the grueling sun. One of the robins mistook Otus' straw-like hair for a nest and settled in, but Otus didn't even notice as he was so intent on the card game he was playing. His overalls, that had been shabby and frayed at the bottom, almost seemed to be mending themselves. The holes were patched up and the pockets, their accommodations on these travels, were still in mint condition. He had no other clothing yet these clothes maintained their shiny blue color and smelled like sunflowers on a spring day. Otus bent down sneakily displaying the cards to Aurora, angling them so that Mrs. Xiomy couldn't try to get a peek.

"What do you think?"

Aurora threw up her hands in frustration, covering her face in her hands. "I think it's hopeless."

"That bad, huh?" Mrs. Xiomy grinned and threw down her hand. "Full house."

Mrs. Xiomy stood up ready for her victory dance but froze as Otus revealed his hand. A straight flush!

"You're either so cute that I was distracted or you are the best bluffer I've ever met."

Otus smiled brightly as Mrs. Xiomy crawled onto his knee. He stooped down so that his face was eye level with Mrs. Xiomy's. She gave him a big kiss on the cheek and Aurora shook her head at him, knowing that was the prize he had wagered for.

"I'll play you next," Otus's eyes danced, holding the cards out to Aurora.

She laughed and said, "I am not as easy to swindle kisses out of. I need to swindle powers out of something in this lake. What am I missing?"

Otus patted her on the head to comfort her and took off into the woods to see if he could locate any meat for dinner. Boreas slid out from under Babs and stood up, stretching his long limbs. He dug his already muddy sneaker into the ground and looked up, shielding his eyes with his hand as if to see something across the lake. He walked past the Professor who was in a meditative state, drawing circles in the sand with his walking stick.

Boreas grabbed his backpack and flung it over his shoulders. "I guess you guys are happy rotting away here waiting for some miracle to happen, but I am hungry and I haven't slept in a real bed since we left Candlewick. I say let's get out of these woods and live in a civilized place while we can."

The Professor laughed, still concentrating hard on drawing his circles, "This isn't civilized enough for you? People pay top dollar to have a lakeside resort."

Mrs. Xiomy jumped up and grabbed the Professor's book and started flipping through it. "How far is this luxury hotel you want us to go to?"

"My father owns a cabin in Crown Pointe not too far from here. See that lighthouse across the lake?"

Boreas pointed across the water and everyone squinted to make out an antiquated marble lighthouse on the opposite side of the lake. It looked 15 miles away, at least, and appeared more like a silver tower than a lighthouse.

"Dad, Jonathan and I used to come here when we were kids to go fishing. Well, Dad and Jonathan would fish and I'd just wait for them back at the cabin. But there are plenty of beds and my dad always kept it well stocked with supplies."

Mrs. Xiomy jumped up and down in glee, "A real mattress! I can feel it now. I agree with Boreas. I think we should go."

Aurora shook her head. "Sounds great, Boreas, but you forgot one important thing. Can Otus fit in this cabin of yours? No! So forget it. We're stuck here, so just deal with it."

Mrs. Xiomy stood up, her mind still envisioning a mattress for her to sleep on. She put on her teacher voice and proclaimed, "I call for a vote."

The Professor nodded as he slapped a mosquito that was biting into his skin. "I second the motion."

Babs stood up, brushing dirt and crinkled leaves off her clothes, and laughed with malice, "What democracy? This is Aurora's show."

Aurora whirled around abruptly. "And what is that supposed to mean?"

Babs started to walk towards her like a snake, slithering with each step as she advanced. "Come on now, everything has been what you wanted, that's how we ended up here at this lake. And now that Boreas has an idea you dismiss it without even thinking about it. We should rename ourselves the 'Aurora followers'."

Aurora's mouth dropped open flabbergasted as Babs walked toward Boreas, who was soaking his feet in the water. She massaged his shoulders and seductively kissed the back of his neck.

Disgusted, Aurora whirled toward the Professor and Mrs. Xiomy. "Is this how the rest of you feel?"

They didn't respond.

"Let me remind you that I am not the enemy here. The Common Good Army is out there."

"Well if they were really out there why haven't we seen anyone since we came back from Australia?" Babs stated with a twinge of irritation in her tone. "If you are all so special and important to them wouldn't they have armies swooping down to arrest you? We haven't seen anyone!"

She stood and walked right up to Aurora. "I think you are mad at the world and are dragging us all down with you, leading us to these God-forsaken places, getting us nearly killed and all for nothing! I want to go to the safe haven. There at least I know what I'm fighting for."

Boreas stood up and put his hand on her shoulder. "Babs, stop it. That's enough."

She shrugged him off. "They are keeping us both prisoners here, Boreas. We're all their prisoners."

"You, Babs, can leave whenever you want!" Aurora cried out, anger emblazoned within her. "In fact, I insist on it. But he has to stay." She jabbed her finger into Borcas's chest and looked at him imploringly, "We are in this together."

Babs grabbed his arm and tugged him toward her. "Well, I'm not leaving without him."

Aurora grabbed his other hand and started to tug at him like a game of tug of war.

"Well, sorry to disappoint you but he's staying with me."

Boreas shook his hands free from both women and cried out, "Stop!"

He grabbed Aurora by the hand and led her away from the group.

"You need to get a grip! You're just annoyed that you're not getting your powers. You don't need to take it out on Babs."

She shrugged him off of her. "She's taking it out on me! You keep taking her side and I thought we were in this together!"

Boreas bit his lower lip and exclaimed, "When you say 'in this together' what does that mean exactly? You shot my idea down back there without even considering it. That's not what a team does."

Aurora took a deep breath and wrestled her hair in her hands and stared out into the water at the lighthouse in the distance. Sure, she wanted a mattress to sleep on and an actual pillow to rest her head. But they had to stay together, Otus needed them.

"I don't know what I'm saying," she said, "all I know is that Babs can't be trusted. And now she's trying to make you choose sides."

"Maybe because Babs actually cares about what I have to say."

Aurora couldn't hold back anymore, "Or it's because she's using you Boreas and you're too blind and stupid to notice."

Boreas laughed, his laugh resounding like a siren blaring on that shoreline. "You know what you sound like?"

"What?"

He grabbed her body and pulled her close to him, "Like you're jealous."

He looked deep into her eyes and she felt her body go numb as he held her. She sighed, lost in his eyes that were penetrating into hers and she found herself trying to fight the temptation, knowing he was fooling her, trying to confuse her like so many people before. He didn't care for her. He was going to make fun of her and trick her like all of those people back at Candlewick High. Anger built within her and she pushed him away from her, freeing herself from his tantalizing hold.

She yelled, "You are not even half the man that Jonathan is."

He stepped back, stung by her words.

"What did you say?"

She didn't hold back any longer, "You heard me. Your father was right...everything he said about you at the Independence of the Last Straw barbeque was right. You are nothing compared to your brother."

He bit his lower lip and he raised his fist as if he was going to punch her. He slowly opened his hand and his palm was red from the clenched pressure. He turned his back on her, walked over to the campsite, grabbed his shoes and stuck them haphazardly on his feet. "I am going to my father's cabin before I say or do something I am going to regret. Anyone coming?"

Babs smiled in triumph as she grabbed her bag and followed behind him. The Professor hobbled over and stood beside Babs, holding onto his mahogany walking stick as if prepared for a fight.

Mrs. Xiomy looked from Boreas to Aurora until she picked up her bag and looked at Aurora with pity in her gaze.

"I am sorry Aurora, but this time you're wrong."

She took her place behind Boreas until it was just Aurora standing on her side of the camp, the fire dying down and the smoke encircling her solitary form like a shadow.

Aurora screamed out, "Fine! We don't need you. Otus and I can take care of ourselves."

Boreas scribbled something onto the sand, "that's the address to the cabin. Tell Otus he can come meet us there if he wants to get the hell away from you."

They marched over to the pier where they unhooked one of the rowboats stationed there. They all piled in and pushed off, with Boreas and Babs taking the oars and paddling away from camp. Aurora sat on the edge of the abandoned wooden pier that was rotting away. She watched as her travelling companions rowed toward the silver lighthouse in the distance, half expecting them to turn around and realize their mistake. The boat rocked up and down over the waves, until they disappeared over the horizon. The last image she had was the determined face of Boreas rowing away as the captain of the ship that was leading the others away from her.

The water splashed aggressively against the wooden beams beneath Aurora. She hung her bare legs over the side. The cool wind combed through her hair that was hanging down loose over her shoulders, having grown two inches since that July. She was in desperate need of a haircut; she had never had her hair so long before, her mother always said that her face looked less round with her hair above her shoulders. But her mother was not here to scold her and tell her to get a haircut. She was on her own and she felt so utterly alone. How she wished that her mother was there and missed the sound of her voice — even when she was nagging Aurora about her hair.

She continued looking out into the horizon, gray clouds congregating above her. In the distance she watched as leaves floated on the surface of the water and drifted past her carried by the hands of the wind and waves. There was the after taste of regret and guilt stuck in the base of her throat. She felt a tear slide down her face, wishing anger hadn't put those words in her mouth. She couldn't forget the hurt and anger in Boreas's eyes after saying what she had said. What was happening to her? She had become a different person ever since the incident at the barn. Ever since she had witnessed Boreas and Babs share that kiss beneath the weeping willow.

She picked up a gray rock on the pier and flipped it over and over again in her palm. She then gripped it tight, stood up, got a good running start and then flicked her wrist and the rock flew out from the epicenter of her palm. It skipped three times across the lake's surface, grazing the water slightly with each hop before plummeting beneath the gentle waves.

"You don't want to do that," a voice squeaked near her. She whirled around in a hurry, half expecting Boreas in front of her, but no one was there. Confused, she turned back toward the edge of the pier and peered into the water where she saw the reflection of a young boy. She quickly whirled around again, looking for the real boy behind the reflection, but there still was no one there. She peered again into the water and there was the young boy's face smiling up at her. He had speckled freckles over his cheeks and his hair was cut short into a Mohawk. He had a fisherman's raincoat on and his smile was missing two front teeth. Aurora put her hand out over where his body should be, but there was only air. At that, she froze, not sure what to make of this illusion transpiring in front of her.

"How are you doing this?" She whispered, unaware if she was just speaking to herself or if she was hallucinating.

The young boy's voice spoke again and she watched his lips move through the reflection in the water.

"You don't want to disturb Champ."

"Who is Champ?"

He looked from left to right, his face moving in and out with the waves. "The monster that lives in the lake."

If only this figment of her imagination knew that a giant was living in the woods near where they were standing. She closed her eyes, expecting the apparition to disappear but the face still floated below her.

"Don't worry, he's my friend, but he doesn't like rock throwing, it disturbs his sleep."

"What are you?" she whispered, wanting to flee, but curiosity again got the best of her. "Are you a ghost?"

He laughed heartily with the innocence of youth. He pulled out a yellow bucket rain hat and fixed it over his eyes, the hat so big so that it slumped down over his forehead.

"My name is Swanson, but Champ told me you were here. He told me who you are."

She sat thinking of all the things that she was; a control freak, an agitator, jealous, a know it all, a fat loser who forced the only people who ever cared for her to abandon her. She flung her hands over her face and cried out, "I am nothing."

The boy waited for her sobbing to subside while a crisp wind encircled her body and dried the tears off of her face.

"Champ says you are more than that. Champ says he will visit you tomorrow at sunset."

Then as quickly as the boy had appeared, his reflection vanished.

Aurora jumped up and screamed into the water, "Swanson? Swanson where are you?"

She heard her name being called and she dropped down onto her stomach to try to see the boy's face in the blue mirror below. But the voice was not coming from the lake it was coming from behind her. She turned and there was Otus standing at the foot of the pier staring at her wide-eyed, holding fish in his arms; enough fish to feed six.

"What happened?" Concern and fear immediately resonated from his voice.

She slowly got back to her feet, the sun starting its descent behind her so that she glowed ominously amidst the dramatic backdrop.

"We are on our own now, Otus."

☆ ☆ ☆

Later that night, Aurora was still mystified by what she had seen and heard from the boy, Swanson, in the lake. She couldn't make sense out of his message about the monster Champ that resided in the lake and knew about her; knew why she was there. She returned to camp with Otus beside her and filled him in on the events of the day. How she had single-handedly caused the rest of the group to head out toward the lighthouse.

"I have a bad feeling about that lighthouse." Otus said. "I don't like the way it is flickering at me. I think we should try to bring them back."

Aurora slumped down beside the extinguished fire to throw more wood on it to reignite the flame. "Well, Boreas left you the address. Said you can find them if you want to get the hell away from me. Otus, I'm such a screw-up!"

She blew under the wood and a small flame began to flicker, gray smoke seeped through the edges as the fire fed hungrily on the wood. She leaned back and looked up to the stars, at the North Star that was pointing in the direction they ultimately would take toward the arctic and the Aurora Borealis.

"Otus," she said slowly, as the giant lay down to star gaze beside her. "Can you tell me where you came from?"

Otus took a deep breath and sighed, vapor escaping from his lips. He readjusted his position on the sandy ground and faced her. His voice started shaking from the cold as he said, "I am made from flesh and blood just like you, Aurora."

"But, who are your parents?"

He shook his head as the fire crackled, embers flying up in the night sky. "I never met my parents. It was just me and my brother Ephialtes. We were the only ones of our kind, or that we knew of. I wish I had known my parents. Maybe when I prove my hypothesis it will make sense. I have a feeling the answers are at the Northern Lights. Maybe then we will find the answers we are all longing for."

He took a deep breath while the fireflies danced in the sky, doing cartwheels in the air. They were like a glimmer of light in that darkness, a glimmer of hope.

"Boreas will come back," Aurora said assertively. "I know he will. If it's his destiny, then somehow he will forgive me. Or else we'll hate each other all the way to the Arctic together."

Chapter 11

Mistaken Identity

Boreas felt his muscles straining as he rowed, mustering all the strength he had left to pull the oars through the water. It was a brisk night with only the stars and the red blinking light from the roof of the lighthouse as his guides.

"Almost there," he grunted between clenched teeth as they sailed across the lake through the darkness of night.

Mrs. Xiomy sat across from him pulling the oars in sequence with him. She had relieved Babs who was now resting her muscles but acting as a look-out. The Professor complained that they were taking too long as he had calculated that they should have reached their destination by now. Boreas was keeping his focus on the cabin that was waiting for them, a place where they could hide out in comfort and be free of the headaches that were attributed to dealing with Aurora. He wondered whether she and Otus would come after them and asked Mrs. Xiomy the same question.

"No," she answered. "They will not leave until Aurora has acquired her powers."

"As if that would ever happen," he thought, picturing the two of them sitting around the fire cooking fish. He envisioned Aurora coming up with some cockamamie story of why he and the others had abandoned the mission. Boreas hadn't abandoned the mission, but that's not the story Aurora would tell. Otus would believe her too, he always believed her.

Boreas looked out into the darkness, where he thought he could see a small flame in the woods, but knew it could only be his imagination. They were so far away that any fire Aurora had built was out of sight. She would make sure that no one was able to see it, not even those who knew where to look.

The boat finally coasted to a stop along the sandy shore in front of the lighthouse and they all jumped out. It felt so good to stretch their legs as each grabbed a side and pulled the boat up onto the shore. They flipped it over and tried to hide it in the bushes, covering it with leaves and anything else they could salvage to protect the boat from view. Wiping his sandy hands on his jeans, Boreas whispered to the others to follow him. They continued past the lighthouse that had only been a speck in the distance a few hours before and now was looming over them, the beacon of light blinding their eyes as they looked up into the glass roof.

Boreas had forgotten what it was like to be in a town. As they walked down the cobblestone streets, houses had lights on and the sound of televisions blared through their walls. Some tourists were inhabiting a local bar and singing wildly into the night. Boreas smiled, it felt so good to be around other people again. He held onto Babs's hand as she rested her head on his shoulder. It felt nice to be normal again.

"We're almost there," he said excitedly as he saw the cabin at the far end of the street. A wave of relief swept over him. He used to dread his summer vacations to this place with his father and brother, but now he felt such excitement at the four walls, beds, technology... He was salivating just thinking about the modern conveniences they had been without for so long. Mrs. Xiomy held onto the Professor's arm and even they had more of a bounce to their step as they made their way down the lane. Boreas felt like he might even start whistling. When they reached the door, he looked under the flowerpot where he knew his father kept the spare key. He stuck it into the keyhole and turned the knob. The door squeaked open and they dashed in to escape the gnawing mosquitoes that were lingering outside. The door slammed shut behind them as Boreas reached for the light switch.

Just then an alarm sounded and they all jumped as blaring noise erupted around them. Red lights flashed and Boreas quickly grabbed the knob to the front door to flee, but it was sealed shut. He was struck with an intense amount of pain and his body violently shook from the electric volts passing through his body. He fell to the floor as Babs dashed to his side, crying his name.

"What is going on?" Mrs. Xiomy cried out as the Professor scurried through his suitcase, finding something that he clasped in his hand.

"Nobody move!" a voice cried out from the corner of the living room. A flashlight blinded them as its beam searched from face to face.

The light was flicked on and Boreas stared into the eyes of none other than his father, Henry Stockington. Beside him, holding a gun, was his brother Jonathan, standing tall and proud beside their father.

"Nobody move or we will kill you."

His father spoke with such anger and coldness. Boreas struggled to his feet, holding onto Babs for support as he regained his bearings. He felt betrayed as his family stood there literally holding a gun to his head. He felt like the entire floor was giving way underneath him. He didn't know what to say as he not only walked right into this trap, but also dragged the rest of the group down with him.

"The last thing I expected was for my family to turn against me."

"Shut up, Boreas," his father barked at him, his icy blue eyes glaring into his son's. His blond hair was filled with white highlights and his thick rimmed glasses were fixed over his pointy nose. "I disowned you as soon as you turned against the Common Good. How did you think I would react once I found out that my son broke into the library? Or when I found out that my son has been fleeing across the countryside as a fugitive with plans to overthrow the establishment? I cannot believe that my son would do this. No son of mine would do this to his father, to his brother, to his country!"

"What country?" The Professor butted in, still clasping something in his fist. "The country you believe in doesn't exist. Your country has turned against you."

Mr. Stockington turned to the Professor and said, "The Inspector warned me that you would be with them. Professor Gassendi, the Professor who turned traitor and caused the prison breakout and fire at the Candlewick Prison ten years ago. The Inspector is going to be very happy to find you again."

"The Inspector is coming here?" Mrs. Xiomy's voice trembled.

"He'll be here by tomorrow," Jonathan boasted, cradling the gun in his hand with his blond hair tied back in a ponytail. His long hair made him look more like his brother than he ever did before, Boreas with his long, wild hair and unshaved face. "The alarm alerted him that we have you."

At a sound, Mrs. Xiomy turned to the open window and cried out, "Common Good soldiers are coming up the stairs now!"

The Professor caught Boreas's eye and opened his hand slightly to reveal a small glass canister. Boreas recognized the glass canister as the one containing the sleep serum that the Professor had showed him in the cavern. Boreas knew that he had to distract his father and quickly.

"Well, Dad, I guess I have disappointed you yet again. But you failed me by never mentioning that my mother is still alive!"

At that, both Mr. Stockington and Jonathan turned to Boreas and the gun nearly slipped out of his brother's hands.

"How dare you say that!" Mr. Stockington exclaimed. "Leave the dead buried."

"I would, but the dead don't normally talk, do they, Dad?"

Jonathan lowered his pistol even more, "What do you mean? You talked to her?"

Just then, the Professor hit Mr. Stockington over the head with his cane and shoved a rag soaked in sleep serum against his nose. Mr. Stockington sunk to the floor and the Professor used the father's body as a shield against Jonathan who still held a gun. Boreas didn't give Jonathan a second to think, attacking him while Babs grabbed the gun that had fallen to the ground. The officers smashed in the door and held their guns up, confused by the scuffle transpiring before their eyes.

"Stop," an officer shouted and fired once in the air as a warning.

Boreas and Jonathan froze as blood dripped from Boreas's nose and Babs put down the gun reluctantly. Mrs. Xiomy stood with the Professor over the sleeping body of Mr. Stockington.

"What happened here?" The officer demanded, pointing at the sleeping father. Boreas recognized her as the brawny female officer with the husky voice from the library break-in, Officer Pelican.

Boreas was devising a plan in his mind, and jumped up, saying, "They attacked my father, arrest them immediately!"

Jonathan stared at him in disbelief, "What are you doing?"

Just then a tall, paunchy, blond-haired officer entered the cabin. Boreas recognized him as the other officer from the library break-in, Officer Woolchuck. He was the officer who nearly peed in his pants when Otus lifted him off the ground.

"The perimeter is secured," Officer Woolchuck spoke with his distinctive Brooklyn accent. "Which one of you is Boreas Stockington?"

Jonathan and Boreas both pointed to each other, "He is."

The officers shook their heads in disbelief. "Answer us. You can't both be Boreas. Wake up the father."

"I think he's in a coma." The Professor sighed, taking off his hat in regret, "will probably be out cold for a couple of days. You know how these things happen."

"I think something really fishy is going on. Now, you..." the officer pointed to Babs, "Answer me, who is Boreas? Fess up and we'll let you go free."

She turned to Jonathan and said, "Well, obviously it's him. We've been intimate for a couple of weeks now."

Jonathan stood up and shrieked, "I am not Boreas. This is my little brother," he grabbed Boreas by the ear and forced him to his feet.

Boreas laughed, saying, "Please, who are they going to believe, Boreas? You, or your girlfriend?"

"I never saw that girl before in my life!"

"Enough!" Officer Pelican screamed. "We'll take you all down to the prison. I am sure the Inspector will find out who is telling the truth and who is lying."

Several other officers entered and handcuffed each of them, even the sleeping body of Boreas's father. They were ushered into a

Common Good vehicle with the siren blaring and red lights flickering wildly.

Jonathan whispered into Boreas's ear, "You are not going to get away with this. The Inspector is not someone to play games with."

"You have no right to speak to me," Boreas scowled. "You stabbed your own brother in the back."

"You have a lot more to fear than that," he threatened and the car doors slammed shut.

Boreas watched as the cabin disappeared out of sight. He peered around at his compatriots and realized that he had gotten them into this mess. *If only he had stayed with Aurora and Otus!* But they were safe on the other side of the lake, unaware that he and the others were in trouble. It was up to Boreas to get himself out of this mess.

They pulled up to the prison that looked more like an old, dilapidated fort that was now being used for the Common Good's purposes as a jail. They were pulled out of the Common Good vehicle and told to line up in a row. Boreas kept his head down when Officer Pelican and her oafish partner Officer Woolchuck passed by, hoping they wouldn't recognize him from the library. Boreas was actually happy that his hair had grown long and that he had not had a chance to shave in a week. He looked very unlike himself and more similar to his more handsome and rugged brother. His wrists were losing circulation from the handcuffs and he wondered how long he could put on this act. He whispered to the Professor, "How long will that sleep serum last?"

"48 hours. We have two days to get out of this mess before your father wakes up and makes the identification. You have two days to stay Jonathan. Once they know you're Boreas then we are sunk."

They walked through the fort that was lit by candlelight and appeared more like a torture chamber than a cell. They heard cries echoing throughout the dimly lit chambers and Boreas felt his throat go dry as they were forced to keep walking by gunpoint. They were all pushed into a cell and the Professor's suitcase was confiscated. Boreas had managed to hide the conch shell that his mother had given to him inside his shoe. If they were going to find Aurora and Otus again, that might be their only hope.

Officer Pelican came in, turned to the group and smiled. "I know one of you is the brat Boreas that we have been chasing all across the East Coast, but we want to be 100% sure before we present you to the Inspector."

Jonathan stepped forward and thrust his head back so that the blond strands over his eyes were whipped off his face.

"Quiz me," He demanded sternly. "I am Jonathan. I have been helping you for the past two months to track down my brother by hiding out in the cabin and rigging it so that when he came, we could snatch him. I am not the traitor."

The officer turned to her partner and they both shone the light in his face. They had Jonathan's picture and said, "It does look like you, but it looks like the other one too. If we bring the wrong one then we'll never hear the end of it. We'll have to do a DNA test."

"That'll take like 2 days," her partner whined.

"I know the Inspector," Mrs. Xiomy said slowly, "he might kill you if you're wrong. He has killed people for less than that."

Officer Woolchuck gulped and nodded his consent. They called in the clinic phlebotomist who stuck a needle into each of the boy's arms, drawing three vials of blood. Boreas watched as his blood was drained from him giving his enemies the identification that they needed. He turned to Babs who avoided his gaze. She was staring at the officers who were whispering in a corner, contemplating their fate. Boreas took a deep breath, knowing this charade couldn't last for much longer as the vile of blood was carried out the door to be tested.

"You," Officer Woolchuck pointed at Babs again. "Where is Aurora Alvarez?"

She shrugged. "Aurora, who?"

"Don't play dumb with me. She's the one with the giant. Where is she?"

Babs shrugged again. "I think we're a little too old to believe in fairy tales, don't you agree, Officer?"

Officer Pelican smacked her across the face so hard that a hand-print was clearly visible on her cheek. "Don't mess with me, girl. I am going to smack every pretty feature off your face until there's nothing left."

"Leave her alone!" Mrs. Xiomy wailed, huddling over Babs.

Officer Woolchuck grabbed Mrs. Xiomy's chin in his hand and shook it violently in his grasp. "I know you," he said harshly, "you're David Xiomy's wife. What are you doing mixed up with these kids and this old, blind Professor?"

"We were on a field trip."

He stuck his fingernails into her skin until blood oozed down her arm like red tear drops. "I think you are breaking teacher-student relations." He turned from Boreas to Jonathan and jeered, "You have a thing for young boys?"

She spat and saliva sprayed across Officer Woolchuck's face. Woolchuck took his sleeve and wiped it across his brutish face before he hit her across the jaw so hard that she went flying against the brick wall with a loud 'smack!'

Officer Woolchuck made a fist with his hand and then, like a sadistic nutcracker, cracked each knuckle as if each joint symbolized his prey in that cell.

"Does the real Boreas want to step forward? Because we'll keep this up until you do. You may not have a friend left once we're through with them."

Jonathan turned sharply to Boreas whose face remained stoic, though internally he was in agony watching his friends tortured before his eyes. The Professor's words kept him silent for he knew that once they found out that he was the right Boreas, the others were disposable. They would have found what they wanted, him, and the others would simply disappear, like so many of the Common Good's victims. The Common Good's motto was to sacrifice the few for the many, but they seemed to have no problem sacrificing multitudes. Boreas kept a poker face as they continued their attacks, doing his best to block out the screams as the night drifted onwards without an end.

The Sacred Hour struck and the officers reluctantly had to abide by the law and honor the hour with sleep. After freeing the prisoners of their handcuffs, the officers warned that they would return with more fire and brimstone unless the real Boreas stepped forward. The door slammed shut with a thunderous bang behind them.

Once he was sure the door was shackled and locked from the outside, Boreas couldn't contain himself any longer and ran to Babs' side. She had borne the brunt of Officer Pelican's wrath with a nasty bruise over her left eye and her arm badly injured. Mrs. Xiomy was unconscious from the amount of pain they inflicted on her, her jaw had blown up to the size of a balloon and the Professor was tending to her wounds. Jonathan paced the room with his ear against the door and his long ponytail shifting back and forth as if it were a pendulum swinging.

He stopped suddenly and blurted out, "Just give him up already! What are you trying to prove? You're all going to get killed defending him!"

The Professor stood up slowly and carefully on his bad leg. "You do not know who your brother is. Why did you think they were after him? Just because of a silly library break-in? Be sensible."

"Don't bother, Professor," Boreas said as he smoothed the hair out of Babs' eyes and kissed her forehead. "He just sees me as his little brother who can't amount to anything; not like he can."

Jonathan marched over to him and stooped down beside his brother. "You are letting your friends get hurt because of this stupid game of mistaken identity. Look at what the officers did to them!"

Boreas closed his eyes trying to shut out his brother's words. He saw the cuts and the bruises inside his mind and couldn't block them out. He heard the wails and the cries of pain and knew that he was to blame. Jonathan sniffed loudly, knowing his words were causing a wound to fester within his brother.

"You always think about yourself! Not about your friends, your family…"

"Don't talk to me about family, because I don't have any!" Boreas cried out as it felt like the walls were closing in on him as Jonathan's shadow towered above him.

Jonathan threw his hands up, aggravated and paced the floor again. His towering frame caused shadows to reach upwards toward the ceiling. Babs rocked back and forth and pleaded for water. The others looked at each other, helpless, for there was none to give. Boreas banged on the door, crying out for someone to give them water, but his plea fell on deaf ears.

"They are going to starve us or make us die of thirst unless you do something, Boreas."

All the pain, the guilt and the heartache intertwined into an instinct for Boreas to charge his brother; they collided and Boreas threw Jonathan against the wall. He grabbed Jonathan by the shirt collar and pinned him against his chest as Jonathan tried to push back. Boreas dug his shoes into the cobblestones and leaned against his brother with all his strength. With clenched teeth, he boomed, "I am not Boreas, not today. You got that straight? Now help me find a way out of this mess or we're all going to be killed."

Jonathan stood flabbergasted at this side of his brother and tried to push back, but Boreas held him with the diabolical courage that conquered any fear he had once possessed of his older brother. He stared Jonathan down with impenetrable fortitude. Jonathan looked around and his eyes fell upon the anguished faces of the Professor, Babs and Mrs. Xiomy.

"Fine!" Jonathan succumbed and Boreas relaxed his hold. Jonathan took the opportunity to smack him off like he was swatting a fly, "but for their sake, not yours."

Boreas wiped the sweat from his brow with the back of his shaking hand. He had never tackled his brother before. Boreas was always told that he was the weak one in the family. He had always believed it, until now.

Mrs. Xiomy regained consciousness and whispered to the Professor. "You know the Inspector, he will kill us all. Boreas is no match for him. At least, not yet."

"Don't be afraid, he can't see that we're afraid."

She nodded, wiping the blood off of her cheek. "I think those officers knocked out one of my fillings."

The Professor started to laugh and she joined in, though not for long as her ribs started to hurt and she was forced to wrap her arms around herself to try to hold back the pain.

Boreas felt his way around the brick wall, trying to look for something, anything that might be their salvation. A small window stood about 5 feet above him with moonlight streaming down. He called Jonathan over to him who was still in shock at Boreas's surprise attack and show of strength. He asked his brother to hoist him up on his shoulders so that Boreas could peer through the window. After a moment of contemplation, Jonathan stooped down and let

Boreas wrap his legs around his neck and sit on his shoulders. Jonathan lifted him so that Boreas was able to grab ahold of the iron bars leading to the outside world. The fresh air was invigorating as a cool breeze wafted through the bars. The moon was illuminated over the fort and he was looking down from the 2nd floor window to a large courtyard approximately 100 feet wide surrounded by armed soldiers and security cameras stationed at every angle. Beyond that, they were surrounded by a moat with a single draw-bridge that had two armed guards at the foot of the bridge. He stopped to think, "What would Aurora do?"

A plan started to form in his brain. It was crazy and most likely would never work, but they had to try. He asked Jonathan to bring him down and then relayed it to the Professor and Mrs. Xiomy. They shook their heads saying it was too risky and too dangerous.

"No, absolutely not!" The Professor declared outright. "You have a nearly blind man, two injured women and a brother who we still don't know which side he's on, and you think this is going to work?"

Mrs. Xiomy agreed. "I like the first part of the plan, but there are too many things that can go wrong with the second part. I mean, don't get me wrong, it's still better than any ideas that were drumming through my brain."

Jonathan was sitting in a corner, quiet, when he suddenly exclaimed, "I think it will work!"

Boreas shifted his position to stare at his brother who crawled and joined them in the circle, "I mean, what is the alternative, death?"

"A pretty serious alternative," The Professor quipped.

Boreas and Jonathan turned to the others in unison and together worked out all the details, going over each point of the plan to ensure precision. The lives of everyone in that room depended on it.

Chapter 12

Champ Encounter

Aurora held the jacket tighter around her as she sat down at the edge of the pier, waiting for Swanson to manifest again. It was nearing sunset, she felt foolish and hoped that she hadn't had a nervous breakdown the day before. She may have only seen an illusion in the water. Otus was sitting on the shoreline behind her, he was afraid to walk onto the pier for fear that his weight would damage the already weathered wood. He was chewing on a piece of grass, biding his time as the golden ball started its descent over the horizon making the water sparkle like diamonds and the sky above them streak with purple and orange; the colors of the Common Good. "How appropriate," Aurora thought bitterly.

"Are you sure he said sunset?" Otus called out to her, spitting the blade of grass a mile into the lake where it floated atop the waves.

"Yes," Aurora called back, her face focused on the water but no image of a little red-haired boy with a Mohawk appeared before her. Aggravated, she didn't heed his advice and took out another stone from her pocket and let it sail as far as her arm could throw until it dunked beneath the water of Lake Champlain. The lighthouse flickered in the distance. She thought about Boreas comfortably lying in his bed in the cottage with their other companions laughing and joking as she sat here like a fool waiting for something to appear out of nowhere.

"There are things in this world that we cannot explain." Her father's voice echoed in her mind as she recalled raking leaves with him in their backyard the autumn before. Her mother had gone off with her friends, Rose and Gabriella and had left herself and her father alone for the weekend. They had raked the leaves into two big piles and she had jumped into one pile as her father laughed at her. She didn't care that the leaves were scratching her skin. She just laid there while the clouds drifted past, oblivious of her presence. The scent of rotting leaves stung her nostrils as her father had sunk into the leaf pile beside her.

"You have conquered the leaves, Aurora Alvarez," her father had called out to her. "You are the Heroine of Candlewick. What are you going to do now?"

She laughed and felt her body sliding further into the damp leaves that were a multitude of colors; cider-brown, honey-yellow, blood-orange red. She then thought about the novels she had read and said slowly, "There are no heroines, Dad. None like me anyway."

Her Father looked up into the sky and pointed at a cloud drifting past, "That cloud never existed before today, but yet there it is shifting and changing before our eyes. Anything is possible, Aurora. I have seen things in this world that I cannot explain, but they exist just the same."

Aurora closed her eyes on that pier remembering how safe she had felt in her backyard, surrounded by leaves with her father's voice so comforting and serene. She wished she could be more like her father. He would tell her that she wasn't going crazy and would provide a sane explanation for what she had seen in the water the day before. But her father was not here and instead of an ally, her mind was her enemy, re-enforcing the idea that she was insane every second she sat on the edge of that pier.

The sun was continuing its descent beneath the lake, as if it was drowning and spraying off colors into the atmosphere as its last hur- rah. She giggled to herself, remembering how she used to watch the sun setting when she was a kid and cry thinking it would not reappear. But then, like magic, it was waiting for her when she opened her eyes in the morning. That was the extent of what she had considered magic. Now that she was older and wiser, she knew that the earth revolved around the sun and the sun never sunk into the ocean or crashed into houses or mountains. It was just an illu- sion, there wasn't any magic. She stood up, turned toward Otus and shook her head at him.

"I must have willed myself to see something supernatural because that's what I hoped I would see."

Otus stood up resolutely and waited for Aurora at the edge of the pier as she walked towards him with her head sunk low.

Just then a wooden beam broke off under her feet. The plank fell into the lake with a splash and Aurora jumped back just in time to not fall through the hole. Then another wooden plank broke off, and then another all around her. Aurora screamed out to Otus who told her to make a run for it. She started to run but then two more planks in front of her broke off and fell into the water below and she staggered to regain her balance.

"What is happening?" She cried out in shock as the pier was breaking apart beneath her and she was still far away from shore.

Otus was eyeing the area below the waves and cried out to her, "There's something in the water!"

She felt her heart about to burst from her frantic running. She made it to the last plank still attached to the beams and she was desperately trying to keep her balance, putting her feet in a ballerina's plié, to keep from falling lopsided into the water. She gasped as she saw a shadow of what appeared to be a long eel creature in the water circling her from below.

"Aurora, don't move!" Otus cried out to her.

Suddenly, a gray tail darted out of the water like a spear and wrapped itself around Aurora's ankles, forcing her down into the depths of the blistering cold water. She struggled to free her legs from the strangling clutch of the slimy fish but it clung to her and yanked her further and further beneath the water. She was losing sight of the surface and didn't know how much longer she could hold her breath. She struggled to grab the knife out of her pocket, but the tail squeezed her body tighter so that her hands could do nothing but hang limply over the thick carcass with no way to get underneath. She saw something swimming toward her like a torpedo and her eyes lit open in the cloudy darkness as Otus attacked the creature, slamming his massive fist into the rubbery side. It relaxed its hold on Aurora slightly; just enough for her to maneuver her hand into her jeans pocket and pull out the knife. She jammed the sharp blade into its side, and the creature let out a sharp cry as blood oozed out of its tail. Its long body kicked her square in the mouth and she was flung sideways, just enough for her to grab onto Otus' arm as he skyrocketed toward the surface. She felt like her lungs would burst but just then, they leapt through the surface of the water. Life sustaining oxygen filled her lungs as she took a desperate breath. She gasped in relief, thinking she was safe, until she felt it grab her by the left leg and start pulling her down again.

"Otus, help!" She screamed, trying to cling to his arm but she was sucked down into the water again. It didn't dive deeper this time and for a moment Aurora was relieved that at least she could breathe, but all too soon she saw her fate. It was taking her toward what appeared to be a whirlpool, with water swirling around and around.

She stabbed again at the tail with the knife, yet it still clung forcefully to her leg. Bone splitting fear consumed her as they continued to get pulled closer and closer to the whirlpool, and began to spin around in a dizzying circular motion. She scanned the area frantically, looking for anything to grab onto but only saw the crashing waves. As her head bobbed above the water she spottedOtus attack the snake-like monster. The monster let out a high-pierced screech but wouldn't release its hold on Aurora. All three of them were entangled together as the pressure pulled them towards the center, spinning their bodies around and around as if they were being flushed in a giant toilet. Aurora closed her eyes, taking one last breath as she was sucked down into the vortex.

✫ ✫ ✫

Aurora opened her eyes as if coming out of a dream. She raised her hand, confused as she didn't expect to be able to move her body when she was dead. Around her was the most beautiful place she had ever seen. A huge cascading waterfall stood before her eyes and deposited water into an aquamarine lagoon. She glanced up expecting to see the last remnants of the sunset, but above her was not sky. Water and fish suspended above her like everything was upside down. She was standing on the lake floor and beautiful seashells were piled up beside her like vines leading up toward the lake above her. She blinked her eyes, not believing this surreal experience, and then she took a deep breath. To her astonishment she could breathe! She gazed upwards again at the water magically hovering above her head. It was like she was sealed off in a separate room on the bottom of the lake, but this was impossible. She felt something touch her shoulder and whirled around to see Otus beside her. He took a hold of her hand, it was a comforting gesture, but it didn't stop her body from shaking.

"Where are we?" she asked, mystified.

Otus pointed and she turned her head to behold the sight of a massive, long eel-like creature lying in the pool where the waterfall was spraying water onto its belly. Its head only had two slits for eyes and its tail that had nearly choked her was wrapped around into a coil and was thick and scaly like a serpent. She turned and saw a young boy swimming up to them from behind a rock, still wearing the raincoat and his Mohawk hair still as red as she remembered from the reflection.

"Swanson!" She called out petrified. "Stay away from him; he just tried to kill us!"

"Nonsense," Swanson laughed, his boyish eyes grinning. "I told you Champ would meet you at sunset!"

Aurora watched as Swanson went up to the eel and rubbed the tip of its head and then sprayed it with water.

"That's Champ?"

The eel-like monster came up onto the sand and slithered its way toward Aurora. Otus stood up, ready to attack as Aurora called out, "Tell your pet to stay away from us or Otus will smash its head in."

Champ slithered up to them and started to dig in the sand until he brought out a conch shell. He left it in front of Aurora who turned to Otus in disbelief. "It's the same conch shell you have. The one Mrs. Taboo gave you to signal to us back in Candlewick."

"She was here," Swanson said grinning. "Champ gave her the conch shell."

Aurora got excited and turned to Champ. "Then we are in the right place. I knew it! Otus! Champ can help me get my powers!"

Champ signaled for Aurora to put the conch shell to her ear by moving his head from side to side like a rattlesnake being charmed. She picked up the pink conch shell and held it to her ear, expecting to hear the sound of the ocean but instead it was the sound of a voice.

"Don't be scared, Goddess of Dawn. I sensed your presence."

It was like the echoing waves were speaking to her through the conch shell. She turned to Champ, whose slitted eyes were staring at her intently.

"I cannot speak to you except through the magic of the conch shell. I cannot give you your powers. You must become reborn in these waters; to be immersed in the power you must renew as the sun rises anew this morning. The true power will then live inside you and will ignite when you need to bring light into the darkness of the one who cannot see."

"Who is this one who cannot see? Is it the Professor?"

The echoed voice swelled inside her mind. "You will be tested and you will spread your light over the darkness. It will be up to you to pass these tests or else all is lost and your giant will be destroyed."

"When will this happen?"

"When you find yourself forced to kill the God of the North Wind."

The conch shell fell from her grasp and hit the sand beneath her feet. She quickly scrambled to pick it up but only the sound of the waves rocking back and forth sounded inside her ear cavity.

Swanson stood up, whistled, and Champ returned to his side. Aurora and Otus watched as the sea monster crawled back toward its place under the waterfall.

Swanson put his rain hat over his head, "I believe that's everything you wanted to hear."

Otus turned to Aurora, "Are you alright?"

"There must be some mistake." She said, feeling her body sink to the ground as she looked up at the fish swimming above her like she was the one in the aquarium and they were gazing down at her from earth. A lone crab crawled up to Otus and onto his lap, not fearful of these strange inhabitants in its abode.

"Did you get your powers?

She looked up at Otus's concerned face, and the rainbow of water that was encircling above them.

"Not yet, but soon. I think it's time we returned to shore."

Swanson nodded and led them both into the waterfall.

"Champ will bring you both back to shore. I have one more message for you, Otus. Mrs. Taboo said if you made it this far to tell you she will be waiting for you when you reach Hyperboria. She believes in you."

Otus thanked Swanson, who then splashed under the waterfall, disappearing like a figment of their imagination. Champ wrapped his body around Otus and Aurora, but this time she didn't fear the species that was holding them. She even felt bad about stabbing his tail with her knife, but saw that he had mended himself. Then, like a bullet being shot out of the barrel of a gun, the creature travelled up the waterfall and back through the vortex. It travelled through the drain that sucked them into the whirlpool... until they were back floating on the peaceful waters of Lake Champlain with the sky and stars once again above them. Champ unwrapped his tail from around their bodies and left them along the shoreline by their campsite.

Otus smiled down at the creature and said, "I am glad to know I am not the only one left of my species out there. Together we are two giants and we are friends."

The creature coiled in the air then dove beneath the waters, disappearing from sight. Aurora, mystified, turned to Otus and said, "Did Champ say anything to you as well?"

Otus smiled. "He didn't need to. Now let's go back to camp and dry off."

Aurora nodded and together they walked back to their campsite. She turned around once and caught sight of Champ jumping up into the air like a dolphin, twirling his slender body and diving once more into the depths of the water, leaving hardly a splash as he returned once more into the lake; his home. She would be returning to that lake at sunrise, ready to be reborn in those waters that now slept so soundly. Yet, she feared what those powers would make her do. She filled Otus in about what Champ had told her as they sat beside the fire. She just failed to mention the last part to him. Failed to mention the part where she would have to kill the God of the North Wind... Boreas...

Chapter 13

Combined Efforts

M rs. Xiomy wailed at the top of her voice, "Open up! Please! Open the door!"

Officer Woolchuck stirred awake and his eyes flickered open. The sun blinded him from the skylight above, indicating the Awakened Hour. Banging erupted from within the cell of his prisoners followed by another piercing scream. Officer Woolchuck stretched and his breath stank as he blew it into his palm, but he ignored the stench and found the key in his pocket. He groaned, "Stop your ranting. I'm coming!" He opened up the door, looking refreshed and extra muscular that morning. He was still wearing his police uniform from the night before and his black gloves were stained with dry blood — their blood. "Eager for another ass whooping?"

Mrs. Xiomy ran to his feet and hugged his knees. "Help me! Please help me! He is here!"

Officer Woolchuck peered around the room but all he saw were the same 5 prisoners from the day before. "Who is here?"

"The giant!"

The officer tripped back over his feet in fear as Mrs. Xiomy continued to hug his knees. "The-the-the… giant? Where is he?"

"He was just here. He said he is going to eat us all for breakfast. Please, you have to help us!"

Mrs. Xiomy was holding him so close in a bear hug and the officer shrieked, "I thought you were friends with him."

"No, he is crazy. He is going to kill us all. The giant and Aurora scour the night looking for people to cook in their giant oven, especially officers. Don't you see him? Look out the window!"

The officer ran over like a frightened puppy and jumped up, grabbing a hold of the bars and pulling himself up to peer through the bars of the window. Jonathan and Boreas both pounced on him, each grabbing a leg extended in mid-air, so fast that the officer didn't see what hit him. They pulled him down so that his body hit the floor, hard, and they covered his mouth with one of Jonathan's smelly socks. Jonathan then put a choke hold on him until he lost consciousness and slumped down onto the floor.

Boreas grabbed the gun from Officer Woolchuck's holster and Babs peered out the door, giving the thumbs up sign that the coast was clear. Jonathan stripped the officer of his uniform and when Jonathan was dressed and ready, they smeared mud on his face to disguise his features. Jonathan had the others hide behind the curtain then cleared his throat, and spoke into the radio. He impersonated Officer Woolchuck's voice to a tee. "Hey, Pelican! Where the hell are you? Need you to come to the cell immediately. They are about to reveal who Boreas is."

Mrs. Xiomy gave Boreas a look of shock and Boreas smiled, "My brother can do impersonations. That's how he gets away with cutting class most of the time."

"Let's just hope the rest of this charade works," Jonathan said, standing up straight, the uniform adding ten pounds on his figure and he already had the blond hair that he stuck unruly into the helmet of the uniform. If you didn't look too closely, it could be Officer Woolchuck.

Officer Pelican came running in as Jonathan buckled over and fell to the ground just outside the cell.

She cried out, "What happened? What happened?"

He pointed to the open door and she took out her weapon and entered the cell to survey the surroundings.

Babs stepped out holding the gun and Boreas and Mrs. Xiomy surrounded the Officer on each side.

"Drop your weapon!" Boreas demanded.

"What is this?" Officer Pelican stammered. "You'll never get away with this!"

Babs continued pointing the gun at her head as the officer dropped the gun to the ground. Mrs. Xiomy grabbed the radio and the second gun. The Professor took his index finger and held it up, telling her in a melodic voice to follow his finger. He then snapped and she fell into a hypnotic trance.

"Ancient techniques for the weak minded," he smiled.

The door slammed shut behind the two officers and they locked it in place.

Jonathan scampered to his feet and took two pairs of handcuffs and pretended to handcuff the others together.

"OK," Boreas whispered. "Now you need to lead us like we are going to meet the Inspector in another part of town. Now hurry!"

"What about Dad?"

"Dad's on his own at this point. We need to get out of here."

They proceeded slowly down the narrow corridors lined with cells marked with "X's" with the sound of other prisoners crying out for help as they passed. Jonathan held Boreas in a head lock and led him down. The female guard at the end of the corridor was busy typing on the computer. She continued typing but said offhandedly, "What is wrong with your face?"

"Had a run in with this lad who confessed he is Boreas. Taking him to the Inspector back at the cabin where he requested questioning."

"And what about the others?" she continued typing with her eyes still glued to the computer screen.

"They have also been summoned for further questioning. Officer Pelican is behind me and will verify my story."

"Why don't I radio her now?" She said, her fingers released from the keyboard and reached for the radio in one fluid motion.

Jonathan mimicked the same exact annoying & condescending laugh of Officer Woolchuck. "I don't think you want to do that."

"And why not?"

He looked left and right continuing to hold Boreas in the neck grip. "Because she is going number two, if you know what I mean. Too much Indian food last night, her stomach can't handle it."

"Oh," the guard grimaced, disgusted and put down the radio. "In that case I'll wait for her to come out then. Head down to the gate and wait for us to administer clearance."

Jonathan then winked at her through the mud that was smeared on his face and with a smile said, "Why don't you grant us that clearance now? I'll make it worth your while when I'm back later tonight."

Her face turned the color of the burgundy sweater she was wearing. "Why, Officer Woolchuck, this is so unlike you. And all this time I thought you were interested in your partner…"

"Pelican has nothing on you," he smiled again and she got flustered and signed a sheet of paper granting him clearance.

"See you later," she called out to him as they walked through the security door and continued down into the courtyard.

"Brilliant," Boreas said admirably. "For the first time, I'm glad your charms actually work on women."

Jonathan shushed him and held him tighter in the head lock as they headed down the narrow corridor leading to the courtyard.

"This is the hard part."

They got through the clearance with the swipe of the card and entered the courtyard where the place was swarming with Officers just having their morning coffee and chatting with each other about the day's activities. Jonathan, disguised as Officer Woolchuck, continued to lead them through the courtyard, keeping his eye around him as did Boreas and the others. The Professor, holding down the rear position, held the bomb that he was able to build out of a few supplies he had hidden in his gigantic goggles, something the officers had failed to search. Right when they were about to hit the door, he let it drop. A huge explosion sounded and smoke filled the courtyard, giving them the cover they needed to make a run for the bridge. The two guards protecting the door ran toward the commotion and the space was free. They were about to make a run for it when an alarm sounded and a voice screamed through the radio that Mrs. Xiomy was holding, "Code Red! Code Red! Five escapees! …one impersonating an Officer, two teenagers, an elderly man and a woman in her mid-thirties. Stop them immediately!"

"Our cover's blown!" Boreas realized that Officer Pelican and Woolchuck were now freed. The bridge was immediately sealed and the Officers that had been oblivious a moment before now took out their guns and was charging toward them. Boreas was about to surrender when Jonathan grabbed his arm and diverted them toward stairs leading down into the basement of the fort. Babs, who held the gun, went first and called out to the others that the coast was clear.

After shedding the barely fastened handcuffs, Boreas took the conch shell out of his pocket and made his way down to the damp basement.

"There's no way out!" Boreas cried out, exasperated.

Jonathan pushed past him and knocked over a huge wooden shelf that was lined with guns and ammunition. The shelf banged against the floor and the bullets rolled past their feet. "When the Inspector took over this fort I overheard that they had built another emergency exit down here. A secret tunnel to escape from if the fort was seized."

Babs and Boreas stood guard with the guns as Mrs. Xiomy and Jonathan examined the wall inch by inch looking for any sign of an air duct. They heard commotion above them and Babs cried out, "Hurry!"

Footsteps were sounding above them and they were trying to break down the locked door. Babs stood at the foot of the staircase holding the gun in her good hand, ready to fire if necessary. Mrs. Xiomy's fingers scrunched through the cracks of one of the wall panels and her mouth opened wide like she had won the lottery. She cried out that she had found it! Jonathan and Boreas put their weight against the panel she had found. They heaved their shoulders against it and the wall gave way and opened wide. Boreas pushed Babs toward the opening and she grabbed the flashlight in the Professor's hand.

"Come on!" She shouted, starting to lead the way through the looming tunnel before them. The guards had just broken down the door and were making their way down the long winding staircase, their footsteps rushing down the steps like a stampede.

Boreas shot the gun into the air to stall the incoming cavalry.

"Go!" Boreas cried out.

Mrs. Xiomy and Babs started to run, holding onto the Professor to guide him through the dark narrow tunnel. The guards were nearly upon them, seconds away from reaching the last step. Boreas knew that they would never get far if the army swarmed in after them through the tunnel. Jonathan was waiting for Boreas to go in first but Boreas pushed Jonathan inside and whispered hurriedly.

"Find Aurora and Otus. They are in the woods by the broken down pier."

"I am not leaving you," Jonathan cried out, trying to pull Boreas into the tunnel after him.

Boreas shook off his brother, looking deep into his eyes. "I'm the one they want. They won't pursue you if they have me. Now go!"

Jonathan picked up the conch shell and threw it back at him right before Boreas slammed the wall door shut. "So you can find us!"

The door slammed shut behind his brother and Boreas stuffed the conch shell inside his sock. He took a deep breath as he turned to face the onslaught of officers stampeding down the stairs. They all held guns up at him as he stood with his hands above his head. He noticed Officer Woolchuck strutting down, wearing only a nightshirt and boxers.

"Guess we won't need to wait for that DNA test after all, Boreas."

Boreas gulped as his face was lifted up roughly by the Officer's large calloused hands against the blinding flashlight. "And perfect timing too, since the Inspector is here and waiting to meet you."

"Good, I've been waiting to meet him too and watch him fire you for indecent exposure. Nice boxers!"

Officer Woolchuck handcuffed him and viciously grabbed him by the hair and began to drag him by the roots. Boreas winced from the pain.

"You, Boreas, have embarrassed me and this unit for the last time." His rancid breath as he spit out those words made Boreas nauseous. "I can't wait to watch the Inspector torture you."

Without another word, Officer Woolchuck hit Boreas hard in the face. He plummeted to the ground like a losing boxer sprawled out in the center of the ring and darkness overtook him.

Chapter 14

The Soul Extractor

Boreas awoke with his head throbbing uncontrollably. He put his hand over his left eye and felt a huge bump. The room he was in came into focus; another cell, this one resembling a small, suffocating box. He didn't know how long he was out for, but he hoped Babs and the others had gotten away. He felt the conch shell still in his sock where he had hurriedly stashed it. Jonathan had told him to use it to find them again. Boreas feared he would never get the chance.

The door opened wide and shafts of light burst into the room; his eyes burned due to the adjustment. Half expecting to see the Inspector, he was taken aback when the face of his father came into focus. His father's tall frame stood there gaping down at his son, shining a flashlight into his face. He then turned back toward the guards who stood behind him and remarked coldly, "Yes. I identify him as my son, Boreas."

"You know the consequences if you are wrong."

"I am not wrong." Mr. Stockington declared forcefully. "Now go tell Inspector Herald that Boreas is ready for him."

Boreas watched as his father stepped forward, one foot in front of the other and knelt down beside his son. Boreas glared at him, spitting out, "I hope you're happy now."

Mr. Stockington shook his head at his youngest son and whispered, "You did this to yourself, Boreas. I made a choice, my country before my family."

"You are just like her."

"Like who?"

Boreas's eyes squinted menacingly. "Like mom."

Mr. Stockington stood up. "So it's true. She is alive."

Boreas nodded.

His father paced up and down the small cell, lost in his thoughts until finally he cried out aggravated, "She's a fool and you are just like her. Every time I look at you I see her and it kills me. So alike... I loved your mother. I loved her more than anything in this world. But I was always second to her. I could never be him, I could never be David and that's who she loved. She told me but when he was killed, I thought, 'now, she will be mine'. She *will* be mine, but I was wrong. She will always be his."

Crestfallen, he slumped back into the shadows of the room and Boreas closed his eyes, wishing that there was something he could say to make his father see him for himself.

"Dad, did you not once think that I wasn't mom or Jonathan, that I was just me? You have been comparing me to them all my life and all I ever wanted was for you to be my dad. Now be my dad, and help me!"

Mr. Stockington knelt down and took his son's hand in his. He put it against his face and Boreas felt wet tears falling from his father's eyes.

"I'm sorry, but I can't. I just hope that Jonathan can be forgiven, that he won't be caught in the stigma of your betrayal."

Boreas took a deep breath and looked up at the ceiling so as to not look at his father. Fighting tears and holding on to the last ounce of pride that he had left, "so you are just going to let him kill me?"

Mr. Stockington marched to the door and looked back once more at his son. "If it's what's best for the Common Good, yes."

The door slammed shut behind him.

✡ ✡ ✡

"What are we doing here?" Analise whispered urgently, not liking how she was transported to this fort near Lake Champlain. Ambassador Alvarez was in the room unpacking, preparing for the interview that would take place the following day.

"I just take orders, Analise," Jake whispered, eying the empty corridors, the fluorescent lights flickering. "I don't know why he changed his mind and wants to do the interview here."

Analise wanted to pull her hair out of her head. All week she had been working around the clock preparing for this interview in the Candlewick Government Building and now everything had changed. They had to email out a dozen notices of the new location. And to make matters worse, Ambassador Alvarez complained the entire trip over while in the helicopter, expressing that she felt this humidity was not going to be good for her hair.

As if reading her thoughts, Ambassador Alvarez popped her head out from the room with her hair done up in big curlers and her face covered in a mask of some green goop to supposedly help smooth her complexion for the cameras.

"Analise, make sure you arrange for my shoes to be shipped here since I left them back in Candlewick. I especially want my lucky red heels. I won't be able to do the interview without them."

"Yes, Ambassador Alvarez," Analise smiled, sweetly.

Ambassador Alvarez closed the door behind her, whistling some melodic tune.

Analise whirled back around to Jake and whispered, "She is driving me crazy! You'd never know her daughter is in severe danger."

Jake smiled slightly, taking the sunglasses off his eyes and cleaning the lenses with a handkerchief from his uniform pocket. "Just make sure you keep an eye on her. The Inspector doesn't like to change plans unless there's a good reason. And I am afraid I know what that reason is." He leaned in, giving Analise a kiss on the cheek. "Please be careful."

Shocked by his sudden display of affection, she looked deeply into his owl eyes and for a second she was speechless. She snapped out of her stupor. "Well, I can handle the Ambassador. You handle the Inspector and find out why the hell he changed our plans when the others were more convenient for him."

He nodded, placing his sunglasses back over his eyes. "Fine, I will take care of it. You practice those interview questions."

Jake hurried down the corridor, feeling his watch buzzing, summoning him to the execution block, where they interviewed and executed major criminals of the IDEAL and the Common Good. He wondered and feared who was facing this type of criminal trial and hoped his suspicions would be proven wrong.

He knocked on the door, and he heard the Inspector growl "Come in." Jake took a deep breath. The Inspector was not in any mood to discuss why the interview had been changed. He could make up something to appease Analise later.

✧ ✧ ✧

Inspector Herald whirled around to see the First Lieutenant, his protégé, march inside. He walked in, young and confident, not fearful in the Inspector's presence, one of the attributes he admired about the young man. He reminded the Inspector a lot of himself at that young age, angry at the world and willing to sacrifice even his family to uphold the IDEAL's way of life.

"You sent for me, Inspector?"

"Yes I did, First Lieutenant. You brought Miss Jones and Ambassador Alvarez here with you?"

"As you commanded," Jake nodded. "Though Miss Jones wasn't happy the interview location changed at such short notice."

"She'll soon be getting the story of her life."

The Inspector smiled his crooked smile, licking the edge of his chipped front tooth.

"So," the First Lieutenant said, "What's so important that you sent for me?"

Inspector Herald reached into the opened old fashioned leather suitcase that had been confiscated from Professor Gassendi. He cautiously picked up a green vile and couldn't believe that the soul extractor serum was finally once again in his grasp. He couldn't wait to inject the serum into Boreas Stockington and watch it manipulate his soul. He wasn't technically breaking his promise to Henry Stockington when he promised he wouldn't kill the boy. In fact if all went as planned and the soul extractor worked, the boy would become their biggest ally. Of course, there was the slight possibility the serum could kill him, but that was a risk the Inspector was willing to take.

He suddenly remembered he wasn't alone in the room and held up the vile so that the First Lieutenant could bask in this glorious moment.

"Fifteen years ago we used modern technology against anti-quated torture techniques. We turned the very person against the people he loved. This is true power. And it worked! The Common Good defeated IMAM and the religious protesters, turned brother against brother. The Professor, in working toward proving the existence of a soul, had miscalculated his triumphs. He had unwillingly concocted the greatest weapon in the history of mankind and Boreas Stockington will be the first victim in over a decade."

The First Lieutenant took a step back and then recovered. "So you have captured the boy?"

The Inspector eyed him curiously. "Of course we captured him. No thanks to those ridiculous officers that you have trained, they nearly lost him again. But this time I will use him to get to the giant. He will have no choice but to succumb to our wishes and end this chase once and for all."

The First Lieutenant took a deep breath and replied, "What do you need me for?"

"After I administer the serum, we will use Boreas to lure Aurora Alvarez and the giant to us. I will need you to work with the team to prepare them to take down a giant."

The First Lieutenant looked as if he was reaching for his gun, eyeing the serum in the Inspector's hand, as if he was contemplating fighting him for it. But the Inspector must have been seeing things, because the Lieutenant's hand went past the gun holster and reached up to his forehead with an obedient salute.

"Consider it done."

The Inspector held the liquid substance, knowing he was holding the fate of Boreas's life in his hands.

"This must be what it's like", the Inspector said bemused. "This must be what it's like to be a God."

Boreas was led by two armed guards into what appeared to be a dark chamber. His left eye was black and blue from where he had been punched by Officer Woolchuck and he was strapped down to a chair that had been used for electrocuting its victims. He held his breath as he realized he had been brought into a torture chamber, used against some of the most prolific criminals of the Common Good. Officer Pelican had revealed that since the bombing of Plymouth Tartarus, the IDEAL agreed to broadcast some of the executions on national TV, as a warning to other traitors out there that this would be their fate; to create fear in their hearts. He recalled what Mrs. Xiomy told him about the Inspector's tactics of torture. He would stoop to any means necessary to get what he wanted.

The door swung open. The chair was fastened with its back to the door and Boreas only heard the sound of footsteps approaching from behind, slow and steady against the floor. The door swung shut and was locked. Boreas closed his eyes, trying to not panic, Aurora and Otus depended on him now. They needed him to stay brave.

Boreas struggled with the straps that held his hands and feet in place, but they didn't budge. He was a prisoner in this chamber and he didn't know if he would come out of it alive. A voice sounded behind him, and spoke like a viper in his ear.

"So you are the troublesome Boreas I have heard so much about."

Boreas swallowed hard and responded, "And you are the psychotic Inspector *I've* heard so much about."

The voice laughed behind him, like a humorless, asthmatic wheeze. The footsteps encircled him and came up beside him on his left. Boreas turned and was face to face with eyes the color of coal. Patches of red and white scarring covered his face and his bald scalp. Where eyebrows should have been, there were just pale outlines left and his nose was square and disfigured from plastic surgery. Only the lips of his mouth were still intact.

"Take a good look at me," he said smiling, his front tooth broken in half. He traced the scar under Boreas's chin and smiled. "You too have faced death, haven't you Boreas?"

The cold touch of his hands caused Boreas to shudder as the Inspector kept smiling at him, digging his fingernail slightly into the wound where Boreas had been sliced by the knife of the Great Secretary back in Plymouth Tartarus.

Boreas took a deep breath. "You don't scare me."

The Inspector curled his tongue and put down the suitcase on the table beside him. "This face taught me a lot about human nature, Boreas. It taught me that everyone feels pain, even the bravest of men and women. But you Boreas, you who have faced death do not fear it. However, you have been inflicted with emotional pain, pain that will be to my advantage in finding your friends, Aurora and the Giant."

"I don't know who you are talking about."

The Inspector laughed that wheezing laugh that made Boreas sink lower into his chair. The Inspector unclasped the suitcase, lifted the lid and exposed the Professor's weapons inside.

"How is the good Professor? Not much longer to live, I fear. He is better with finding weapons than cures I am afraid."

He held up the neon-green vile and a syringe and Boreas felt his heart beating rapidly as he stared at the soul extractor, the substance the Professor had said proved the existence of a soul. The Inspector filled the syringe and squeezed it so that part of the serum shot out the top. His disfigured face was illuminated by the brightness of the vile substance glowing in that chamber of darkness.

"This may kill you," he said, exposing his jagged tooth as he advanced toward Boreas. Boreas did not take his eyes off of the serum, as if hypnotized. "But I hope for both of our sakes that it doesn't do the job too quickly."

"I'll never lead you to them. Never!" Boreas declared outright. At that, Officer Woolchuck punched him across the jaw. The Inspector put his hand up and the Officer stepped back obediently.

"You will lead me to them." He took the syringe and held it up in front of Boreas's face that had beads of sweat dripping down his forehead. "If you survive, this serum will extract the part of the soul where all your pain and hate is confined and you will help me trap your friends, unwillingly. Unless…" he licked the lower edge of his tooth, "you tell me right now where your friends are and save us from this experiment."

Boreas looked directly into the Inspector's eyes and then at the serum. He swallowed hard, closing his eyes, but even in the escape of the darkness of his mind, the image of the Inspector's face was still outlined; he could not escape. The outline transformed into

Aurora's face, smiling at him, saying that he was not alone, that they were in this together.

"What will it be, Boreas?"

His eyes opened wide and smiled back at the Inspector and stared into his inhuman face, the coal eyes digging into his own.

"I hope it kills me then."

The Inspector struck the needle forcefully into his forearm and Boreas cried out in pain as the serum was pushed into his bloodstream. The First Lieutenant was standing by the door to hide from Boreas and turned away, not able to watch while Officer Woolchuck looked on the Inspector's handiwork admiringly. Once the entire serum was depleted into Boreas's body, the Inspector removed the needle and carefully placed it on the desk. He then took out Boreas's file and started speaking in a slow and steady voice, unwavering — like a hypnotist.

"You, Boreas Stockington, are a disgrace to your Father. He turned you in without even once trying to plead for your life. He said that you were a disgrace to this country for turning against it. You, Boreas Stockington are a disgrace. Your mother, she chose to leave you and fake her death because she wanted nothing to do with you. She chose the life of a fugitive rather than to care for her child, her precious baby. Your brother, he is more of a man than you'll ever be, he should be the one with this destiny, not his weak younger brother. You could never live up to him, you are nothing compared to him. Your friends, the Giant and Aurora, where are they? Where are they to help you when you need them? The giant knew that you and the girl are disposable. You had no say in the matter, fighting for something you don't even believe in. Boreas, you have been used and now they expect you to die for their cause. Die for it. You are meant for more than that, you are meant to help us stop them, stop them before they ruin the only good thing that this world has left."

He paused, turning to the boy with his head face down, his hair disheveled and hanging loose over his face. The Inspector waited impatiently to see some sign of change in him. He was still breathing heavily, so that meant he had survived the initial test. Now to find out if the soul had been extracted.

"Boreas, will you help me destroy the Giant once and for all?"

Boreas looked up, his eyes bloodshot and his nostrils flaring. "I will lead you to him."

Chapter 15

Serum Replicas

The First Lieutenant banged on the door, fearful he would be caught in this section of the fort, designated for media personnel only, but he didn't care and kept banging on the door madly.

The door opened slightly and Analise stood there in her nightgown, her hair tucked under a red scarf and her brown eyes droopy with sleep.

"Analise, I need your help."

Her eyes popped wide open in shock, as if she just awoke and realized this was not a dream. "Jake? What on earth? You're crazy. Don't you realize this is dangerous? You shouldn't be here."

"He has Boreas."

She quickly pulled him into the room and closed the door shut behind her, putting her finger to her lips to shush him. Analise then quickly tiptoed over to the Ambassador to make sure she was still sleeping soundly.

"Yes, I heard they captured him," she whispered. "Now get the hell out of here before the Ambassador wakes up and gets us both in trouble."

"Herald administered some drug to him and I saw it. The boy is bewitched or something. He is going to lead the Inspector to Aurora and the giant."

She put her ear against the door, afraid there were people lurking outside. "I swear if the Inspector finds out you are here we are as good as dead. You know that, don't you?"

He stood up, brushed his hair out of his eyes as beads of sweat dripped down his forehead. "He made samples of the soul extractor serum, I saw him holding a vile. He cannot have this kind of power. He will truly use this power for evil. I need you to destroy the samples."

"And exactly how do you think I am going to do that?"

He took a seat on the bed and took her hands. "I need you to sneak into his chamber. That's where he is hiding it. I will distract him as long as I can but I need you to go in and steal it and then destroy it."

Analise stared into this troubled man's eyes, knowing what was at stake if they failed. She took his trembling hands into her own and replied succinctly, "I will do it."

He removed his hands from her grasp and stood up. "OK." He handed her a key and closed her palm over it. "Get dressed and head over to the Inspector's room in five minutes. I will go to his chamber now and distract him."

"What about Boreas?"

"Boreas is out of our control right now."

She nodded as she pulled out a pair of jeans and a t-shirt from her drawer. She started to put them on as she called out, "Jake, if we get caught, Mary..."

"Don't, Analise. I know what could happen."

He looked back at her one last time to give her a reassuring nod then put his ear against the door, listened, and then opened it slightly to ensure that no one was eavesdropping. He disappeared back into the darkness of the hallway. Analise threw on her shirt and jeans and followed suit despite the fear trembling through her body. She had to remove all doubt, she knew what she had signed up for and it wasn't just to be another media lackey. She had memorized each hallway in the fort and knew exactly which one the Inspector would inhabit during their stay. She heard voices echoing down the hall and was glad she had grabbed her USB flash drive, which stored the media footage she had been editing. If stopped, she could pretend that she needed help editing a story.

She took a deep breath as she saw two shadows heading down the side of the hall and tensed as she recognized the voice of the Inspector. She threw her body against the wall, trying hard not to breathe, fearing that any sound she made would cause the Inspector to become suspicious. She counted to ten and then forced her legs to move, sliding her feet along the wooden floor. She finally reached the Inspector's door, but she didn't know how long Jake would be able to stall. She took the silver key out of her pocket and looking to her right and left, jammed it into the lock and quickly turned it. The door gave way. She squeezed through and closed it abruptly behind her. The Inspector's room was cold and empty. Though they were in a fort, there were hundreds of TV's that lined the room. Each of them was powered on, with the sound on mute. They cast an eerie glow in the barren room. She quickly started searching the shelves, trying to find a suitcase or something that would house the serums that he had copied. They had to be somewhere. She searched under the bed and in the closet, but was coming up empty handed. She knew that he wouldn't have hidden it in plain sight. *Think like him! Think like him!*

It was then she remembered the Inspector raving about David Xiomy, about how he had killed him. In that desolate room, there was a statue of the famed protestor in the corner. It was made of bronze, his back facing them as he was being led away by the Common Good soldiers. She walked over to it and put her hand on it. The statue turned, revealing a hidden door in the wall. She quickly ran to it and opened the door when an alarm sounded! Lights started flashing, but the serum was facing her and she didn't know what to do. Just then the doors behind her flew open and soldiers rushed in, pointed guns at her head and ordered her to get to the ground or they would shoot. She did as she was told and knew that it was all over for her. Mere seconds later, the Inspector entered the room followed by Jake who looked absolutely menacing. The Inspector eyed Analise and ordered the guard to shut off the alarm. The guard administered a code and the noise dissolved. Analise lay on the floor with her hands in front of her and the Inspector's shadow looming over her.

"What is this, Analise Jones? I didn't expect you in my quarters tonight."

"I wanted to surprise you," she said quickly. "I wanted to show you my media footage personally to get your feedback."

"So you broke into my room?" he asked, not convinced, shaking his head at her.

She tilted her head up and said in a flirty tone, "I just wanted to talk to you...alone."

She didn't know how she was going to keep up this act. She was hoping Jake would intervene, but he was glued to his spot beside his Inspector. He wouldn't intervene for her, she was on her own. How did she get into this mess?

"So you broke into my safe?"

"While waiting, I was curious about the statue of David Xiomy. I didn't know why you would have this in your room? I turned it to get a better look and then this wall panel just opened up. I was as surprised as the guards when the alarm sounded and nearly burst my ear drums."

The Inspector offered the girl his hand and she took it. His hand was clammy while he was, most likely, testing her pulse. Try to stay calm, she ordered her pulse, but she didn't know if her heart was cooperating.

He then felt her backside, lingering where the USB flash drive was nestled in her back pocket and he grinned. "I would like to watch this footage of yours, Miss Jones, tonight. First Lieutenant."

"Yes," Jake replied brusquely.

"Take the suitcase out of my room and lock it in my office tonight."

"Yes Sir."

Jake took the suitcase and marched out of the room. She had caught his eye and it was then that she knew this had been his plan all along, that she would get caught and now be at the mercy of the Inspector. The Inspector continued to keep his hand on her backside, massaging it softly with his fingers.

"You can leave us," he ordered the guards, licking his upper tooth seductively. "I have business to take care of."

The door closed shut behind them and it was just Analise and the Inspector alone. The TV screens flickered off her face and she hoped the eerie light disguised her fear of what would happen next. The nightmare continued as he slowly undid the belt around her waist.

The door knocked again and the frantic voice of Ambassador Alvarez was screaming on the other side. "I need to speak with Analise Jones immediately. I am having a panic attack. I cannot go through with the interview tomorrow. I cannot…I will not."

The Inspector bellowed for the guards to take her away, but Analise hastily said, "We cannot reschedule the interview. Too many people are waiting to hear her story…they will question you and your motives if she doesn't go on the air."

He licked his front tooth as if in thought. He then bent down and handed the belt to Analise with a sly smile. "Don't think this is over, Miss Jones."

Analise grabbed the belt out of his hands and ran to the door, where Ambassador Alvarez was standing there in her nightgown, like a crazed psychiatric patient.

"I am here," Analise said, putting her arm around the small petite woman.

"I cannot go on tomorrow, Analise. I absolutely will not unless you talk some sense into me. I swear I don't know what to wear, my shoes aren't here yet…"

The Inspector's eyes were fastened on Analise until they rounded the corner and were safely in her room.

As soon as the door was locked, Ambassador Alvarez turned to Analise and held her in her arms. Analise was completely surprised by this sudden change, but let this woman hold her, comforted in her motherly embrace.

"My dear, I thought I would be too late."

Analise felt her throat go dry as her heart resumed its natural beating. "But how did you know to come? I thought you were asleep. I didn't know you had heard my conversation with Jake."

"Jake saw that I was awake," she said slowly. "I am sure he wanted me to hear, just in case anything went wrong. I am glad I was there in time."

Analise took her hands and squeezed them gratefully. "Thank you," she said feeling a tear fall from her eyes, realizing what could have happened if the Ambassador hadn't arrived at that moment. "I don't know what I would have done…how I would have gotten out of there if you hadn't…"

"I did so much wrong with my Aurora," the Ambassador said with tears brimming in her eyes. "I want to do right with you. It's like I have Aurora back with me….like I am helping her the only way I know how."

Analise smiled, "You are helping her, and now you know Jake and I are trying to help her too."

The Ambassador patted her hand lovingly, then wiped the tears from her eyes. "Look at me, what a mess. I will have dark circles under my eyes tomorrow now from all this crying. I don't think I can do this interview, not now that I know Boreas Stockington is going to lead the Inspector to my daughter…what are we going to do?"

Analise took a deep breath, resolved to not let the Inspector win. "We do the interview tomorrow. We try to give Aurora hope."

Chapter 16

The Hunter

The water resembled crystal clear glass, reflecting light off its surface like a prism. Aurora removed her clothes, her naked body shivering as her toe dipped into the cool shimmering substance. She slowly immersed herself into the liquid, the sensation causing her body to go numb but homeostasis began to kick in and she swam to speed up the process. She dipped her head into the water, drowning out the world around her as a slight buzz filled her eardrums. She opened her eyes to reveal a hazy world where seaweed, plankton and other organisms collided with her skin and for a split moment, she felt one with them. She felt her lungs urging her to breathe and she fought the temptation by diving downward into the void below. She raised her hands in front of her and they were floating, lifeless and weightless. Even her body felt lighter than air down here, defying gravity. She floated further out into the lake and her lungs were ready to burst when she finally adhered to the demands of her body and reversed her route, advancing upwards toward the light at the surface. She hit the invisible divide between her world and the watery world below as her head rose above the surface. Aurora flung her hair back as if in slow motion and her lungs filled with oxygen once more. She felt invigorated and alive like a baby taking its first breath.

Ducks soared downwards across the orange sky at dawn and skidded across the water, splashing in her direction. She laughed in delight as they landed so gracefully, resting and floating wherever the waves would take them. So carefree... they ignored her existence and continued bobbing along past her as she floated on her back, her entire being exposed to the sky and the rising sun. There was no one here to judge her or laugh at her naked form. Here she was perfect, floating along like the ducks, closing her eyes and letting the waves take her where they wished, ebbing up and down, completely at peace. She listened to the sounds of nature like the ducks quacking, the crickets singing, the frogs croaking, the dragonflies buzzing and dancing in the sky, swirling and twirling around each other like they were dancing a waltz to the morning serenade.

This is what it meant to be reborn, to start anew, just as Champ had instructed. She immersed herself in Lake Champlain like how she had begun her journey into this world, unclothed and renewed out of her mother's womb. As the early morning sunrays stretched their hands over her luminous body, she felt as if she could do anything, as if the sun was being absorbed into her blood and her fingertips and her skin. She closed her eyes and hoped that the power prophesized by Pierre Gassendi was filling her, but she wasn't exactly sure how she should be feeling. She thought if a strange reincarnation was occurring that she would know, but all she felt was free and alive. She watched a duck flapping its wings and sprays of water dripped from its dark brown body as its green neck stretched and it took off. It soared upwards into the morning sky; its little body rising to the height of the trees, just like her it was free and alive.

A gunshot erupted from the woods and the duck spun and spiraled toward the ground like a meteor, vanishing behind the leaves and out of Aurora's line of vision. Without a second thought, Aurora swam as quickly as her arms could go, like a propeller swishing through the water, until she reached the shore. She pulled herself out of the lake and back into the chill that struck her naked body with great force. The shock of the cold did not slow her down as she ran to the oak tree where her clothes were still hanging. She shook them out, then clasped on her bra, and threw her shirt over her head, her hands missing the open sleeves as she kept turning to see if the hunter would emerge from behind the trees. Her legs scrambled back into her panties and jeans and zipped them closed as she hid behind the oak tree, her hair dripping and her breath caught, not sure if anyone had seen her. The leaves gently rustled around her and she felt her body shrinking backwards down the slippery slope, her senses alert and her body ready to react. She found her way back to camp. Otus was alert and put his finger to his lips to quiet her. She stood still, knowing the hunter was close by.

Otus sprang from his hiding spot and landed with such force that the ground shook and the hunter fell, the gun blasting off a shot that lodged deep into the oak tree above Aurora's head. Otus extended his hand and with a roar grabbed the hunter into his grasp and yelled, "Gotcha!"

The hunter froze in fear as Otus carried him into their camp. He was like a speck in Otus's hand. In the hunter, she saw something that made her heart skip a beat. Otus was about to fling him like a boomerang when she yelled, "Otus, no!"

Otus paused as she ran towards him, "Aurora, he just tried to kill us!"

The hunter fell to the ground, shaking in fright with his back to them. He had his blond hair tied in a ponytail that hung down his shoulders and he was wearing a metallic jacket that clung to his broad chest. What had caught her eye, however, was the silver stud earring in his right ear.

"It's Jonathan."

Saying his name out loud caused her throat to go dry. She licked her lips, quickly fixing her hair that was still drenched, squeezing it out and smoothing it with her hand. Jonathan rolled over and lifted his face toward Otus as he tried to find his voice. His face revealed a bruise over his left eye and black scruff on his cheeks. He was much thinner than she remembered but he still had the beautiful turquoise sparkle in his large oval eyes. His lips were still thick and sensual and she couldn't believe that she stood within arm's length from him in the middle of nowhere. He smelled of pine needles and his hands were calloused. She saw bruise marks on his knuckles as well, as if he had been in a fight.

His eyes didn't leave Otus's face as he said in his deep baritone voice, "You are a giant!"

Otus's left eyebrow raised in suspicion as he tilted his head giving Aurora a look like, "Very observant. Who on earth is this guy?"

It was then that Jonathan's eyes followed his gaze and landed upon Aurora who stood there gaping at him in shock and surprise.

"Jonathan, what are you doing here?" she stood beside Otus, like a mouse in comparison to her counterpart.

He scrambled to his feet, his ponytail shifting to his shoulder as he stood up to his full height, nearly two feet taller than Aurora. He was breathing heavily and still very badly shaken when he said, "Boreas told me where to find you."

"Boreas." Aurora said hurriedly, shock plastered on her face. "Where is he? Is he okay?"

Jonathan turned to Otus and exclaimed in frenzy, "I need you to come with me now. I have Babs, Mrs. Xiomy and the Professor all at our camp. The Common Good has captured Boreas."

Aurora felt her hand cover her mouth in horror. She turned to Otus and they both read each other's mind.

"Take us to them now."

✧ ✧ ✧

Aurora felt like a part of her had been ripped out of her body.

Jonathan relayed the story to them as they were flying over the wilderness; Otus rode the wind like he bore wings. Jonathan explained the plot to capture Boreas and that he had been stationed at the cottage with his father to help capture Boreas and turn him into the Common Good at the command of the Inspector. He spoke of their capture and the mistaken identity, his father going under the spell of the sleeping serum and not able to do the identification, the torment in the jail cell and the escape. Aurora and Otus listened without interruption and she just couldn't believe that both Jonathan and his father had turned Boreas into the Common Good. She couldn't believe that family would do that. Once the story had been told, she inquired about her own parents fearing that they too were conspiring against her. Jonathan shook his head and said that all he knew was that the Common Good had arrested Mr. Alvarez and confiscated a lot of the collections in the Alvarez house following the library incident. They had burned all of their possessions in the middle of Wishbone Avenue as a statement. Aurora felt sick to her stomach as she thought about her nightmare… of her house burning down. It was as if her subconscious knew that her family's possessions were being destroyed, all of their collections burned away as if they never existed.

"But what about my mom? Is she alright?"

Jonathan looked at her solemnly, holding onto the overalls pocket for dear life. "I overheard something in the prison that your mom is now an Ambassador for the Common Good."

Her mother an Ambassador for the Common Good? No, it was impossible. Aurora felt betrayed. Had her mom turned against Aurora, and her father? Or was this another ploy by the Inspector to show that he had the control. That he had his mother and father's lives in his hands.

They reached the lighthouse where Jonathan told them that their friends were hiding out. They figured that they would be safer in a conspicuous place since no one would expect them to go and hide there. It was already past the Awakened Hour and Otus had to quickly drop off his passengers and then sink beneath the lake to hide out until they called him. They couldn't risk him being seen by the Common Good, especially if there was a brigade out looking for them. They didn't know what Boreas had told them, but they had to assume the worst. Aurora proceeded with caution, not sure yet if she could trust Jonathan, especially after he had confessed to having turned against his own brother. She remembered her wish upon the star back in Plymouth Incarnate and her father's warning in her head that she had ignored, "The wish may come true, but not in the way one expects".

Her wish had come true. Jonathan was with her, and not Boreas.

The lighthouse was made of solid marble and was used more as a memorial than as an actual lighthouse. The light was turned on this year in memory of the lives lost in the Battle of Lake Champlain during the Last Straw where family member was pitted against family member as each side fought for their cause. The side of the Common Good and the IDEAL wore their indigo and orange colors proudly and had the entire government militia on their side. The rebels had whatever weapons they could find, rocks, guns, sticks, and attacked valiantly against bombs and modern technology. Their means of protest was different from IMAM's followers who believed this fight was to be won by peaceful measures. Both acts of protest were demolished when the Inspector took his place in government.

Aurora recalled the newspaper article they found in the library about Mrs. Xiomy; her face the epitome of pain and anguish as her husband was dragged away from her by armed officers of the Common Good. Her loved one was torn from her side and she never saw him again. Aurora felt that same anguish in her own heart, thinking she might not see Boreas again. The last words they had spoken were so horrible and Aurora tried not to think about them as they advanced toward the lighthouse, trying to blend in with a number of tourists who were visiting the lighthouse.

"We'll wait for lunch time when most of them will leave and go to the town. Then we'll be able to get in unobserved."

Aurora nodded and adjusted her backpack strap that was digging into her shoulder. She walked through the manicured gardens and saw carved name after name. They were separated by Rebel and Idealist. The Rebels were written on the cobblestones on the ground so that visitors had to walk on their names and their legacy. The Idealists were carved on a giant green marble tablet magnificently displayed in front of the lighthouse and covered with beautiful marigold plants of pumpkin-orange, maroon and fluorescent-yellow. There were also two beautiful red geranium plants at the base. A quote was written above the names, "For those who supported and died for a better world, a world free of religious adversity, who believed in our plight to free the world of the divisions that divide us." *The IDEAL* was all that was carved as the owner of that quote.

Aurora looked down at the names of the people who had fought bravely for their beliefs against greater odds than she could imagine. She stooped down and dusted off one of the cobblestones, removing a fallen crinkled brownish-red maple leaf to reveal the name "Henry Yorkshire". She stared at that name for a while and thought about how Henry had a mother, a father. He could have been someone's husband or brother or uncle. And here he was, now just a name covered by dirt and dust, nearly forgotten under the footprints of those who could still stand.

"I won't forget you, Henry Yorkshire", she whispered solemnly. She picked up the maple leaf and twirled the stem in her fingers until she crushed it in her grasp, the pieces of the leaf scattering over the marigold bushes like ashes.

The tourists started to disperse as the sun was at its zenith overhead and Aurora's stomach began to growl that they were at the lunch hour. They waited patiently as the last guard left to get a bite to eat and then they ran and slipped through the door that led into the lighthouse.

They slammed the door shut behind them and a voice boomed out saying, "This lighthouse is off limits. Please leave immediately!"

Aurora recognized the voice of the Professor and screamed up the spiraled staircase, "If that's your cover than you are all in worse shape than I thought."

Mrs. Xiomy's head peeked out from the top of the steps and her blond hair draped down over her shoulder like Rapunzel as she cried out, "Aurora! I'm so glad it's you."

Aurora clamored up the stairs and Jonathan followed closely at her heels. As they reached the top of the lighthouse, she was attacked with a hug by her teacher. Behind her Babs stood clutching a hand gun, the nozzle pointing down now, but Aurora realized that if someone else had happened upon them then the gun would have been their first line of defense. She nodded at Babs, not forgetting that she was the reason they had left their camp to begin with. Babs walked toward the opposite end of that tiny space, staring out the window that provided a view of the lake and the memorial below. The Professor appeared more disoriented than usual and she realized that he was without his suitcase and his medicine. All of their clothing was covered with dirt and blood and Aurora knew that it was a miracle they were still alive after having been captured by the Common Good.

Mrs. Xiomy told their tale about how Boreas had slammed the tunnel door shut behind him, sacrificing himself in hopes that the Common Good wouldn't go after the others. They followed the tunnel which ended up leading them to the other side of the moat, which was not being guarded. They hid in an abandoned summer home until it was nighttime, stealing food, clothes and additional provisions. Mrs. Xiomy and Babs were still very weak after being tortured by Officer Woolchuck, so Jonathan had decided to search for Aurora and Otus while the others hid in the lighthouse to gain back their strength. Nothing was safe and they didn't know who were spies and who were tourists so they couldn't risk getting caught now that they were recognizable.

"We're not exactly an inconspicuous group," Mrs. Xiomy admitted, ending her anecdote.

Aurora peered out one of the windows of the lighthouse and knew that Otus was down there swimming beneath the lake, waiting for her signal. She flicked the light two times, as if there was a sharp wind tampering with the flame. That was her signal that she had found the others and that they were safe.

"Now," she took a huge breath, fearing her own question, "how do we rescue Boreas?"

"We…don't." The Professor slurred, as the untreated Multiple Sclerosis was affecting his speech and causing his other symptoms to get progressively worse.

Babs bit her lower lip and said softly, "He's probably already dead."

Aurora recoiled as she remembered what Champ, the sea monster, had foretold. Aurora put her hand against the glass pane and watched her fingerprints making marks against the glass. She coughed and stammered, "That's not how he dies. I mean, I think Otus and I would sense something if he was dead."

"He took…took it," The Professor stammered, his face as white as a ghost. "He… took it…and he's not going to give it back."

"Give what back?"

"His suitcase" Babs interpreted.

The Professor wobbled unsteadily toward the window, muttering obscenities under his breath.

Mrs. Xiomy whispered to Aurora so that the Professor couldn't hear. "He hasn't been the same since we got out of the tunnel. Without his medicine, he needs to be in a hospital."

Aurora shook her head assertively. "We are all in this together, like it or not. And we have to rescue Boreas."

Mrs. Xiomy removed her arm from around her pupil's shoulders. "I am sorry, Aurora, but Boreas is on his own."

"We can't just leave him in there to be tortured, or worse."

Mrs. Xiomy wrestled with the loose strands of hair across her face and exclaimed, "If we go back into that fort now we will all be captured and the Inspector will have won. He would have you and Otus and the mission would have failed and millions of lives would be destroyed because of it. Do you think that is what Boreas wants?"

"Without Boreas, millions of lives will still be destroyed."

"You don't know that."

Aurora sat down huddled in a corner and Jonathan took a seat beside her. She quickly looked up to see his face so close to her own and felt his warm breath on her skin. He lifted the sunglasses off his face and sat them atop his head. She felt so vulnerable in his presence and closed her eyes, hoping that he would get up and go away.

"I can't believe you wanted to turn us all in to the Inspector," she said to break the uneasy silence.

"Correction, I wanted to turn in Boreas. My father and I thought he was a traitor to our country."

"And you didn't think that maybe he wasn't?"

Jonathan laughed, one of those laughs that used to give her goose bumps in Candlewick High. They still gave her goose bumps.

Jonathan continued, "My brother has been doing everything he can to humiliate our family, and now this charade. If the fate of the world is in my brother's hands, then I pity the world and the mockery of it all."

Aurora eyed him suspiciously. "What do you mean the mockery of it all?"

He gulped and shifted his position so that he was now sitting on his hind legs, fixing his jacket closer around his broad chest. He blew a strand of blond hair out of his eyes, but it just went back into place, wafting to the left side of his forehead. "I just mean the two of you, on this mission. It is a little absurd, don't you think?"

Aurora used the ledge for support and stood up, "The mission, or us?"

She whisked herself away from him and stood by the torch, warming her hands by the flame, trying to warm the goose bumps off her skin. He came up behind her and she could smell his scent of honey suckle and pine needles; she sucked in his aroma. He was beside her, so close that his shoulder was touching against her own.

"I am sorry, that came out wrong. This whole mission thing is hard to grasp. Why of all the people in this world were you and my brother chosen? It should have been me instead of him."

Aurora looked up into Jonathan's pristine face and said, "Boreas said the same thing."

Taken aback, he nodded and put his sunglasses back on over his eyes and adjusted the zipper on his jacket.

The fire was a good distraction so Aurora continued to warm her hands, closing her eyes, trying to forget about Jonathan and instead think of a way to rescue Boreas. Otus could storm in and grab him, but there was too much risk. Otus could be killed, or captured, and then where would their mission be? Mrs. Xiomy was right. Otus could not interfere.

They could go through the tunnel and hope they didn't barricade the door into the dungeon. They could lure the Inspector out of the fort by saying they would make a trade. Would he buy it?

Each solution felt more hopeless than the next, but Aurora kept frantically thinking of ways that they could rescue him. She started bouncing ideas off of the others who shot them down, left and right. Babs was getting frustrated by her suggestions and was becoming more sarcastic with each of her responses. Aurora ignored her and continued pondering and stammering out idea after idea. She had to find a way to save him, because if the tables were turned and she was in his shoes, she would hope that they were thinking of ways to save her from her horrible fate.

Right when it appeared that she was running out of ideas, something sounded faintly in the far midst of her mind.

"What was that noise?" she whispered, ushering the others to be quiet. It sounded again, like a fog horn playing over and over again.

"I don't hear anything." Jonathan bellowed and they all yelled at him to be quiet.

Aurora ran to the window and peered down. Her eyes wandered over the beach, searching frantically for the source of the noise.

"It almost sounds like a conch shell, but Otus wouldn't be playing it." She said out loud.

"Boreas has a conch shell," Jonathan said excited. "I threw it back at him before he slammed the wall door shut in the fort. It was a small white shell, with an orange tint, I think."

"The gift from Fawn!" Aurora exclaimed, nearly tripping over her feet as she flew down the spiraled staircase.

She waited until the coast was clear and then snuck out of the lighthouse, closing the door behind her. She ran past the manicured gardens, over the cobblestone names and past Henry Yorkshire. The conch shell played again, and it sounded closer than before. She spotted a brook straight ahead with a cobblestone bridge above it. The conch shell was sounding in that direction. She took off toward the bridge but heard footsteps behind her. She glanced back nervously but it was just Babs flying behind her, her long braid swinging back and forth as she ran to catch up. Aurora reached the brook first and splashed through the water, her pants getting soaked but she continued racing forward, the current pushing against her, and she zigzagged around the large rocks in her way. She tried to strain her eyes to see if there was anything moving beneath the large cobblestone bridge. The bridge curved upwards in a horseshoe shape above her head, which created thick shadows within the inner crevices. She stopped midway, knee-deep in the water and waited for the conch shell to sound again. The soft rustling sound of the water gushing under the bridge was all she heard until Babs splashed into the water, kicking her feet up as she advanced cautiously toward Aurora.

"It might be a trap." Babs warned, keeping her finger on the trigger of the gun.

Just then the quiet was interrupted by a rough, stoic voice. "Well, it took you long enough."

Aurora dove toward the voice, swimming as fast as her arms could go under the bridge. When she resurfaced, there, holding onto the side of the bridge for dear life, was Boreas. He was bruised and beaten up, with a dark bruise imprinted over his left eye. Dried blood stained his cheek and he was completely drenched, the conch shell cradled in his left palm. Aurora and Babs swam to his side and they hoisted him up so that he could lean on them for support. Babs kissed him tenderly as they carried him to land, but Boreas was too weak to kiss her back.

They rolled him over onto his side as he started coughing up blood. He said urgently, "It is not safe here, they will see us. Where is Otus?"

"Otus is safe, the others are too. How did you escape?"

He shook his head and took Babs by the hand and squeezed it gently. Babs stroked his hair out of his eyes and tears were falling down her face, and they didn't appear to be fake.

"I thought you were killed," she stammered, one tear streaming down her cheek and landing onto Boreas's bruised wrist where they had shackled him.

"Close to it, my father interceded and told them I should be tried in Candlewick. They were moving me and put me in a van. I was beaten pretty badly so they didn't handcuff me, big mistake on their end because when we hit a ditch going over the bridge, I broke open the door and threw myself out, landing in the water and played dead. They presumed my body was washed down the brook and hit the rocks. That's when I took my chances and hoped you would hear me calling you through the conch shell. I figured if anyone could hear it, you would, Aurora."

She nodded, surveying the bridge. "They didn't search the bridge after you jumped in?"

He sneered at her, getting to his feet. "Doubting me already, Aurora? I thought you would be relieved I was alive."

Babs gave Aurora a dirty look and continued to guide Boreas through the backwoods where they would wait for nightfall to sneak back into the lighthouse. Aurora cursed herself, the guilt again overwhelming her as she watched Boreas hobble through the woods toward the lighthouse. She kept glancing back at the brook and then back at Boreas, who she thought had been hobbling on his left leg just a minute before, but was now limping on his right leg. She tried to cast the idea out of her mind, but something was gnawing at her. The Inspector, who had risked so much to capture Boreas, would he have given up that easily?

Chapter 17

Truth or Dare

Aurora stood at the edge of the lake at the Sacred Hour. She felt numb all over, digging frozen fingers into her pockets. The rain was falling onto her body like hornets stinging her skin and she felt frantic, like there were eyes spying on her from all directions. She blew into the pink conch shell, the gift from Champ, softly and steadily and immediately she saw bubbles in the lake about 20 feet from where she stood. Rising out of the water, like a whale, was Otus. He swam toward her, spitting water up into the air like he had a spout. He stood up, towering above her and water dripped down over his bare chest. It wasn't safe even at this hour for him to be out here and she immediately ushered him to follow her. She led him into the shadows of the town, away from the lighthouse where the others were situated. The canopy of trees helped to block some of the onslaught of raindrops and she turned to Otus and finally felt safe to share the good news.

"We found Boreas, they are taking care of him but we need to move quickly. He escaped, but I fear that the Inspector would not give up looking for us this easily. We need to move."

Otus stood awkwardly, registering this information, "He escaped?"

She nodded, sensing the doubt in Otus's tone. The same doubt lingered in her mind. Something wasn't right with this situation, but she was resisting her inner voice that was telling her to run and escape from this place.

"I sense that we are in danger." Her gaze lingered on the top of the lighthouse, where Boreas was waiting for their return. "I can't imagine the Inspector just let him escape, without having this whole island swarming with Common Good guards."

Otus wiped the hair out of his troubled eyes and was shivering as he stood there dripping wet in the cold. "I don't have a good feeling either, but Boreas would not turn us in."

She remembered what Mrs. Xiomy had said about what happened in the fort. Boreas had sacrificed himself to save the others. He wouldn't turn against them, at least, not willingly.

"I still think we should move out tonight. Do you feel up to it?"

Otus nodded, but they both thought the same thing. Where do they run to? Aurora still didn't have her powers. Without the powers, what hope did they have of continuing on the mission? The trees moved eerily above them, swaying with the wind and her mind was swaying along with it. She felt at a loss and didn't know where to go or what to do.

"Otus, I didn't tell you this before, but Champ told me something that you're not going to like. He said I would get my powers when I had to kill the God of the North Wind."

Otus peered down at her, his mouth open in disbelief.

"That's impossible!" he said, the words shaking. "We are in this together, Aurora! That's the only thing I know for certain. All three of us need to be there at the Northern Lights to stop the Geometric Storm. The prophecy..."

"The prophecy led us to a dead end, Otus! Look at us. Boreas almost died and if we're not careful, we are going to be next. I don't know what kind of joke this prophecy is, leading us into the hands of the enemy and leading us to Champ who told me... I don't know what to do or who to believe! I am starting to think this is all just a story. A story that people have believed is real. Believing a story! Just a story!"

Otus picked her up, but Aurora couldn't make eye contact with him. The rain drops grazed against her face as she peered up at the dark clouds above her, and at the solitary light from the lighthouse illuminating the world around her. *What had the world ever done for her?* Here she was risking everything to save lives of people she didn't even know; people who didn't care about her or her mission. She should be in school, studying towards a career, living with her parents on Wishbone Avenue away from this nightmare. She thought of all the books in the library, of all the stories that people used to believe and die for. Risk everything for. *What was it about these stories that made the world stop and fight for them? To die for them?* She thought about Plymouth Tartarus. She thought about the Sistine Chapel with the God-like figure holding out his finger and starting life with a touch of his hand, with light. Life didn't start that way, and yet it had been depicted and believed for so long. Immortalized.

Otus held her in the palm of his hand and said softly, "I think humans want to believe in something to make sense of why they are here. To believe there is a reason to their existence. These stories depict people who did the impossible. The impossible makes them worth remembering."

Aurora thought of the man Henry Yorkshire whose cobblestone was immortalized by the lighthouse. "Humans also do impossibly horrible things to each other."

Otus nodded. "Humans will never learn. They haven't learned yet and they have been on this planet for hundreds of thousands of years. They will never learn that we all are faced with the same battle. Good versus evil. There is good and evil in all of us, it is a constant battle that we all face. Yet, it is the stories of men and women who conquered that battle on the side of good that we wish to remember, believe in, to emulate. We wish to believe that there is a better place without fear, without pain, without death. There are so many ways for a human being to die—old age, illness, by human hand, fluke accidents, natural disasters. And yet you wake up, every day, and take life for granted. And your bodies can only take so much pain, but yet so many overcome and continue to fight because there's only one life. And you find the beauty in it—somewhere deep inside you find the strength to do the impossible."

Aurora's eyes were glued to Otus' determined face that looked far off into the distance, as if he was gazing upon a beacon of hope that illuminated his path—his destiny. She stood up and said, "I believe you are doing impossible things, Otus."

He looked down at her, his face sparkling as the drops glittered on his features. "I wish I was a human, even if it is for just one day," he whispered.

"And why would you want that?"

He put her gently down on the ground and said slowly, "Never mind. Let's get the others before the Sacred Hour is over. Like you said, it's time we left this place."

They maneuvered their way through the darkness and the rain toward the lighthouse. Otus camouflaged himself against a large oak tree outside the structure while Aurora raced onwards, dripping wet and hoping the others were ready for their quick getaway. She banged on the door three times and waited, but no one answered. She banged again and still no one came to the door. She opened it up and heard a loud commotion escalating from the top of the stairs. She heard a scream as a body was flung down the stairs. Jonathan rolled one step at a time and landed at Aurora's feet. Horrified, Aurora dashed to his side and looked up to behold Boreas at the top of the stairs cracking his knuckles with a menacing scowl plastered on his face and fury shining through his eyes like a flame. She felt a pang of fear overwhelm her as she helped Jonathan struggle to his feet. Boreas was about to come down the stairs when Aurora screamed, "Boreas, stop!"

The fire extinguished from his eyes as he looked down and caught her gaze. He took a step backwards and Mrs. Xiomy and Babs hurried down to help Jonathan, nearly skipping two stairs at a time. The three women helped Jonathan climb back up the stairs, letting him lean against them for support.

"Let me at him," Jonathan cried out. "He has never beaten me and I am not going to let him gloat!"

"This is not the time or the place for your brotherly squabbles," Mrs. Xiomy demanded, aggravated. "Do you want us all to get arrested again?"

"What happened?" Aurora exclaimed, out of breath from helping Jonathan up the last step. They put him down and Babs examined his leg. Boreas grabbed Babs by the shoulder and shoved her backwards.

"Get away from him! You're my girlfriend, not his!"

Babs looked at him, rubbing her shoulder and she cried out, "What has gotten into you! He's hurt, Boreas, and unless you are a doctor, shut up and let me examine him!"

"You are not going anywhere near him!" He grabbed her by the shoulder and Babs took out the gun and held it up.

"You are not to touch me again!" She cried out in between a sob. "We're through."

Aurora stared blankly at the madness ensuing before her. Babs and Boreas just broke up, the Professor was off in his own world, and Aurora felt like she was on the threshold of disaster. She had to take control again, even though she had no idea what she was going to do next.

"Otus is waiting for us! We are leaving immediately!"

Boreas tensed up. "Where is he?"

"Outside. We are leaving this place now!"

Jonathan managed to get to his feet. Babs diagnosed him with only a slight sprain but luckily he was able to walk on it. Boreas watched him uneasily and Aurora went over to the Professor and tried to lead him away from the wall.

"I can't see!" The Professor confessed, crying. "Completely blind. The goggles can't help me anymore. Beyond help. They took it. I can't believe he's back!"

"We'll get you help!" Aurora promised blindly. She wasn't sure if there was help to be had, but she didn't know what else to say. She just had to get him away from the windows. The Sacred Hour was ticking away and they hadn't made any progress evacuating the lighthouse.

"We need to go to Candlewick!" Boreas stated.

Everyone turned to him, stunned at his outburst.

"Candlewick? You are more nuts than the Professor!" Mrs. Xiomy exclaimed.

Aurora was holding the Professor by the arm and started to head toward the stairs when Boreas jumped in front of them, his body blocking the way out.

"We have to go to Candlewick," he repeated, like a he was hypnotized, his eyes wide open and alert, and his mouth over-emphasizing each syllable.

"A trap," the Professor said solemnly. "I may be blind, but I'm not stupid."

Boreas continued to block them as they tried to get around him. "Aurora, we have to go there or else your parents will die."

Aurora froze, her body tensing up as she cried out, horrified, "What do you mean?"

He took a deep breath. "I heard the Inspector talking to my father. Your parents are going to be tried and sentenced this week unless we stop it. Your mother is the new Ambassador of the Common Good. After her TV interview they are going to fly back to Candlewick where they are going to stage a conspiracy and execute your parents for conspiring against the Common Good."

Aurora felt like she had just swallowed sandpaper. Her parents were to be sentenced to death, because of her? She pushed Boreas out of the way and made her way cautiously down the steps, guiding the Professor and trying to keep herself from tumbling down. It felt like the room was spinning around her like she was caught in the whirlpool in Lake Champlain once again. She had to talk to Otus; he would know what to do. If anyone would know, he would.

Otus was overjoyed to see everyone safe, especially Boreas. However, the warm welcome Otus was expecting was not returned.

Aurora felt sick as she was raised up into the overall pocket. They needed to go somewhere to think, but Boreas didn't give her that chance, taking charge immediately.

"Otus, we need to go to Candlewick. Aurora's parents will be sentenced to death if we don't stop it."

Otus didn't wait for them to say anything as he jumped up into the air and flew off southward, in the direction of Candlewick. "We will be there in two days," he proclaimed as they took off at lightning speed.

Babs cried out, "No. We must go to Plymouth Incarnate. We need Fawn's help; she will know what to do!"

Boreas cried out in protest, but Otus changed route, heading now toward Plymouth Incarnate.

Mrs. Xiomy held Aurora in her arms and said softly, "You will be faced with the same dilemma as I was, Aurora. Remember what happened to the person I loved. The Inspector will do whatever he can to get what he wants and he wants you, Boreas and Otus. Don't forget that."

She nodded slowly, watching the stars whirl past her as she thought about her father, and making the wish with him when she was a child. She couldn't let the Common Good kill them. Not if she could help it.

She wished she had her powers already, but Boreas was still alive. At this point, looking at his arrogant face leaning over the side of the overalls pocket, she was willing to kill him to save her parents, the two people in her life that she loved more than any others. If there was a choice, she knew what she would choose.

Chapter 18

Racing Against Time

urora was once again standing on the shoreline of the Hudson River in the epicenter of the wilderness. Aurora gazed out at the shimmering water, remembering that where she stood was the same spot where the memorial service was held for all those who had died in Plymouth Tartarus. It was the same spot where she had realized all those fallen, including her friend Eileen, were never going to see another birthday, or another sunrise. It was this same spot where Aurora, Boreas and Otus were determined to continue on their journey to the Northern Lights, and where Fawn had wished them goodbye and had presented Boreas with the conch shell. She dug her foot in the dirt and remembered it all so vividly, yet so much had transpired since that day. Summer had transitioned into autumn, and though the spot was the same, the place that was now called Plymouth Incarnate was deserted. The rebel community was nowhere to be found. Aurora and her team had all separated to search for any signs of life, but to no avail. Fawn's words came back to haunt her, "You won't be able to find us again. We will find you if you need us."

We need you, Fawn, Aurora thought with all her strength. Nobody manifested before her eyes. She was on her own. She looked into the water as a tear trickled down her face, but only her reflection stared back. They were once again on their own against the Common Good who held her parents at their mercy. She felt utterly helpless, defenseless against them.

"Why? Why is this happening?"

"Hello again."

Startled, Aurora gazed down into the water and there was Swanson smiling up at her through the water with his missing tooth and hair styled in a Mohawk. She leaned down and put her hand into the water over Swanson's face, not believing he was really there. All she touched was water but he giggled as if she was tickling him.

"SWANSON! What are you doing here?"

"Champ says hi. He can't leave Lake Champlain though. He has limits, but I don't."

"I need to find Plymouth Incarnate. I need to find Fawn. Do you know how we can find them?"

He looked left and right and then thought long and hard. "Plymouth Incarnate... If I were them I would be inside the rocks."

He pointed up and Aurora turned and followed his finger with her eyes high above them to large rock formations formed by glaciers all those years before. "Inside the rocks," she repeated. She turned back to the water, but Swanson had vanished. She blinked, half expecting him to return but once again he was gone.

She jumped up hurriedly and cried out for Otus, but forgot he was off fishing and hunting with Jonathan. Mrs. Xiomy and the Professor were looking for herbs to help alleviate some of the

Professor's M.S. symptoms. They had to search the rocks, even though it sounded way too daunting and she sounded ridiculous just muttering it to herself. She felt uncomfortable standing there alone in the wilderness and hurriedly walked back to camp expecting to find Boreas and Babs there, but only the fire welcomed her back.

Just then she heard a scream. She spotted the gun sticking out of Babs's backpack and she grabbed it on impulse, the weapon feeling foreign in her hands. She cautiously walked toward where she had heard the scream, expecting the Common Good to pounce on her from behind the trees at any minute. Her heart was doing summersaults in her chest and she tried to prevent herself from hyperventilating. Where was Otus? Was she the only one who had heard the scream? She dodged in and out of trees, the gun feeling heavy in her hands. The trees cleared and she found herself in a clearing with long overgrown grass that reached to her knees and grazed her legs. Staying hidden, she overheard voices shouting from the midst of the clearing.

"We are through, Boreas!" Babs's shrill-like voice echoed. "What don't you understand?"

"I don't believe you!" Boreas cried out, grabbing Babs' arms. Babs kicked him with all of her strength. Boreas didn't look fazed and knocked Babs to the ground, twisting her arm behind her, making her cry out in pain. "No one breaks up with me, you hear me! Espccially not for Jonathan!"

"You are deranged!" Babs shrieked. "I don't want you or Jonathan, you jealous bastard!"

Aurora couldn't stay silent any longer and jumped into the clearing, pointing the gun at him and cried out, "Boreas, let her go!"

He looked up at her with wild eyes, like a demon amidst the yellowish-brown grass. He sneered at her, "Go away, Aurora!"

Babs yelled, "Aurora, shoot the bastard!"

Aurora fired once in the air, then pointed the gun at Boreas's heart and called out, "Get off her now!"

Boreas unwillingly released his hold on Babs who slapped him hard across the face and then scampered off, looking scared and confused.

"Boreas, what the hell is wrong with you?"

Aurora was speaking to something deep within him, not the monster staring back at her.

"Nothing's wrong with me," he spit out, moving closer toward her, like he didn't care that she held a gun pointing at him. "For the first time I see clearly and I am not going to let Babs break up with me and go after Jonathan. I won't stand by and watch her…and you…be infatuated with my brother!"

Aurora felt stung by his words, but calmly said, "Boreas, you can't force Babs to go out with you again."

"I wasn't forcing her to do anything, damnit! I was just making her see reason."

Suddenly the ground shook, knocking both of them off balance, causing them to fall. Otus emerged from the woods, his shadow towering over the two teenagers. He scooped up Aurora and in the ruckus she dropped the gun. Boreas scampered off like a wild animal, until he was out of Otus' reach.

"You can't kill him, Aurora! I don't care what Champ said!" Otus scolded.

She scanned the area, trying desperately to find Boreas in that clearing. "I wasn't going to kill him. He attacked Babs. He has changed, Otus. Something happened to him when they caught him, it's like they changed him into a monster."

"You wouldn't be yourself if you were caught by the Inspector too," Jonathan added, out of breath having finally caught up to Otus. He picked up the gun and placed it in his jacket pocket. "He has ways to torture his victims that you can't even imagine."

Aurora shook her head. It wasn't that. It was like Boreas was a different person. Like something evil had possessed him, and she couldn't put her finger on what it could be. Otus continued to scold her, but she didn't listen. Her thoughts were on Boreas and how she had held a gun pointed at his heart. Her hand trembled as she remembered the feeling of power she had as she contemplated pulling the trigger, the power to take a life. The power of life and death gave her the power of a God. Perhaps that was what Champ meant. In order for her to be a goddess, she needed to take a life, Boreas's life.

Otus put her down and Jonathan put his arm around her. Aurora rested her head on his shoulder and felt safe in the arms of this man, her ideal. He would never attack a woman like Boreas had done. He was holding her now and she smiled sadly wishing that he saw her the way she perceived him—as beautiful.

He was stroking her hair and she wished that he would do that forever. He whispered, "I wish the Inspector had tortured me instead of him. He can't take the pain like I could. He's trouble, like my father said. He doesn't think about anyone else but himself."

Aurora shook her head. "But that's not true. Since this journey began, Boreas has sacrificed so much for us....for me. He saved my life, I can't believe I almost contemplated taking his."

Jonathan continued stroking her hair, "You did what you had to do to protect Babs."

As much as she didn't want to break away from Jonathan's embrace, Aurora realized she had to go find Babs and make sure she was okay. She searched the woods but really felt like she needed to run away from this madness.

She wanted to pretend that her parents were safe and just go back to Jonathan holding her, stroking her hair, being there with her. It was everything she had always wanted. But when he opened his mouth, he was so confident, too confident. He was always berating Boreas as if to validate that he was better than his younger brother. He didn't have to prove that to Aurora. As far as Aurora was concerned, any feelings she had for Boreas were long forgotten. She could never care for that monster she saw in the field. *But why then could she not forget that he was also the Boreas who had given her a rainbow?*

She found Babs sitting beside a waterfall, her hair hanging loose over her shoulders, her face opaque and pale. Her feet were wafting in the stream at the base of the waterfall. Aurora sat beside her and put her arm around her. The running water was comforting as the silence grew between them, with Aurora waiting for Babs to speak first.

"I thought I loved him." Babs said softly, the rushing water making it difficult to hear her words, "But he has changed. Ever since he escaped from the Inspector, he's not the same person I fell in love with."

Aurora watched as Babs sunk her head into her hands, her hair flowing over her pale and freckled face, massaging her bruised wrist where he had grabbed her.

"He's not the Boreas I know," Aurora admitted, finally.

Babs dried her tears and then said, "I saw Fawn. She won't let us find Plymouth Incarnate. Not yet. She said that it's not safe for them to make themselves known."

Aurora jumped back and felt her body tense up. "Fawn said that? Doesn't she know that we need her?"

"Do you blame her?"

Aurora looked down into the water where she half expected to see Swanson's face again. Plymouth Incarnate was somewhere inside the rocks. It was for her to know, not the others. She would be coming back to this spot, but as she feared, she was on her own.

"Did Fawn tell you anything else?"

Babs looked up at her, her eyes puffy and fearful, "She said that we are in danger."

Aurora laughed, like Babs was reciting a line from a horror movie. "Tell me something I don't know."

"I don't trust either of them, Jonathan or Boreas. I have a bad feeling that something is waiting for us in Candlewick. We can't go there."

Aurora closed her eyes, wishing for a sign, anything. "I have to go. If Boreas is telling the truth and my parents are in danger, I have to try to save them."

Babs took her hand and said the words Aurora feared, "And what if Boreas is lying?"

Aurora didn't say anything. She stared into the water, watching it drift over the rocks and boulders in its path. It appeared so calm and peaceful, but it was disintegrating the rocks, eroding them piece by piece, having more power than the sturdiest and strongest rocks in the river.

Babs stood up and said decisively, "I believe that you are the Goddess of Dawn. I know that we may not see eye to eye on a lot of things, but Eileen trusted you and Eileen was a better judge of character than I ever was."

Aurora clasped at the cross that hung over her heart, the gift Eileen had given her as she lay dying in Plymouth Tartarus, a victim of the Common Good. They had once again abused their power by not permitting people to freely believe what they wished. She held this cross, this piece of gold around her neck, but what it symbolized was something larger than the two of them could ever understand. It was something worth fighting for, somehow…

"Thanks, Babs," she said hugging her former nemesis. "In case something goes wrong, there's something I need you to do for me."

Babs and Aurora headed back to camp, their arms filled with dried leaves and sticks to feed the dying fire. When they arrived they found Mrs. Xiomy busy mixing together some herbs she found in the wilderness to help treat the Professor, who was becoming more forgetful with each passing moment. Otus and Jonathan returned with five striped bass fish and Aurora got to work cleaning, gutting and slicing them into filets before cooking them over the fire. Boreas skulked in shortly after, just as an ominous breeze pierced through Aurora's skin. They all sat around the campfire in complete silence while the fish cooked over the flickering flames.

Aurora stood up, the fire blazing and illuminating shadows on the ground. She served fish to each person, not sure who to trust or who would follow her on this foolish mission. She threw the fish on Boreas's lap. He did not make eye contact with her and she preferred it that way. She took a bite of the striped bass and let the fresh flavor fill her mouth. She swallowed and addressed the group.

"I can't ask any of you to come with me – you have done so much already – but I have to go to Candlewick. I have to try to save my parents, even if it might be a fool's mission. Fawn is not far and I am sure that she and the others will make themselves known in due time. The Professor is not well and he needs to stay here. Hopefully they have something that they can treat him with. Babs, can I ask you to stay here with him?"

Babs nodded and Aurora felt herself getting stronger with each minute that passed.

Mrs. Xiomy said, "I want to go back to Candlewick. I have to see if my dog Newton is alright. He must be terrified since I've been gone for so long. He's a brave dog, though. He is a survivor, that one."

Jonathan shook his head, "If we go back, we cannot go to our homes. They will be expecting that and will be sure to have guards stationed there."

"Well then, give my regards to your parents," Mrs. Xiomy said, scarfing down another bite of fish, "I feel this is a suicide mission. They would never let you just walk into Candlewick Prison and rescue your parents, you must know that."

"You know the dungeon," Aurora said, slowly. "Can you at least draw out a map for us?"

Mrs. Xiomy stuffed another piece of fish in her mouth and said, "I don't think you understand, Aurora, that it's an impossible mission."

Boreas stood up, his long hair flailing in the wind as his body cast an eerie shadow on the trees behind him. "It should just be me, Otus and Aurora. You cowards stay here with my two-faced brother."

Jonathan sprang at him like a tiger, but Boreas was quick, managing to get away in the nick of time, causing Jonathan to fall to the ground. Boreas laughed at his brother in the dirt, calling out, "Look who's the loser now. You're not so tough. We're not at the Spring Formal now. You can't beat me up in front of the entire school anymore."

"You were the one making an ass of yourself with that damn microphone, singing that song and embarrassing me!"

Boreas twisted his face into a vicious smile and then spit out, "So sorry that I was trying to distract everyone from your heinous girlfriend, Hattie Pearlton."

"You leave Hattie out of this. She never did anything to you or anyone."

Boreas folded his arms and nodded his head toward Aurora. He caught Aurora's eye and she felt the fish slide from between her fingers. She tried to hide, mortified.

He snorted and said, "Why don't we ask Aurora?"

The Spring Formal replayed in her mind as all eyes stared at her. The same sick feeling overtook her as she remembered that night.

Boreas walked over to her and put his arm around her shoulder. "Tell him, Aurora. Tell him what a princess his Hattie is."

Instinctively, Aurora unraveled herself from Boreas's arm. She turned to Jonathan and said sheepishly, "I don't know what he's talking about. He's just mad and taking it out on everyone."

Jonathan nodded, "He just wishes he was me, he always has and always will."

Boreas jumped to his feet and laughed raucously.

"Aurora, there's your knight in shining armor. Take a good look. But no, don't look at me. Why would you? I'm just the boy with the microphone who took a punch for you at the dance. But I forgot that you prefer punch being thrown in your face, especially from one Hattie Pearlton."

Aurora gasped in horror as Jonathan turned toward her, his face illuminated by the flames dancing on the crackling logs. Otus stood up and grabbed Boreas before he had an opportunity to escape.

"You apologize! Apologize to Aurora or I swear I will fling you across these woods so fast you won't know what hit you."

"Shut up, Otus! Whose side are you on anyway? Last I heard I was the God of the North Wind. So put me down or I swear that I'll destroy your mission before you can even say the words '*Common Good*'."

Otus turned beet red and steam started to come out of his nostrils like a bull. Otus lifted Boreas up onto the highest branch in the forest and left him up there. Boreas screamed down, "This is just fine with me! I prefer being away from the likes of you!"

Jonathan snapped his fingers as he remembered, "I forgot that Hattie threw that punch on you." He shook his head with a smile grazing his lips. "I mean, I know she likes to play around with you and all. But wow, I can't believe I forgot about that. Every time I think of that night I just think of beating up Boreas."

Aurora swallowed hard and said, "Yeah, well Boreas didn't deserve that beating, Jonathan."

She left Jonathan to his memories and asked Otus to lift her up to the tallest limb beside Boreas. Otus reluctantly agreed. Boreas was clutching to the limb with his head down as if he were sleeping, but she knew he would never dare to fall asleep up here. She looked up and felt so close to the sky. She felt like she could reach up and grab a star to give to the boy before her to try to wake him up from the trance he was in.

"Boreas," she said, her voice carrying over the rustling of the leaves and the bellow of the wind.

"Like I told Otus, I prefer to be away from all of you."

"Well, I won't bother you for long. I just wanted to say thank you."

His face scrunched up in disgust, but he didn't respond. It looked as if he was fighting something in himself. She put her hand on his shoulder, but he grabbed her wrist and twisted it hard. Pain escalated up her arm and a surprised shriek escaped her lips.

"I didn't do it to warrant your thanks. So just forget it."

"Boreas, you're hurting me."

He continued to twist her wrist to a point that she thought he might break it. She wrestled with him, putting as much of her weight against him as she could, but he wouldn't release his hold. He leaned over her, his eyes like hollow, black pin points staring down at her. She froze in shock. His once captivating eyes were now void of all the emotion and passion she used to see when she locked eyes with him.

"What did the Inspector do to you?"

At the mention of the Inspector, Boreas released his hold and his hand went to his mouth. He clenched his nails between his teeth. The void in his eyes cleared like clouds floating past the moon. A lone cricket chirped in her ear as Boreas was lost in his thoughts, clenching his eyes shut as if he was fighting a battle within himself. She stared down at the group loitering beneath them, at the Professor wildly ranting and drawing circles with his walking stick, the circles seemingly symbolizing their mission to the Arctic; to the Northern Lights. The lights felt so far away and she closed her eyes, worried that they would never see them. The next day she was going to embark back to where they had started this journey, back home to Candlewick, and she didn't know what would happen once they crossed over the border of her hometown.

She pictured Candlewick in her mind. She could see her house on Wishbone Avenue so vividly. She could see the ruby-red house across the street where she had found Otus. She could see Mrs. Xiomy's ostentatious, purple Victorian house at the end of the cul-de-sac, overrun with botanical plants and flowers, and hear the barking of her chow, Newton, whose slobbering tongue would run all over their faces.

They had been so young then, so naïve and unsure of the world. When did they grow up? When did she grow up? Her mother always said it would happen before she knew it. Now she knew it and wished that she could go back in time; things were simpler then. The worst thing she had to deal with back then was Hattie Pearlton. How trivial that all seemed now, when she thought about the obstacles she would face to try to save her parents. What would the Inspector do to her if she was caught? Mrs. Xiomy kept saying that Boreas was lucky to be alive. Aurora wasn't as sure of that as she looked over at Boreas, thought of his hollow eyes and how he had attacked Babs. Otus had said that there was good and evil in everyone and that we were all in constant battle with ourselves. But as she remembered Boreas's dead eyes, she wondered if evil did exist. If it did, did it now reside within Boreas Stockington?

After much coaxing and coercing, Aurora managed to get Otus to carry Boreas down from the tree limb with her. Otus told Boreas the story of his brother Ephialtes— The Giant Warrior. Ephialtes thought he could change the world by fighting everyone, including his brother with his fist and his sword. But one giant fighting against the world just made him a giant fool and he ended up getting stuck under a rock which no one could ever move. Though he banged on the rock, causing earthquakes and tremors with his fists, the rock remained stationary and without friends there was no one to help him in his hour of need. He was to be trapped there with his vengeful and violent thoughts throughout eternity.

"So you're saying that I should trap Jonathan under a rock?" Boreas replied once the tale was done.

At that, Otus picked him up and flung him into the river so that he was drenched from head to toe. Babs gave Otus a high-five and called out, "Thank you! He was in desperate need of a bath. He was stinking up the whole camp."

Boreas rang out his shirt, dripped back toward the camp and skulked off to a corner. He stripped down to his boxers and dug into his bag for a change of clothes, throwing on a navy-blue hoodie and jeans.

"Stupid giant," he muttered under his breath. He quickly searched his bag where there was a secret zipper compartment that housed a vile of sleeping serum, still in-tact. It was housed in a small plastic bottle and he hid it back in his bag, zipping it up non-chalantly. There was just enough serum to make the stupid giant sleep for about 10 minutes. It would be enough time for the Inspector to close in and capture him. Boreas smiled secretly with the knowledge that his plan was working out perfectly. Of course he knew that Aurora would drop everything to try to rescue her parents. Against all reason and logic, she was letting him entice her to go back to Candlewick. She may suspect that he had changed but she didn't believe that he would stoop so low as to set them up.

Well, they underestimate me for the last time, he thought, knowing he would have the last laugh. He threw his backpack over his shoulder and headed toward the others. He spotted Jonathan with his bag flung over his shoulders, like he was coming with them and immediately hatred filled his veins.

"Who invited you?" Boreas cried out.

"Well, I didn't want you to have all the glory of this rescue mission." Jonathan smiled the condescending smile that reminded Boreas too much of his father. It was a feature that he didn't share with the rest of his family. "Besides, you should probably stay. It doesn't seem right that the three of you should all be heading into the Inspector's clutches, since you're the ones needed to fulfill the prophecy."

The Professor blurted out, "It's a trap, you imbeciles!"

Mrs. Xiomy gave him a soothing head massage, "Let's all remember what happened the last time you three split up, we ended up in jail."

Aurora and Babs were off to the side talking and Boreas watched them out of the corner of his eye. Babs still hadn't forgiven him for that little episode earlier but he didn't care. Soon enough they would all be under arrest for conspiring against the Common Good. Only Boreas would be spared. The Inspector said he would be spared.

Boreas watched in dismay as Babs sauntered over to Jonathan with a bag of berries in hand.

"For you to think of me while you're on the road," she said sweetly, giving him a kiss on the cheek. She then handed him a bag filled with berries, while watching Boreas out of the corner of her eye. Jonathan put his hand on his cheek, confused, and was about to thank her but she was already walking away, her hips moving from side to side seductively. Boreas felt a pang of longing but shook it off. He had more important things to occupy his thoughts than Babs' curves.

Otus called out, "Climb aboard. We have a rescue mission to get to!"

Aurora gave Mrs. Xiomy a huge hug and at her urging, promised that they would be careful. The Professor pointed at the circles on the ground that he had drawn and called out, "Your powers, Aurora, don't forget your powers!"

Boreas watched Aurora's crestfallen face as she nodded and kissed the Professor on the forehead. "You take care of yourself and if we can smuggle you some medicine, we will."

Boreas bent down and found the gun in Babs's bag and snuck it quickly under his jacket as the others were saying their pathetic goodbyes. He zipped up his jacket, the gun not noticeable under the extra padding. It was an added precaution since he had to deal with Jonathan now as well. A bullet could silence bravery very easily.

"Come on," he called out in a singsong voice, climbing up the rope and into the pocket of Otus' overalls. "Time is a wasting."

Jonathan and Aurora nodded and followed suit. Boreas hoped that Babs wouldn't notice the missing gun until they were out of ear shot. For the first time, he was thankful none of them had a cell phone; modern technology would have been such an inconvenience to his plans.

Boreas turned to Aurora, "So what were you chatting about with Babs?"

Aurora continued waving to Babs, Mrs. Xiomy and the Professor as Otus took off with a running start and a giant leap into the air to begin their journey to Candlewick.

"Just girl talk, it's not meant for Stockington ears."

Jonathan started popping berries into his mouth. "Berries anyone?"

Boreas slumped into a corner of the pocket and thought to himself, *I hope he chokes on them.*

Chapter 19

Candlewick

Otus ran throughout the Sacred Hour and they reached Candlewick right when the Awakened Hour was approaching. They were on Main Street but the stores were still closed, their window panes shut like the eyes of the sleeping tenants. A slight crack formed in the street where Otus had landed. Aurora expected the Inspector and his officers to surround them from every angle, but so far they seemed to be alone. Nearby was a gigantic hole in the cement where an old warehouse once stood. It had been blown up, apparently. It was one strike against them already as that warehouse was going to be their hideaway until they could break into Candlewick Prison.

"What do we do now?" Jonathan whispered as they stood gaping at the devastation. The sun was beginning its ascent as Aurora tried to think of another place that they could hide out until darkness approached. The warehouse and a cave were the only places she knew in Candlewick that were large enough and likely abandoned so they could hide Otus and not attract attention. However, the cave they saw was surrounded by Common Good soldiers. As she was racking her brain for an idea, she saw her face plastered to the window of a bagel store. It said, "Wanted, Aurora Alvarez, Fugitive of the Common Good. Reward."

There was another one and then another one on the store beside it. There was not one of Boreas, however.

"Guess I'm not as photogenic as you are," Boreas nudged her.

Aurora traced the outline of her picture through the shop window and shook her head in disbelief. They had been wandering away from society for so long that she had forgotten that she was a fugitive in her own town. Even this place she called home was just as foreign as the other places she had travelled. She tore the wanted poster down and crumpled it in her fist. "I have to think of everything, don't I? We'll have to go to the ruby-red house."

Boreas slapped her on the back forcefully, "Brilliant, Aurora!"

Aurora rubbed her back where he had slapped her but she didn't have time to pout as they immediately took off toward the ruby-red house. As the sun grew larger in the sky, they turned the corner and landed on Wishbone Avenue. The street was unrecognizable to her. Where she had imagined trees in full bloom she was met with autumn's destructive fingertips at work. The trees were barren except for a few straggling leaves that hung limp and withered on the branches. Dead bulbs and withered flower petals were buried beneath the crinkled and brown leaves. It felt like they were marching in a funeral procession with death surrounding their every step.

She gasped as they reached #17, her house. The number and the mailbox were each hanging lopsided, creaking back and forth in the wind. The white paneling was now charred and hanging loosely from the foundation. The roof was caved in at the center and she saw remnants of her parent's collections burned on the front lawn. She bent down and picked up a nearly dismembered beanie baby, the USA special edition, and a Lou Gehrig baseball card that fell apart as she tried to lift it from underneath broken Christmas records. She knelt down, staring in disbelief at the remnants of her childhood home, her past. At the window that had been her room, the curtains were drawn as if she was at home getting ready for school that morning and then running down the emerald carpeted staircase to greet her father as he read through his history magazines. She looked through the pile, searching desperately for any sign of the magazines that were so precious to her father, but they were all gone. It was as if her heart had been burned to embers with all of those memories. She thought she would cry as Otus picked her up and cradled her in his palm, but no tears fell from her eyes. She cherished those memories much more now.

"They can destroy this, but they haven't found a way to erase my memory", she firmly said through clenched teeth, "As long as I have that, they cannot take my parents away from me."

Otus watched as Aurora stood up on his outstretched palm, looking out at the house that was a symbol for her fight against the Common Good. She clutched onto the beanie baby, her mother's favorite. Determined, she put it into her backpack; red and blue stars were barely visible on its stomach since the white fur was charred black and nearly brittle to her touch. It was a piece of her mother she would carry with her as they embarked on their mission to save her.

Just then a front door screeched open and they whirled around as Aurora's neighbor, Old Mr. Harold, walked out of his house, following his morning routine. He stretched upwards and hacked up a lung. Bounding out the front door was Newton, Mrs. Xiomy's chow dog. He started sniffing and barking in delight in their direction. Otus was still struggling to open the sewer grate that led to the secret passageway into the ruby-red house as Newton continued barking raucously at them, his tail wagging in glee. Old Mr. Harold was desperately trying to quiet down Newton, oblivious to the giant on Wishbone Avenue.

Hurry, Aurora thought, fearful Newton would give them away. Just then she remembered that their hand prints needed to be on the grate simultaneously for it to open. She grabbed Boreas's hand and placed both his and her own over their inscribed handprint on the sewer grate. Otus put his enormous hand over his own handprint and the sewer grate mysteriously turned and revealed the dark opening below. Otus scooped them up and jumped down the narrow hole, magically fitting through the narrow opening, right when Mr. Harold turned in their direction. Aurora breathed a sigh of relief that he hadn't seen them. She was also glad she would be able to report back to Mrs. Xiomy that Newton was in safe hands.

The ruby-red house was eerily quiet as they reached the bottom of the narrow corridor. Otus turned on a light which revealed the giant basement that Aurora and Boreas had stumbled upon by accident on the Independence Day of the Last Straw. The large painting of Old Mrs. Taboo still stood on the wall, her sinister smile suggesting she knew something that they didn't. The huge bed was still there and the bowls where Otus had made the rat stew were still sprawled on the floor, unwashed. The scent of mildew and rotten rodent remnants was overpowering.

"Ugh, we are not going to be able to stay down here for long," Boreas said as he pinched his nose shut.

Otus stared at him and shrugged, "Smells fine to me, but then again, I used to live down here."

Jonathan stared at the gigantic room in awe. "I have never seen anything like this. Hattie would never believe it. We used to make out behind the bushes and at times thought we heard sounds, but she always thought that it was just me trying to scare her."

Aurora felt her heart sink at the sound of Hattie's name. Even after everything she had been through, Aurora still felt sick to her stomach thinking about her old bully. Aurora tugged on her hair nervously, knowing Hattie was close by, and knowing that Jonathan knew it too.

Otus plopped them down onto the massive mattress and Aurora felt her body bobbing with the old mattress springs. Aurora pulled out the map of Candlewick Prison that Mrs. Xiomy had sketched for her prior to leaving Plymouth Incarnate.

"We need to figure out our strategy," she said, spreading out the map on her lap. "First we need to make sure that they are in the Candlewick Prison. Second, if they are there then we will need to infiltrate the prison somehow."

Jonathan snapped his fingers excitedly, aggravating Boreas since snapping was another thing he couldn't do that his brother could.

"Hattie's father works in the prison. He might be able to help us find out if your parents have been moved."

Aurora grimaced at the mention of Hattie's name and Otus caught her eye.

"Is that alright with you, Aurora?"

"Wh-Why would I have a problem?" she stammered. "I mean, if Hattie's father could help us that would be great, but I would prefer if we didn't get her involved... Too much danger, you know..."

Boreas slid down off the mattress and headed toward the kitchen. "Though it stinks in here, I am still desperate for a drink of water, anyone else thirsty?"

Otus nodded excitedly like it was the best idea he had ever heard. He bounded off to follow Boreas, probably also happy to see his old kitchen again.

Aurora was alone with Jonathan when she said, "How are we going to contact Hattie's dad?"

Jonathan flexed his muscles and flashed a smug grin, "Hattie would do anything for me."

Aurora nearly gagged and had the thought that she would give herself up to the Common Good before she had to face Hattie Pearlton. But she had to suck it up, especially since Jonathan was right. Hattie could be their only hope to find out where her parents were for sure. She swallowed her pride, whatever was left of it, and gave Jonathan the go ahead. Jonathan's face brightened and he jumped to his feet.

"Otus, I need a lift!"

Otus came bounding back into the room, and Aurora had to hold onto the mattress for dear life to avoid tumbling to the floor. Otus chugged his water and threw the cup against the floor where it clanged repeatedly like bell chimes.

Otus lifted up Jonathan who called down with a sly wink, "If I'm not back in 15 minutes, then I am probably still busy negotiating."

Otus took his cue and climbed back up through the secret passageway. Aurora tried to clear her mind, but it kept going back to Jonathan's negotiation methods. She screamed internally; mad at the twist of fate that made them have to involve Hattie Pearlton in their scheme. It was as if the world was conspiring against her, leading her back to Candlewick and making her witness Jonathan's love for Hattie. Not to mention forcing her to deal with Boreas who still was an unpredictable force. She buried her face in the mattress, wanting to suffocate herself. She didn't know which Stockington brother irritated her more, but it was a close contest.

Aurora closed her eyes until she heard the sound of footsteps below her and the drip - drip of liquid onto the ground. Reluctantly, she peered down over the edge of the mattress to behold Boreas walking beneath her. He was swaying back and forth under the weight of a gigantic goblet filled with water. It was a sight for sore eyes, but he was pouring more water on himself then he was drinking. She thought it would be easier if he just dove into the goblet to drink. He put down the goblet and attempted to reach the rim in order to pull himself up. She slid down the bedpost, landed on the ground and gave him a boost. After the third try, he managed to grab onto the rim of the goblet and pulled himself up. He leaned over and slurped in some of the water, nearly falling headfirst into the goblet swimming pool. He jumped down from the top of the goblet and wiped his mouth with the back of his hand.

"So my perfect brother once again saves the day. Why am I not surprised?"

He took a pair of scissors out of his backpack and began to cut at his hair that had grown to the length of his shoulders. He was butchering his hair but he wouldn't accept Aurora's help. He insisted that he didn't trust her. She laughed at his ridiculous efforts to cut his own hair. He looked like an idiot. She wished Babs could see him now, she would be happy that he was no longer her boyfriend. When he had finished, he looked like a porcupine with uneven strands sticking out in every direction.

She held her hand out to him and said, "Are you finished being a stubborn jerk?"

He looked at himself in one of the puddles on the floor and winced, handing her the scissors reluctantly. She trimmed around his uneven strands, pulling his hair extra tight so that he yelped each time. She smiled and continued to trim his black strands, smoothing them out with her fingertips.

"It's so strange being back here," she said, breaking the silence.

Boreas clenched his hands so tightly that they turned a shade of mauve. "I know."

The scissors snip - snipped and she felt like she was trimming the hedges with her father. She asked Boreas to turn and face her. When he did, she tried to spike up his hair over his forehead like he used to do. He didn't look like his brother now. He looked like the Boreas she remembered, the one who danced with her back in Plymouth Tartarus at the gala. He was the Boreas that felt the world spinning out of control with her but kept in perfect rhythm with her during that one dance. She snipped one small uneven strand above his eyebrow and smiled at him.

"Now you look like your old self." She put the scissors down, the metal blades clanging against the floor as she leaned back against the bedpost, facing him.

He blew a loose strand out of his eye and the coldness and hatred resumed its place. She was once again staring at a stranger. The Boreas she had known did not exist any longer. He had been destroyed, like her house on Wishbone Avenue. The foundation was the same, but it had been altered by the Common Good.

Otus returned carrying Jonathan who was pale and bleary-eyed. Aurora and Boreas were shocked at the transformation from the heroic confident man who had been there 15 minutes earlier to this.

"Jonathan, what happened?" Aurora cried out.

Jonathan's mouth opened and yet nothing came out. Finally he said, "Hattie's father is dead."

Disbelief settled in as Aurora listened to the words. Jonathan had raced over to Hattie's house and had snuck in through the bedroom window, like he had done so many times before only to catch her crying in the arms of Tony Hyacinth, the senior linebacker on the football team. Hattie had yelled at Jonathan that they were over, that Jonathan had up and vanished months earlier without sending a word or even commenting on her Facebook page. When Mr. Alvarez was arrested, Hattie's father had stood against it. The Inspector had

Mr. Pearlton arrested, tried and convicted. He had been sentenced to death two days earlier.

"I wasn't there for her," Jonathan said, anguished. "She was crying in Tony's arms because I wasn't there for her!"

Jonathan kicked the goblet causing the water to splash out and make a large puddle on the floor that seeped into the cracks in the concrete. "I can't believe they killed him!"

"We have to find a way to save Aurora's parents before they suffer the same fate," Otus said, grabbing a long black trench coat off of a hook.

Jonathan nodded solemnly, the room swaying around him as the reality of their situation settled in. "Well, she did make one thing very clear. Aurora's parents are in Candlewick Prison. Hattie said that tomorrow morning there would be justice, that Aurora's parents would be killed just as her father was, at the Awakened Hour."

Aurora stood up with rage boiling within her. She couldn't believe it, but she felt sorry for Hattie. Despite the bullying, she didn't want anyone to have to suffer. Here she was, in the same boat as her bully, but she hoped and prayed that her parents would be spared. She remembered what Mrs. Xiomy had said. She had risked everything to save her husband's life and yet they had killed him anyway. She had told Aurora that she would have to make the same choice, her parent's lives or her own.

The clock ticked away as time was fleeing away from them. She didn't listen as Jonathan and Otus were trying to map out a strategy. She realized that there was no way they would make it in time. Even with weeks of planning, there was no possible chance that they could rescue her parents. If she had her powers maybe she could do something to save them, but she didn't have them. Perhaps Champ was just as confused as everyone else and was just trying to make sense out of something that was never meant to be believed in. Babs said she believed that Aurora was the Goddess of Dawn. Aurora felt just as she always felt, like nothing special. There was no goddess inside of her.

Otus said excitedly, "A surprise attack, right before dawn. That's the only option. It's the only way."

"It's hopeless." She said low at first and then louder. "It's hopeless. Don't you see? The Inspector would be anticipating an attack. He must know that Boreas has told me that my parents will be killed. He will have every guard ready to bring us down. And now Hattie and that boy she was with know we are here. Can they be trusted? They must have already told people that they saw Jonathan. It's just a matter of time before the Common Good Army finds us. We need to get out of here or else we'll be caught."

"But your parents…" Jonathan stammered, map still in hand.

"My parents would want me to be safe" she yelled as tears flowed from her eyes. "They'd want me to stay alive."

Silence filled the room and she couldn't look at them, gazing at anything but their pitiful faces. She settled on the portrait of Mrs. Taboo, the elderly woman's portrait appearing to shake her head in judgment at Aurora's lack of courage. Boreas came up beside her and took her hand in his. She threw her arms around his neck and sobbed into his shoulder. His jacket muffled some of her sobs as he gently rubbed her shoulders.

"It's okay, Aurora." He said, with a hint of compassion in his voice. "We'll think of something."

She dried her tears and took a deep breath, while Boreas stared at her and held her tightly in his arms. She felt safe in his arms, felt like no harm would come to her or her family while he was there. They were in this together, after all. They needed each other to survive.

Jonathan stood up and said, "Hattie did give me something, but it sounds insane to me. She gave me the code to open the prison cells."

Aurora turned to him. "The code to open their cell?"

Jonathan shook his head. "No, it's to open all the cells. It's the master code to control the electricity that locks the cells. I know, insane, right?"

"Wait! This could work!" Aurora cried out. "If we can get in then we can use the code to cause mass chaos and confusion. Then we can free my parents!"

"But how do we get in?" Jonathan chided.

As if a light bulb went off in his head, Boreas exclaimed, "We can get in through the secret tunnel by the graveyard. The same one that Mrs. Xiomy and I used to escape the last time we were in the prison."

"That's crazy, there are guards stationed all around the prison."

"We'll distract them," Otus said suddenly. "We can set off a distraction outside the prison and lure the guards from their posts."

"What kind of distraction?" Jonathan asked.

Aurora smiled, the Independence Day of the Last Straw coming back to her.

"Jonathan do you still have any extra fireworks from the barbeque?"

Jonathan nodded and his face lit up. "Yes, we have a few of the big ones that we didn't have time to light."

"Then we'll give the Inspector a fireworks display he will never forget."

Chapter 20

Dawn Approaching

Night engulfed Candlewick and Aurora and Jonathan dashed in the shadows to the Candlewick graveyard. Jonathan knelt down, a black wool hat covering his head and a black shirt hugging his upper torso. He looked down at the phone they had stolen that he had used to tap into the prison's security system via satellite connection. He could make out the entire interior of the prison and detect soldiers within a 5 mile radius.

Aurora called into her radio, "Boreas, can you hear us?"

"Ten-Four." Boreas's voice crackled back

"We are on the south side. There are twelve guards covering the main door. Are you ready for the distraction?"

"We are in position, setting off the fireworks now!"

Aurora turned toward Jonathan who nodded, knowing the danger of the mission they were embarking on. She was glad she still had four of the stolen detractor bracelets in her schoolbag from when they had been in Machu Picchu. At least those bracelets made them undetectable via satellite, for now.

A loud boom sounded, followed by more as fireworks went off around the prison, exploding into the air as if it was the Independence Day of the Last Straw all over again. Rockets and other fireworks shot upwards and an array of colors exploded across the sky. Aurora's attention, however, was focused on the radar showing the commotion amongst the guards as they all hurried to go after this threat to the city.

Ten of the twelve guards hurried out from behind the prison walls and split up into separate units to search the surrounding area for the source of the fireworks. Jonathan checked his phone and said, "Video surveillance de-activated and nice work, Boreas and Otus!"

"Be careful," Otus's voice resounded through the radio.

Jonathan and Aurora ran through the Candlewick graveyard, passing by the pink marble tombstone of David Xiomy.

Help us through this, Aurora thought as her feet skidded over the damp grass. They raced into the Candlewick brook, splashing through the water into the dark tunnel ahead.

Jonathan took out his flashlight to illuminate the narrow tunnel, hearing the sound of cars rushing above them. Adrenaline was pumping through both of their veins as they continued racing to the end toward the secret door, which led into the prison interrogation room. Jonathan put his ear against the door and shook his head at Aurora; there was no sound from within. Aurora searched madly for the button that Boreas said would open the door. Soon enough she spotted it underneath thick ivy that snaked up the wall. As the door slid open, they faced each other knowing that there was no turning back now.

Aurora followed Jonathan cautiously into the prison interrogation room. He walked to the main door that was slightly ajar. He looked left and right and spotted a guard just around the corner from them. He took out a stun gun that they had found next to the fireworks in the Stockington garage. Jonathan aimed and shot the guard. He dropped to the ground, jerking with convulsions. Jonathan grabbed Aurora's hand and they ran down the dimly lit corridor. The fluorescent lights beamed down on them and for Aurora they brought back horrific memories of being held captive within the depths of Candlewick Prison all those months before.

"The box that controls the electricity should be on the east wing," Jonathan whispered with his face close against Aurora's as they both stared intently at the radar screen. "It looks like there are still about five guards in front of us. Boreas, what is going on out there?"

"They found the fireworks and are remobilizing. You don't have much time."

Jonathan shut off the radar screen and stuffed the phone back into his pocket. "Okay, once we turn off the electricity and free the prisoners, we'll need to get lost in the chaos and wait for Boreas and Otus to signal to us when we can escape back through the way we came."

"With my parents."

Jonathan nodded. "We'll find them, Aurora."

Aurora pushed any doubt from her mind in order to stay focused on the mission at hand. They were going to find her parents. They had to or die trying.

They looked down the long narrow hall and Jonathan signaled to Aurora that the coast was clear. They ran down the dark corridor, seeing faces of prisoners crammed inside the cells. Some were about to scream out, but Aurora put her finger up against her mouth to urge them to be quiet. Then she heard a voice that slithered down her spine.

"Hello there, Goddess of Dawn."

She whirled around to see the sickly, albino face of none other than Max Radar, the IDEAL. He glared at her with his red eyes through the bars and looked so frail and weak that she couldn't believe this was the same man who had tried to manipulate them to join his cause in Machu Picchu.

"Radar?" Aurora whispered. "What are you doing here?"

"The Inspector was tipped off about our hideout. Figured it was from either you or Boreas. Come to join the party?"

Jonathan tugged at Aurora's sleeve to indicate they had to keep moving. She nodded, but couldn't tear her eyes away from the man before her.

"I didn't turn you in. We're here to cause a commotion and rescue my parents."

Radar laughed, coughing up blood. "I believe you, Aurora Alvarez. But be warned. The First Lieutenant is down at the end of the corridor."

Aurora startled. The First Lieutenant was Mary Fray's brother, Jake. He had risked everything to save Aurora's life before, but he also had stood on the sidelines when both Mary and his mother were arrested. Was he on their side now? She couldn't risk it. She had to assume he still belonged to the Inspector.

"Thanks for the tip, Radar," Aurora said.

"Anything for a friend with a common enemy," he grinned mischievously.

Jonathan grabbed Aurora's arm and they cautiously made their way down to the East wing of the prison. They came upon a guard and Jonathan tackled him, knocking him to the ground and Aurora, fearful that he would scream out, grabbed the stun gun and aimed it at the man. She pulled the trigger and he started convulsing.

"Nice shot," Jonathan beamed at her. She blushed slightly but then snapped out of it, handing the gun back to Jonathan as they continued down the hall. Time was running out and they had to punch in that code.

They turned the last corner and came upon a room with voices echoing from within.

"I administered the serum to all ten of them and nothing happened. How do you explain that?"

"You must not have administered it correctly."

Aurora recognized the voices. They were the voices of Officer Woolchuck and Jake Fray, the First Lieutenant. She felt frozen as they eavesdropped on the conversation.

"You may fool the Inspector, but you are not fooling me. You were the last one with the serum, you must have switched it."

"How dare you? I am your superior!" Jake shouted.

"I know a liar when I see one and you have been acting weird these last few months, ever since you stood up for that reporter girl."

"Look, if you have a problem with me then take it up with the Inspector. We have to stay focused."

"The serum should have worked. We both saw what happened to that boy. We all know what it is capable of."

Aurora leaned back, nearly knocking against Jonathan, fearing that her breathing would give her away. As she looked up at him, Jonathan's eyes were glazed with fear but he nodded to her that they had to keep moving. They slowly inched their way, hugging the wall. The door was open, if one of the Officers looked up, they would see them.

Jonathan inched his way past the door and managed to get past unobserved. He motioned her forward, but Aurora urged him to keep going. He had to get to the box, at least one of them had to. Just as Aurora was sliding past the open doorway, the eyes of the

First Lieutenant met hers. She froze, petrified, as he stood there, recognizing her. Officer Woolchuck was still ranting with his back to her. The First Lieutenant pointed his gun directly at Aurora. She stood there immobile, her eyes staring straight at the man who was about to kill her. She kept still with the gun still pointed at her and Officer Woolchuck still talking.

"First Lieutenant, are you listening to me?"

Officer Woolchuck turned around and spotted Aurora.

"What the hell is this?"

The electricity went out and they were in complete darkness.

A loud alarm sounded and bright red emergency lights flashed on. The First Lieutenant lifted his gun and hit Officer Woolchuck on the head, knocking him unconscious and he collapsed to the ground. The First Lieutenant rushed over to Aurora and yelled over the commotion of prisoners opening their cell doors all around them.

"Aurora, this is a trap. Your parents aren't here. It's Boreas; he's going to give up the giant. You have to stop him!"

"Boreas!" Aurora stood there completely mystified. Jonathan raced up to her and they both stared at the First Lieutenant.

"Go, I'll stall for you as long as I can. Go this way!"

He pointed down the long corridor, urging them to hurry.

Aurora didn't wait for him to change his mind as she grabbed Jonathan's hand. They ran as fast as they could now that the alarm was sounding. They hid in a doorway as Common Good soldiers ran past, some being tackled by prisoners who were fighting back. Some prisoners were able to overtake guards and get their guns. Gunshots were heard in the distance as the two teenagers ran for their lives. Aurora was thinking about the First Lieutenant, hoping that he wasn't leading them into a trap, but worried that he was telling the truth.

"Boreas, can you read me?" She cried into her radio. She waited anxiously for Boreas's voice to echo back, but there was only silence.

She grabbed the receiver and called again into it, "Boreas, do you read me? Answer me!" Crackling and static were all that answered her and fear overtook her.

Jonathan called out behind her, "Aurora, what's wrong?"

"Boreas has turned against us!"

"What are you talking about? He probably just can't respond right now."

She didn't wait for Jonathan as she reached the end of the corridor, leading to the outskirts of town. She ran down the hill in rapid pursuit, hoping she was not too late to save Otus. She felt her throat go dry as her legs moved swiftly over the grass. She cursed herself for falling into this trap. Boreas had set them up!

She quickly hid behind a tree as she heard approaching footsteps and Jonathan followed suit. A brigade of soldiers ran past, heading into the prison the same way they had just escaped. She breathed a sigh of relief that the soldiers had just missed them. Once the brigade had disappeared through the prison walls, Aurora and Jonathan ran until they reached the southern overpass where they proceeded with caution as the Sacred Hour was ticking away.

Aurora froze in mid-step as she beheld the body of Otus spread out on the ground, covering a 30-foot radius in an open meadow. Boreas stood over him, a gun pointed at Otus's right temple and cried out, "Stop right there or I will kill him!"

Jonathan nearly collided into Aurora's body as they both stared incredulously at the man who had betrayed them.

"Boreas, what are you doing?" Jonathan shouted. "The guards are going to find us; we have to get out of here right now!"

Boreas stood up, "That's what I was intending all along, brother. You never should have come, Jonathan. Now you are going to suffer the same fate as these traitors."

Aurora was seized with hatred as she stared at the man who had been her friend. He was eyeing his watch and she knew she had to keep him talking to distract him and get the gun away from him. "How do I know that Otus is not already dead?"

Boreas ushered her toward Otus with the revolver. "Come touch him, if you dare. Even if you do overtake me, you are both not strong enough to move him and the Inspector will be here in five minutes, right at the Awakened Hour."

Aurora cautiously walked past Boreas and put her hand onto Otus's chest. He was still breathing, though deeply unconscious. He was sleeping peacefully, unaware of the horrors that awaited him if he woke up in the hands of the Inspector. And that would be his fate, unless Aurora could think of some way to prevent that from happening.

"He's asleep," she called out to Jonathan who was frozen in place, biding his time and waiting for an opportunity to strike. Boreas was still holding the gun up against Otus's temple. Aurora measured the distance between her and the man who had betrayed them and decided that she could attack him. If he shot her, at least Jonathan would be there to finish the task.

"Quit contemplating how you are going to attack me," Boreas chided, ushering her away with the gun. "I know how your mind works, Aurora. I knew you would come to save your parents. You are so predictable. The Inspector and I planned the whole thing. We had to get Otus out of the picture. From there, you would be easy."

"You made him drink the sleep serum," Jonathan called out huskily. "The one the Inspector gave to Dad back in the cottage."

"I put it in his water when we were in the kitchen together back at the ruby-red house. By the time the serum took effect on his big oafish body, we were already in position. Now it's just a waiting game until the Inspector will seize him and you both."

"And you," Aurora called out angrily. "Don't think the Inspector is just going to let you walk away."

"He said I would be spared."

"Just like he told Mrs. Xiomy that he would spare her husband if she gave up the rebels. He doesn't keep his word, Boreas, you must know that."

He laughed arrogantly and kicked Otus in the side. The moon was starting its descent beyond the horizon and the sunlight was beginning to transform the dark night sky into the grayish tint that signaled the start of dawn.

"Boreas, listen to me!" Aurora said, trying to keep his eyes on her. "We are in this together, remember? The three of us... Otus is your friend."

"Our friend?" Boreas bellowed, turning the gun up at Aurora. "He has known all along that we can't win. This has been a suicide mission from the start with Otus putting our lives at stake, and for what? For this fairy tale. Where are your powers, Aurora? If you are so powerful, then stop me."

Aurora felt her body go cold. He was right, she didn't have her powers. She felt like a failure, looking at Otus, who desperately needed the Goddess of Dawn. Otus had been wrong; she was not the right Aurora.

"That's what I thought," Boreas sneered, continuing to wave the gun between her and Jonathan who she had noticed had come a few feet closer to them since Boreas had been talking with her. *Jonathan is going to tackle him*, she thought, eagerly. She had to continue to distract Boreas.

"I never told you about Champ!" She exclaimed. "He says I do have my powers. At Lake Champlain I was re-born in the depths of the lake. I have my powers, Boreas. It is you who doesn't have yours."

Boreas again looked at his watch and then back at Aurora, humoring her. "Oh, really? If you have these powers then why don't you use them?"

"Don't think I won't! You have betrayed us and the way for me to activate my powers is now possible."

"And why is that?"

"Because today I have a reason; I am going to have to kill you, Boreas."

He laughed so heartily that it made her stomach churn as the light was stretching further across the night sky. The Awakened Hour was nearly upon them and they had to act fast. She could see the lights of the prison helicopters and jet planes turning on in unison for the attack. The chaos ensuing within Candlewick Prison was not deterring Inspector Herald from achieving his end goal — capturing Otus. Aurora gulped realizing she was running out of time.

"Don't laugh, Boreas. Champ said that I would get my powers the day I had to kill the God of the North Wind. So, if I have to kill you to get my powers, then I will."

Boreas placed his finger on the trigger of the gun that was still pointed at her.

"What happens if I just kill you now? Then what happens to your powers and the prophecy?"

"If the prophecy is correct, you won't be able to kill me."

Boreas looked at her and there was once again a conflict within him as his expressions churned and his neck jerked as if he were fighting some unknown force buried deep inside of him.

"I will pull the trigger," he said, holding the gun out. The eyes of a monster stared directly into hers. He screamed that he could kill her, that he would kill her. His pointer finger shook as Aurora continued to stare death in the face, thinking that this was the end. The sun created an assortment of colors that reached toward her, holding their rays out to her. *Give me strength*, she thought as her eyes closed shut.

And then the gun went off.

Aurora opened her eyes wide. She was not hit, the bullet had missed her. She looked up at Jonathan tackling Boreas, each of them punching and screaming at the other. Aurora quickly checked to make sure the bullet didn't hit Otus, but he was safe and still breathing easily. The brothers rolled around the dirt, their faces bloodied as she searched for the gun. She found it nearly buried in the dirt kicked up in the fight and picked it up. She looked up to see Boreas on top of Jonathan with his hands around Jonathan's neck, strangling him to death. Jonathan croaked to her, "Shoot him!"

Aurora took the gun in her hands, remembering how it felt when she fired at Boreas the other day to scare him at Plymouth Incarnate. She never intended to kill him. She had to now. She yelled at Boreas to stop or she would shoot, but he continued to strangle his brother, not heading the warning. Aurora cringed as she pointed the gun at him but nothing happened. Her fingers couldn't do it, she just couldn't kill him.

Jonathan's face was turning blue as Boreas continued to struggle to end the life of his brother. She heard the helicopter propellers starting up in the distance, coming to kill them, to stop them from saving this world with what beauty there still was within it. There was beauty and love and that was something worth fighting for.

She dropped the gun. She felt the sunlight streaming into her veins, the same way it had while in Lake Champlain. She raised her hands instinctively and pointed them at Boreas.

As if a firecracker shot out of her fingertips, sunlight streamed out of them and directly into Boreas's heart. He was knocked off of Jonathan, but she continued to hit him with the rays of the sun. He stood there fighting the light until he was engulfed in it completely, his body illuminated, even his hazel eyes shone bright yellow. Power was taking over Aurora, controlling her as she aimed all her love and all that she felt into the heart of Boreas.

She suddenly collapsed, struggling to catch her breath as her body was on fire. Her fingertips still glowed, but the blaze was extinguished. Jonathan ran to her side and nervously reached for hand, afraid that he would burn by touching her. When he felt her skin and it was cool, he put his arm around her and helped her to her feet. "Aurora, are you alright?"

She nodded breathless as she saw Boreas lying face down before her, but she knew she hadn't killed him, that wasn't the power she had been blessed with. She hurried to his side and held his head in her arms. He opened his eyes weakly and stammered, "Aurora. I'm sorry."

The helicopters were closing in on them as she held Boreas against her heart. The sun was now fully arisen. The helicopters were surrounding them and she ran to Otus's side as the sound of the choppers were getting louder and louder.

She knelt down and mustered up some tears that streamed down her face and fell onto Otus's face like morning dew. Immediately Otus blinked and was awakened.

"What happened?"

She pointed to the helicopters and shouted, "We are being attacked!"

She grabbed Jonathan's hand and they were lifted up into the pocket of the overalls.

"Otus, help Boreas up, quickly!"

The helicopters started firing at them, ripping at the ground all around them. Aurora shone light from her fingertips into their windows and blinded the shooters so that they misfired.

Otus took off running across the meadow, the helicopters still firing as she heard a voice through the loudspeaker.

"You are surrounded! Stop or we will shoot you."

Aurora turned and there in a helicopter cockpit was the ghastly face of Inspector Herald.

"It's the Inspector," Aurora shouted to be heard over the cacophonous sound of the propellers.

Otus tried jumping but was blocked off by a jet that came through the clouds, seemingly out of nowhere. Aurora tried to blind the jet but it avoided her rays and was able to fire at them from an even closer distance. Otus was shot in the leg and fell to one knee with a gasp of pain. Aurora and Boreas looked up and saw another jet aiming right for them.

"Otus!" She cried out as the plane screamed toward them. Just when it was about to shoot at them, it made a quick U-turn and shot at the Inspector's helicopter instead. In amazement, Aurora turned to see that the plane was coming back for another attack. Over the loudspeaker she heard the high-pitched voice of none other than Mrs. Xiomy!

"Hello, Inspector! So we meet again!"

Aurora and Jonathan cheered wildly as Mrs. Xiomy and Babs attacked the Inspector. Another plane shot in with none other than Fawn Stockington manning the guns, her black hair trapped under a helmet and sunglasses.

She heard Fawn's voice yell through the loudspeaker, "Stay away from my sons!"

The Inspector continued fighting along with two other planes that had not been infiltrated by Fawn and the other members of Plymouth Incarnate. Otus found enough energy to jump up and grab one of the Inspector's planes by its tail and fling it so that it went flailing into the distance, spinning out of control. At that sight, the Inspector made a quick U-turn and headed back toward the prison where more of his air force was preparing to take-off.

"We have to leave," Boreas cried out to Otus. "He is getting more planes to attack us and track you."

Aurora heeded Boreas's warning. She signaled for Fawn and Mrs. Xiomy to retreat as Otus jumped up in agony. He was desperately trying to lose the two copters that were in hot pursuit of them.

Otus was leaping with every last ounce of strength he could muster, crying out in pain each time he landed on his wounded leg. Aurora and Jonathan held each other as Otus fought with everything he had left to bring his friends to the safe haven. Boreas buried his face in his hands, whimpering, "What have I done?" over and over again. He heard Otus' suffering and knew that it was all his fault.

Chapter 21

Peering into the Soul

Otus was able to lose the helicopters and just managed to make it to the safe haven without being seen. Otus had become very weak by the time they landed by the river. As soon as he hit the ground, Otus collapsed down to one knee, his leg in severe pain, having lost a lot of blood.

Aurora slid down and told the others to mobilize. "We have to get the doctor immediately," she cried out as she examined the wound. It was a direct hit. The bullet was trapped beneath the skin and she prayed it hadn't hit the bone. The doctor came running out from behind the rocks with his medical kit, followed by Babs, Fawn and Mrs. Xiomy who had beaten them back to the safe haven, having landed the plane in a distant clearing. They immediately ran to Aurora's side.

"You were incredible," Babs cried out. "I knew you could do it! I knew you were the Goddess of Dawn!"

"My parents? Are they safe?"

Babs bit her lip and her head turned toward Fawn who removed the helmet from her head, shaking her long black hair out so that it wafted over her worried face.

"They were never there, Aurora."

Aurora fell to the ground. The First Lieutenant had been right, Boreas had invented this entire lie to get her and Otus back to Candlewick.

"Where are they?"

"Your dad is in a prison out west. Your mom is still working for the Common Good government as an Ambassador."

Aurora couldn't believe it. "But Hattie Pearlton said my parents were there in the prison."

"Hattie lied to Jonathan, Aurora. She was in on the scheme. She had been told that her father would live if she cooperated. Unfortunately, the Inspector killed Mr. Pearlton already. There was no chance for us to save him. But Hattie did one noble thing by giving you and Jonathan the code. You helped free many prisoners, many of whom are making their way here to the safe haven."

Two cloaked guards had already seized Boreas and were chaining his legs and hands together. Horrified, Aurora turned to Fawn and cried out, "He was given the soul extractor serum by the Inspector! He was acting against his will!"

Fawn's eyes, the same eyes as Boreas, stared intently at Aurora. "If that's the case, then I don't know who he is now."

"But my powers... I believe they..."

"You believe they have brought out the better part of his soul?"

Aurora nodded, "I thought for me to get my powers, I needed to take a life. But to be the Goddess of Dawn you cannot take a life, you must save a life."

They both watched as Boreas was led away to Plymouth Incarnate to be interrogated. Fawn turned to Aurora and said softly, "The Professor will testify. The soul extractor serum doesn't force you to try to kill another person, especially not a friend or a brother. That's something Boreas already had within him."

Aurora shrugged Fawn's arm off of her. She ran to where the doctor was operating on Otus's leg. She felt like her world was crumbling apart. The Inspector knew that she had received her powers and that she had saved Boreas. And both her father and Mary Fray were in a prison out west, her fight was only just beginning.

Jonathan was sitting by the Hudson River, his ponytail blowing wildly in the wind. He was holding the black wool hat in his hands and he intently gazed out into the wilderness and the purple mountains. A hawk landed mere inches from his feet but he didn't even notice, or chose to ignore it as Aurora took a place beside him. She dangled her feet off the edge toward the water that was lapping lightly against the river bank.

"I just saw my mother," he said without turning to see who it was beside him. It was as if he already knew. "Boreas wasn't lying about something. She is alive."

Aurora sat looking into the world beyond as the hawk raised its wings and flapped majestically against the sky, toward the glistening sun – the sun that now lived within her veins.

"I am sorry you had to find out this way."

He nodded, unbraided his ponytail and let it hang loosely over his shoulder. He was breathing heavily and she watched the contours of his chest rising and falling in rhythm with his heartbeat.

She took a deep breath, "I wanted to tell you earlier that I had asked Babs to follow us. She convinced your mom, Mrs. Xiomy and some other members of Plymouth Incarnate to travel to Candlewick by submarine in order to provide back-up in case things took a turn for the worst. I had a feeling that Boreas was not to be trusted and

I couldn't take a chance. I needed to know we had back-up and couldn't risk telling either you or Boreas because I didn't know who to trust."

Jonathan faced her, took her hand in his, tracing the inner lines of her palm where sunlight had manifested through her skin. "I never would have thought that Boreas would try to kill me."

"He didn't know what he was doing."

"Are you sure?"

Aurora couldn't say. She felt his hand holding hers and instead of feeling uneasy, for the first time she felt comfortable being so near to him. It was so easy to talk to this man who for the longest time she had just admired and loved from afar. And now here he was, holding her hand and gazing into her eyes.

He relaxed his hold and then faced out toward the water again. "Hattie was in on it too, I heard. I should have known not to trust her. It's like everything I knew before doesn't exist anymore."

Aurora squeezed his hand in hers and felt strength surge within her – a strength that she never knew she had. She spoke the words before she had a chance to second guess herself or worry about the consequences.

"I know that some things still exist, Jonathan."

She raised her face and looked deep into his eyes. She wanted him to kiss her, to kiss her and hold her and love her the way she had always hoped he would. After everything she had been through, this is what she wanted – or at least what she thought she wanted. As his face leaned down toward hers she raised her lips to meet his.

"Aurora."

She was yanked back to reality by the sound of another's voice. She turned and Boreas stood behind her. He stood disheveled and broken with chains locked between his legs and the two cloaked men gripping his arms. She looked up into his eyes, the ones that she remembered glowing and passionate, like a window into his soul.

"I just wanted to tell you thank you for saving me." He glanced sadly at Jonathan and then back at Aurora. "I guess you got everything you ever wanted, huh, Aurora?"

Her mouth opened, but no words came as he was whisked away, chains rattling with each step. He didn't look back. She turned toward Jonathan who still had his arm wrapped around her. She leaned against him but felt cold all over, as if Boreas's eyes were still peering into her own.

✡ ✡ ✡

Jake was surrounded by chaos. People swarmed past him, freed from the confines of the prison. High priority prisoners had been freed, and he was understaffed to try to contain them. He heard gunshots behind him and he quickly moved out of the way to get out of the line of fire. Order had been restored, but at a huge price. He passed by many dead guards as well as many dead prisoners. About fifty had escaped, but they were able to contain the others. They had not anticipated Fawn Stockington and David Xiomy's widow, Rana Xiomy, impersonating guards to help the prisoners sneak through the back exit, or them stealing airplanes. The Inspector never saw that one coming.

It was then that he heard the Inspector's voice behind him.

"First Lieutenant!"

Jake whirled around and the Inspector grabbed him by the arm and dragged him into a small room where five prisoners were on their knees. He stiffened when he recognized one of them — his mother.

"What is this?" He cried out, feeling his mother's watery eyes focused on him. He then noticed a green stain on each of their arms.

"Each of them had the soul extractor serum administered to them and do you know what happened?"

Jake tried to stay calm. The Inspector didn't know that he had switched the serum with a dye. He couldn't give himself away.

"I have no idea."

"Look at them!" The Inspector grabbed him and forced him to stare into the face of a man that was trembling. He felt like he was going to be sick. The Inspector grabbed him by the hair and dragged him back to his feet. "There is no change in them, how do you explain this?"

"You must not have replicated it exactly like the batch you used on the Stockington boy."

"That's what they say, but I know it was exact. I know it and that leaves me with one conclusion."

Jake stared into the black eyes of the man above him who toyed with a gun.

"What are you suggesting, Inspector?"

"That there's one way to see where your loyalty lies."

He handed the gun to the First Lieutenant. Jake looked around and saw that the guards had encircled them. One was Officer Woolchuck, holding an ice pack to his head where Jake had hit him with the gun. He realized now that Officer Woolchuck had turned him in. He was on trial.

He heard his mom whisper, "Jake, don't."

What choice did he have? He took the gun in his grasp and felt like all eyes were on him.

"You should know where my loyalties lie," he said slowly, articulating his words so that each one was a dagger thrown at the Inspector. Jake kept eyeing the Inspector as if his glare could cause him to burst into flames.

"If you truly are one of us, then shoot her."

Jake's mouth went dry, knowing exactly who the Inspector was pointing to. He followed the length of the Inspector's arm until his eyes rested on his mother's. She looked pale but strong, her black hair disheveled over a serenely beautiful face. She didn't take her eyes off her son, just kept staring.

"This woman was found guilty of practicing the Jewish faith. I pronounce a sentence of death. The IDEAL has spoken, now let justice be served."

Jake felt his hand trembling, the first time that had happened since he had held a gun. His mind was drumming with thoughts, trying to think of a way out of this. If he didn't shoot his mother, then he certainly would be killed. The Inspector was watching him carefully. His mother whispered, "Jacob, it's okay, I forgive you."

"Mom, stop!" Jake cried out, her words, her forgiveness making this harder. He felt his hand level, relaxing his grip, the way he always did. Just pull the trigger. It was that easy. He had done it countless times before, but not like this. Not like this.

"Kill the traitor!" The Inspector growled, his words like a devil tempting him. "If you are not a traitor yourself, then kill her!"

Jake held the gun, with his finger on the trigger, but his mother was not closing her eyes. They were soft and soothing, looking directly into his, confusing him. Who had he become? Who had the Inspector forced him to become!

With one fluid motion he turned the gun on the Inspector with rage in his eyes.

"You're the traitor!"

Jake pulled the trigger but no bullet fired. Horrified, he pulled it again but it just clicked. The barrel was empty. The Inspector had given him an empty gun.

"No, you're the traitor, First Lieutenant!"

Before Jake could stop him, the Inspector lifted another gun out of his pocket and shot his mother directly between the eyes. Jake cried out, but it was too late. His mother fell backwards, her pupils rolled back behind her lids as the bullet pierced her forehead and blood oozed down her angelic face. Jake ran to her side, holding her in his arms. "No," he whispered.

Jake held onto his mother, her eyes shut now and her body rigid in his grasp. The Inspector towered over him, watching him like a hawk as Jake sat there like a wounded child with his mother in his arms.

"You switched the serum, where is it?"

Jake let go of his mother's lifeless body and spat out, "I destroyed it, every vial. I washed it all down the drain and filled the vials with green dye. You'll never be able to do what you did to Boreas ever again!"

The Inspector grabbed Jake by the collar, pulled him to his feet furious at the man who he had hoped would take his place when the time came. Now, he was a traitor, the one conspiring against him.

"How could you do this to me? After everything I did for you!"

"If you are going to kill me then just do it!" Jake spit out. "I did what I had to do and I wish that damn gun had a bullet in it so it would be your body on the ground and not hers!"

The Inspector grabbed him, pushed him against the wall and punched him hard in the stomach. "Death is too good for you, Jacob!"

Jake fell back against the wall as he fought for breath. It was the first time the Inspector had called him by his first name. The guards held their guns up, pointing them at the man who moments before had been their leader. He was now disgraced, he was no longer the First Lieutenant. Jake waited in silence, expecting the Inspector to sentence him. He was not sure what he was waiting for.

"Yes, death is what you now crave, isn't it?" The Inspector said slowly, dissecting Jake's mind. He reached down, ripped off Jake's First Lieutenant Badge and threw it at him. "You thought I'd let you get off easy by ending your life, but it's not going to be that easy. I won't let it be that easy."

Jake felt fear creep up his spine as he realized the collateral the Inspector still had over him.

"Your precious sister is still alive," The Inspector said slowly.

"You leave her out of this," Jake cried out, lunging forward but Officer Woolchuck grabbed him, tossed him to the ground and shackled his arms. He and his sister were at the mercy of this madman before him.

"I won't kill you, not yet. There's still one last thing I need from you. That retched girl Aurora trusts you. I could use that trust to my advantage."

Jake shook with rage, "What are you talking about?"

"Officer Woolchuck filled me in on how you helped her and the Stockington boy flee."

"Yeah that's why you hit me over the head," Officer Woolchuck growled, twisting Jake's arm behind him, causing him to wince in pain.

Jake fought the pain, trying to buy himself time. "And if I refuse to work with you?"

The Inspector circled him with his hands clasped together and shrugged, "Then I'll make you watch your sister die."

"No," Jake cried out, trying to find a way out of this nightmare. "No, I'll kill myself. You can't force me to do this!"

The Inspector held him up against the wall, staring at the young man who he had trusted with his life. How despicable his former First Lieutenant looked now, just another pawn in his game. "If you die, then I will kill her. That's a promise. The only way Mary goes free is if you do exactly what I say. Do we have an understanding, Jacob?"

Jake stood staring at the lifeless body of his mother, her blood pooling on the prison floor. He closed his eyes, fighting it, not wanting to give in, but he pictured Mary's face, so young and so innocent. He had no choice. He couldn't let her suffer the same fate as his mom. He spoke the words through clenched teeth, "You win, Herald."

The Inspector nodded to Officer Woolchuck who kicked Jake hard in the shin, causing him to crumple to his knees as his leg shattered. He cried out in pain, as the Inspector grabbed him by the jaw and smiled cruelly down at his fallen soldier.

"I always win."

End of Book Two: *The Change Agent*
The adventure continues with Book Three: *The Control*

Acknowledgements

I couldn't have continued **The Hypothesis of Giants** journey without the help and support of so many people. First and foremost, I would like to thank my amazing editor Theresa Goncalves, whose critical eye and attention to detail strengthened this story and challenged me to take the novel to new heights that I never imagined possible. This story wouldn't be the same without you and I am so happy I got to work on this novel with such a wonderful friend! A special thank you to Sue DeVito (Aunt Sue) for being a beta reader and providing an initial critique of this novel. Your encouraging feedback and edits were invaluable. I also would like to thank Roseann Magrane for taking the time to proofread this story in its early development. Thank you to Midnight Whimsy for creating the beautiful cover design for this novel and to Gerik Goncalves for being my website designer and for believing in the series from day one. Thank you to Ken Spencer from the Astronomical Society of Long Island for taking the time to teach me about star charting. I look at the stars in a brand new light now and any inconsistencies on mapping out the stars are all on me, though I can partially blame my creative imagination. Thank you to my amazing family and friends for their unconditional love and support of this series and being my number one fans. Thank you to my wonderful friend Billi Cipriano, who helped with writing the back cover blurb when I failed to figure out a way to describe my novel in 150 words or less. Thank you to my sisters Erin and Cassandra, as well as my brother-in-law Louie for letting me bounce ideas off of them and sending them countless emails during the day to help get second opinions on the cover designs. Thank you to my dad, John, for his unwavering support of my novel and I am so glad I was able to incorporate our character, Officer Woolchuck, into the series. A special thank you to my loving mother Christine, for always believing in me and for instilling a love of reading and writing in me at a young age. I'll be loving you…Always. I would sincerely like to thank my amazing husband Mike for being so supportive of my dream and for being there with me along this writing journey, with this book being especially more difficult since I was pregnant during the final editing stages. I am so blessed to have you in my life and I can't wait to share this story and the series with our beautiful baby girl. Lastly, a special thank you to the readers for all of your support and love of this series. Let's all strive to do impossibly good things in this lifetime.

About the Author

Melissa Kuch is the author of **The Hypothesis of Giants** series. She currently resides on Long Island with her husband Mike and their daughter Lily. For more updates about this series and other works by Melissa Kuch, please visit her website at www.melissakuch.com, or follow her on twitter @kuchmelissa

Made in the USA
Middletown, DE
20 October 2015